Shattered
at Sea

Also by Cheryl Hollon

Published by Kensington Publishing Corp.

Shattered at Sea

Cheryl Hollon

KENSINGTON PUBLISHING CORP.
www.kensingtonbooks.com

KENSINGTON BOOKS are published by

Kensington Publishing Corp.
119 West 40th Street
New York, NY 10018

All Kensington titles, imprints, and distributed lines are available at special quantity discounts for bulk purchases for sales promotions, premiums, fund-raising, educational, or institutional use. Special book excerpts or customized printings can also be created to fit specific needs. For details, write or phone the office of the Kensington sales manager: Kensington Publishing Corp., 119 West 40th Street, New York, NY 10018, attn: Sales Department; phone 1-800-221-2647.

ISBN-13: 978-1-4967-1177-9
ISBN-10: 1-4967-1177-7

First printing: September 2018

10 9 8 7 6 5 4 3 2 1

Printed in the United States of America

First electronic edition: September 2018

ISBN-13: 978-1-4967-1178-6
ISBN-10: 1-4967-1178-5

To
Lujoye Barnes, muse extraordinaire

ACKNOWLEDGMENTS

A writer needs a mountain of encouragement because there are few reasons to write and a million reasons not to write. The dedication required seems unsurmountable at the beginning of every new mystery. I spend many months writing, revising, editing, promoting, and marketing each book. My support group is the reason this book exists.

Many thanks to my publisher, Kensington Books, for continuing to publish and support the cozy mystery genre. Some of my friends were caught in the cruel crosshairs of merging and downsizing publishers. Most were picked up and dusted off by generous professionals in the business. Some decided it was time to strike out alone. Some have decided to leave publishing forever. May success reward those who had to make those tough decisions.

This book is wildly better because of the editing skills of Selena James and Rebecca Raskin. My publicist, Lulu Martinez, continues to support this crafty little cozy series with off-the-wall promotional ideas. As I've met more and more of the large Kensington family, I feel lucky to have such a supportive publishing home.

My literary agent Beth Campbell inspires me to reach higher and dig deeper to make each book better than the last. I am grateful for her guidance. Her success with new clients fills my heart with pride. Congratulations on her recent promotion to full literary agent. She has a great career in front of her.

Bradley and Eloyne Erickson own the glass shop that continues to inspire this series. Their website is www.grandcentralstainedglass.com and they would be happy to introduce you to the fascinating world of making your own family treasures. Check out their class and workshop schedule.

In today's world, children are denied the casual freedoms I took for granted. We played outside every evening after supper and stayed out until the streetlights came on. It was our signal to scramble home. My parents also took us on outdoor adventures like hiking, fishing, canoeing, archery, and camping. We basically ran as free as squirrels. Thanks, Mom and Dad, for such a great start. You instilled in me a lifelong search for new adventures.

I am indebted to a real cruise ship glassblower I met on the Celebrity cruise ship *Eclipse* during research for this book. Jamie Perian was delightfully open about her experiences aboard the cruise ship and behind the scenes. She and her teammates work incredibly hard to educate and entertain the passengers. Some of those passengers book cruises with the sole purpose of buying the glass pieces put up for auction. It was an honor to talk to her. I have taken quite a bit of literary license in imagining this make-believe cruise. If there are inconsistencies in the glassblowing sections, the fault is entirely mine.

I peeked at the archives from my critique group. We have been meeting at my little bungalow once a month for more than eight years. I'm grateful for the pointed guidance I receive in the early stages of a new book. Sam Falco and Christa Rickard are my vigilant guardians, telling me that I can always add more emotion and more tension. Thanks, guys—see you next month.

Having a genuinely supportive family is not as common as one would think. My heart breaks for those writers who must toil alone. My family encourages my writing. They happily attend my events with some evidence of pride and pleasure. I am blessed.

The world's most dedicated writer's champion continues to be my husband, George. He's my first reader, trusted adviser, taskmaster, and long-suffering spouse of an obsessive writer. I love you a bushel and a peck.

Prologue

At sea, cruise ship Obscura, security office

"There's no way he's dead," Savannah shouted at the security guard. "No one saw it. You haven't found a body."

"Miss, that's often the way it is for these cases," said the security guard. "We are proceeding with the investigation. You have no authority here. You're not even related to the passenger."

"But . . ."

"Leave it to us. We're the only authority out here in international waters."

Savannah turned away with her fists clenched and her eyes narrowed to small slits.

Leave it to you? There's no way.

Chapter 1

"It's a terrible time," said Savannah Webb. "I can't take a week off and leave everything to Amanda and Jacob. It feels wrong."

"It's the chance of a lifetime." Edward Morris folded his arms over his chest to reflect Savannah's stance. "The offer is a seven-day cruise in the Mediterranean that begins and ends in Barcelona, Spain. What's a little scheduling sacrifice compared to this opportunity?"

They stood eye to eye and toe to toe for a few moments. Savannah once again appreciated that Edward felt unthreatened by her six-foot height and unusual strength built by years of glassblowing large objects using heavy molten glass.

"What opportunity?" asked Amanda Blake, assistant manager and part-time stained-glass instructor. Savannah and Edward broke apart quickly.

Amanda stood next to them at the checkout counter of Webb's Glass Shop. "I'm always a little

suspect of the word *opportunity*." She finger-quoted.
"It can mean many things."

"In this case," said Savannah, "the opportunity is
to work as the substitute glassblower on a cruise ship
in the Mediterranean."

"That's awesome! When do you leave?" She adjusted the large statement necklace on her generous
chest. It was made of saucer-sized glass medallions
that clinked when she moved. Amanda was always
moving. "How long will you be gone?"

"The problem is that the cruise is for a week, and
since it leaves out of Barcelona, Edward wants to go
a day early so I can meet his family in England. Then
we'll fly out to board the ship on Sunday."

Amanda clapped her hands together. "So, what's
the problem? I can handle Webb's Glass Shop and
the beginner's stained-glass class by myself. Jacob is
perfectly happy over at Webb's Studio. It's only a few
blocks away, so I'm not too far if he needs something."

Jacob Underwood, Savannah's apprentice, had
recently moved to her expanded business site in the
Warehouse District of town.

Edward spoke up. "He's been handling things
very well. Your student clients know about his Asperger's syndrome. He knows everyone who rents a
studio. If a new student wants to rent space, he can
send them over for Amanda to handle the paperwork and payments."

Savannah momentarily tried suppressing a giant
grin, but it forced its way out into a hearty laugh.

"You're absolutely right." She gave Edward a big
hug. "This opportunity will not come around again.

There's a bazillion things to get organized, but I really want to go."

Savannah Webb checked her watch, then looked out the rental car window for the sixth time in thirty seconds. "Are you sure they open this early?" She looked over to Edward who sat beside her on their way to the Miami passport office. They had taken the 7:30 A.M. flight from Tampa Airport, which had meant a 4:30 A.M. wake-up call.

"Our appointment is at 10:45. It's only 9:30. We're in good time." Edward looked back at Savannah. "I still can't believe you don't have a passport."

"Not as many Americans travel outside the U.S. as you Brits; you guys are always looking for holiday trips abroad."

"If you spent one dreary winter in England, you would go mad. You take the sunshine for granted."

"True. Anyway, Dad did so much traveling when he was working for the government. He always said that there was so much to see in this country, why go to foreign parts while we still have so much to enjoy right here? You have wanderlust—not me."

Savannah enjoyed the occasional weekend trip, but most of the time she was perfectly content to kick back in her little Craftsman cottage with Edward and their dog and cat fur babies, Rooney and Snowy.

"It's not only about seeing more sites. It's about experiencing different cultures in a way you can't appreciate without walking around on their streets, eating their food, and facing their weather. You grew up in St. Petersburg, then spent a few years in Seattle at the Pilchuck Studio. Quite a narrow view."

Savannah tilted her head and turned toward Edward. "But I read a lot of books—more than any of the kids I grew up with. All the librarians knew me."

"Doesn't count. You can't smell the spice market in New Delhi without standing there."

Savannah reached over and held his hand. "Okay. I'll give you that point. But you must agree I'm certainly changing my outlook today. This is an incredible opportunity for me. Thanks for helping."

"I only helped with the passport—stuff I know. My travel agent did the rest. Jan is a miracle worker with travel challenges. You're the one that's done the impossible to get everything arranged so you can spend ten days away from the shop." He looked at her slip of paper. "Thirteen? Really?"

"Shush up," Savannah whispered as they sat. "It's my lucky number."

"Number thirteen," the receptionist announced to the waiting room in a strong voice that hinted she had a musical background.

Savannah jumped up so abruptly that she dropped the folder containing her documents all over the floor. She stooped to gather them up and bumped heads with Edward. "Ouch!" She plopped down on her behind and rubbed her forehead. "What are you doing?"

"Trying to help." Edward gathered the papers and slid them into Savannah's bright green folder, then pulled her up by the hand. "You seem flustered."

"Good guess." Savannah felt a flush rising in her cheeks. She looked over to the receptionist who was frowning like a judge sentencing a convicted drug dealer. Savannah resisted the urge to step forward at once. She first straightened her papers. Then she put on her brightest smile and walked up to the receptionist's desk.

"Hi, I'm appointment number thirteen."

"If you're ready, step through the aisle over to cubicle number eight."

Number eight—hmmm. That's lucky in China and unlucky in India. I think I'll lean toward China's belief.

Savannah stepped into the tiny space that held a desk barely wide enough for a computer monitor and a mouse. There was enough room for a guest chair and the passport administrator—nothing else.

"Hi, my name is Margie Adams. Please have a seat, Miss Webb." Savannah smiled and sat. Margie must have been the oldest civil servant in the world. She looked to be nearing ninety, if not already there. However, she was meticulously groomed and had curly white hair, a smooth ivory complexion, and maroon eyeshadow that accented her piercing eyes. "Good, it looks like you have your documents. Hand them over and I'll fire up the application program. We'll get this passport process steaming along so you can go to"—she looked at Savannah's passport request form—"London, England."

"Yes, we have tickets to leave on this evening's eight-o'clock flight from Miami."

Miss Adams was flipping through Savannah's papers and her fingers were flying over the submission form entries. "Everything looks good, Savannah. I always appreciate an orderly mind." She paused.

"Wait. Here's your driver's license, but where's your birth certificate?"

"It should be right there." Savannah reached out for the folder. "May I check?"

"Sure." Margie closed the folder and handed it over.

Savannah flipped through the documents and sure enough, the birth certificate wasn't where she had placed it. Her heart jumped two beats. Without that, there was no way she was getting a passport, flying to London, or boarding that cruise ship. She flipped through the papers one more time. It was gone.

"Excuse me," said Edward from the narrow hallway. "Are you looking for this?" He held up her birth certificate. "The receptionist said I could bring it down."

Savannah gave him cow eyes in relief, took the paper, and put it where it belonged.

Margie stretched out her hand for the folder. "Louise must like the looks of you. She would normally have let this explode into a massive issue, then play the martyr." She grinned at Edward, then turned back to her computer screen. "You can go back to the waiting room. It won't be long."

Edward left and Margie peered at the justification section. "It says that you're going to work on a cruise ship?" She scanned Savannah from top to bottom. "You don't seem like a cabin porter type. What are you going to do? Are you an entertainer?"

"More like an educator." Savannah smiled and leaned forward. "I'm taking the place of an injured glass artist on a cruise ship leaving out of Barcelona. I'll be doing glassblowing demonstrations on one of the larger ships for their seven-day Mediterranean cruise. The poor girl will be released from the hospital in a few days, so I'm only filling in until she returns."

"Glassblowing? On a cruise ship?" She lifted a single eyebrow. "You can't even have candles in your cabin on a cruise ship. How can they have glassblowing demonstrations?"

"It's a special setup. The Hot Shop was designed by Crystal Glass Works to run on electricity instead of gas fires. The techniques are a little different, but they heat the glass in electric furnaces—no fire at all. It will be tricky for me to learn how to work the glass without using a blowtorch, but what a wonderful opportunity to see the Mediterranean!"

All the while, Margie was tapping away into the application form template. It was disconcerting that she could hold a conversation and simultaneously type at lightning speed. Margie filled in the last field and pressed the enter key with a flourish. "There, now let me check one last time for accuracy." She sped through each field delicately flicking the tab key. "Fantastic. Everything looks perfect. I'll submit this to the back-room clerks who will create your brand-new passport. All you have to do is come back here at two today and it will be ready."

"Thank you very much." Savannah grinned like a Cheshire cat. *It appears that thirteen and eight are my lucky numbers.*

She returned to the reception area. Edward stood and splayed both hands palms up. "So? You look happy."

"Yes, we can pick up my shiny new passport this afternoon. I'm hungry."

"Of course, you are. When there are issues, you can't eat. As soon as the issues are resolved, you're starving. I've sussed out the pattern."

They arrived back in plenty of time. Margie nodded and waved to them. They only had to wait a few minutes until Savannah's passport was ready. Then they drove to the Miami International Airport to turn in the rental and check in for the flight to Heathrow Airport. They received special treatment because Edward's parents had upgraded their economy class tickets to business class as soon as Edward told them they were coming to visit. Jan had used her insider contacts to make it happen.

"They must be anxious to make you welcome," said Edward.

"What do you mean?"

"The two of them travel business class across the pond each and every time, but when they send me a ticket? It's crunch class both ways," said Edward.

Squeezing in a family visit before the cruise ship embarked was an opportunity Edward couldn't resist. Savannah was looking forward to seeing Edward's parents again.

The first special treat was the short line for business class passengers at the check-in counter. The second treat was the pre-check TSA line through security, followed by the third treat, a pass to the airport lounge to await boarding time.

They enjoyed a local craft beer accompanied by small plates of finger food. Savannah pulled out the illustrated instruction manual she had received from Crystal Glass Works that detailed the procedures for glassblowing with the electric hot shop on board the cruise ship. She reviewed the handwritten notes she had made in the margins when she took the training class.

When their boarding time was called, Edward and Savannah walked into the business class cabin and Savannah gaped at the size of her personal space. Their large, wide seats were in the center aisle so that they sat side by side yet each had unrestricted access to the aisle. She hefted her carry-on into the ample overhead compartment.

In her seat, the best available noise-canceling Bose headphones were sitting on top of a decent-sized pillow and a quilted duvet. A small amenity kit contained slip-on socks, a sleep mask, ear plugs, moisturizer, toothbrush, toothpaste, lip balm, and breath mints.

As soon as Savannah had settled into her seat, a flight attendant offered her a glass of champagne. "Welcome aboard, Miss Webb. I hope you enjoy your flight."

Savannah turned to Edward who had also received his glass of champagne. They looked at each other and clicked glasses. Savannah toasted, "Good luck to us on the first of many international adventures. Cheers."

Chapter 2

Savannah felt Edward's hand on her elbow as he
guided her through a confusing assault of bright
lights, blaring announcements, and scurrying passengers of every type. She looked at Edward's focused
smile. *He likes this kind of challenge. Relax—he's got this.
Let him shine.*

In minutes, they were outside in the chilly autumn
air. Edward stood on his toes, peered across the
street, and waved his arm. A small red MINI Cooper
car pulled up and a not-quite-so-tall replica of
Edward got out of the car and popped the trunk.

"Hello, you must be Savannah. I'm Ian Morris,
Edward's better-looking cousin." Savannah shook his
outstretched hand and matched his winning grin
with a surprised smile.

"Hey," said Edward, helping to get their two
suitcases and carry-on bags crammed into the boot
with practiced efficiency. "Who says you're the

better-looking cousin? Certainly not my mum, but maybe yours. Savannah, you be the judge."

"Ian, you look exactly like a younger"—she playfully patted Edward's tummy—"slimmer version of Edward."

"Oi!" yelped Edward as he sucked in the start of a beer belly. "I'm going to work this off on the cruise."

Ian scrunched his brow. "From what I've been told, we should all expect to gain at least a stone. I intend to gain mine downing exotic drinks with tiny brollies stuck in them."

Savannah enjoyed their easy banter. "Your parents must be very proud of your achievements to give you this cruise as a graduation present."

Ian's face flashed a dark look, then he grinned. "Yeah, I took a wayward path to University, but I got there at the end of the day."

She gingerly folded herself into the backseat on the left-hand side of the car. It felt odd that she was on the passenger side until they pulled out onto the road.

Her heart leaped to her throat in disorientation. *The cars are driving in the wrong direction!* She blinked several times and calmed herself.

Savannah grabbed the back of the front seat and the hold bar above the top of the window to wedge herself against the sway of the swerving car as it sped around a traffic circle to emerge onto a small country road. "Ian! Did you make that turn on two wheels?"

"Yes, ma'am. I am required to keep at least two wheels on the pavement at all times. Three wheels is harder and four on the ground is just plain boring and I'm not a bore."

Savannah tapped Edward on the shoulder. He turned. "Are we going to survive this drive?"

"Yes, Ian likes to make an exciting first impression, but he settles down as soon as I remind him of the standard death threat he receives if he doesn't start driving like a sane person instantly. Ian. This is your one and only warning."

Ian switched gears and reduced his speed to pace the other cars on the road. Savannah was fascinated with the amount of gear changing going on with Ian's left hand on the gear knob while he steered with the right.

Savannah wedged herself even farther back into the seat. They headed north to a mid-sized town called St. Albans, about twenty-five miles as the crow flies but more than forty as the road twisted. It was the family village where most of Edward's relations lived.

Savannah felt a little disoriented. Her eyes were a bit gritty and she was thirsty. She was right at the point of nodding off when they arrived. She gave her head a quick shake.

This must be jet lag. I never noticed the Seattle to St. Petersburg time difference when I visited Dad.

They pulled into a short driveway in front of a two-story, freestanding house with batten and beam construction on the outer walls. It was the real 1750s deal. The roof was traditionally thatched and all the multipaned windows had fairytale shutters with flowerboxes spilling over with bright blooms and ivy.

The glossy black door opened and Edward's mother

scurried out to accept a kiss on her cheek from her son and then she kissed Savannah on each cheek and gave her a gentle hug.

"Darling, I'm so happy you're here. Welcome to St. Albans." Glenda was plump with a cheerful flush on the apples of her high cheeks. Her smile was easy—it creased her face with crow's feet and dimples—and her eyes were the same shade of green that Savannah loved in Edward.

Glenda Morris was followed by Edward's father, Ronald, who shook Edward's hand.

"Welcome to our home, girl." Ron shook Savannah's hand and placed a quick smooch on her cheek. "We've been waiting for you." He puffed out his chest like a new papa.

Savannah wondered if this was normal or if they were adding more affection to their greetings because she was an American. They hadn't seen Edward in a few months, but they acted as if it had been only a few days.

They went through the front door into a cramped entry that revealed the door to a powder room and a wooden stairway to the upper story. Through an open archway to her right, Savannah glimpsed the living room fireplace. It was the focal point of the room, and there was also a large comfy sofa, two facing love seats, and a coffee table in the center space. The floor was covered by an oriental rug too large for her to see its edges.

Before she could see anything else, the menfolk carried their luggage to an upstairs bedroom and Glenda told them from the bottom of the stairs that they had about an hour to freshen up. Luncheon would be served family-style in the kitchen on the ground floor at the back of the house.

Savannah pulled the laptop out of her briefcase and set it up on an ancient but sturdy table in front of one of the dormer windows that looked out through the sharply trimmed thatch roofing. There was a clear crystal vase filled with pink heritage roses on the windowsill. Beside it was a small china dish of wrapped sweets. *Nice touch.*

Edward walked up from behind, wrapped his arms around her, and buried his head in her shoulder. "They've given us the guest quarters with the en suite bathroom. This is rather special. Mum only lets her parents stay here. I usually get my childhood single bedroom, which is the tiny room next door to this one with the shared bathroom at the end of the hall. What does Mum have up her sleeve?"

"I think she's trying to tell you in the sweetest possible way that perhaps you might be an adult now."

Savannah thought it was a pitch by his mother to acknowledge their relationship. Savannah felt comfortable in her situation with Edward. He lived in her home now with her dog Rooney and his kitten Snowy.

Is marriage really my next step?

Edward screwed up his face. "Oh, that's fine, then." He hugged her tighter and kissed the back of her neck. "Are you still jet-lagged?"

"Mm mm." Savannah relaxed into him for a moment before straightening up. "Nice, but I think it's time to behave. Do I have time to check my e-mail?"

He checked his watch. "Lunch is typically at one o'clock and it's now going on noon. Sure." He walked up behind her and reached around to give her a snuggle. "You already look scrumptious. No freshening up needed for you."

"Mm mm." Savannah turned in his arms, distracted by his attentions, until his words sunk in. She stiffened. "It's after twelve? I need to take a shower and change and I would imagine you would, too. I'll go first and then I'll work my e-mail while you're getting ready. Yikes, there's not much time."

"Relax, Mum doesn't operate on a strict schedule. She's relaxed about family meals." Edward pressed his lips tight. "Her catering jobs? That's an entirely different story."

"Still, I don't want to annoy her in my first hour."

"You won't. I think I'll check my e-mail as well. Nicole has been running things so smoothly that I sometimes forget I actually own the pub."

Savannah stepped into the bathroom for a quick shower, but stood there faced with an undecipherable set of shower controls. She pushed, poked, pulled, prodded the dials in all combinations—no water.

"Edward, I can't figure out how the shower works."

After kissing her on the back of the neck again, Edward reached into the shower. "You have to pull each faucet out, then turn it to set the flow. Good?"

Savannah nodded. "And it's the opposite to turn them off?"

Edward smiled and nodded. "The hot water has another stop for extra hot water—but be careful with that."

After her shower, Savannah towel-dried her hair and mentally thanked her mother for passing on the curly black hair gene that was a genuine one-step, wash-and-dry style. When she got out her toothbrush and toothpaste, that's when she felt her jet lag again. On the sink was a faucet labeled HOT and a faucet labeled COLD. Each faucet had a single spigot. She stood in front of the sink holding her loaded toothbrush. She had never encountered a sink with separate water flows.

She shrugged, wet her toothbrush under the cold water, filled one of the paper cups with a mixture of hot and cold, and brushed her teeth.

Not particularly an earth-changing difference, but Edward was right—you can't get this experience from a book. She stepped out of the bathroom to find Edward cross-legged on the bed typing away on his laptop.

She changed into casual jeans and an I LOVE THE 'BURG T-shirt she had picked up at a fund-raiser. Then she slipped on a brand-new pair of Dockers. The boat shoes were the same type that she wore for work, and due to her public role in demonstrating glassblowing, she felt she deserved a new pair. She needed to break them in as much as she could before the performances started aboard the cruise ship.

As soon as Edward was in the shower, she opened her laptop and signed into the Morrises' Wi-Fi. The first e-mail in her in-box was from Amanda.

Hi Savannah! I hope your flight was smooth and you are settled into Edward's place.

I love housesitting your bungalow. My tiny garage apartment feels even smaller now that I'm experiencing the convenience of having plenty of room for cooking. You have a great kitchen!

Rooney was a little anxious after our walk last night. I think it finally dawned on him that you wouldn't be coming back for the night. Weimaraners are certainly high-energy dogs! Eventually he settled but spent a lot of time pacing from your bedroom to the kitchen and whining at me as if I could magically change into you.

Little Snowy is missing Edward; she's curled up in his reclining chair right now, but I'm managing her loneliness with lots of play and treats. She has these spells of frenetic energy and attacks everything that comes her way. Her new trick is to jump onto Rooney's back. She stalks along the back of the couch and pounces on him when he walks by on his way to your room.

Don't worry! Things are fine. I'll e-mail every day just like you said.

X O X O X Amanda

Savannah felt slightly giddy. She hadn't been aware that she was worried about Rooney until Amanda's e-mail. He was her dad's puppy and Rooney dealt with some abandonment issues after Mr. Webb's death. But Amanda could charm the stars from the sky. She shouldn't have worried.

The next most important e-mail was from her glass shop apprentice, Jacob Underwood. Although he was upfront about his struggles with Asperger's syndrome, he was growing into a great employee and consequently growing out of his apprenticeship role.

> Dear Miss Savannah, here is my report for Friday.
>
> The studio—All students visited their workspace.
> My custom work—The pattern for my commission piece is tacked down on the largest worktable. I have checked that all the special sheets of glass are in stock except one. I have ordered that sheet from the vendor.
> Calls—The phone didn't ring today.
>
> Sincerely yours,
>
> Jacob Underwood, Apprentice, Webb's Studio
>
> P.S. Suzy says hi.

Savannah smiled as she thought of how rigidly reserved Jacob had been when she took over Webb's Glass Shop at the beginning of the year. Suzy, his service beagle, was a big part of his growing confidence and maturity. He had no idea how grateful Savannah felt that he thrived by working on stained-glass restorations.

She also felt the guiding hand of his juvenile-court-judge mother in the structure of this e-mail. It must have cost him some pride to ask her for help. All eighteen-year-olds hated that.

Edward is taking his time in the shower.

They had been living together for a few months. It

happened after an investigation into the death of her high school boyfriend. She had to admit that it was a struggle at times to be considerate of a partner. She felt he was worth the effort.

She skimmed through the rest of her inbox and filed most of them away for later. Edward stepped out of the shower. "I'm running late. I nearly fell asleep under the running water. Go on down. I'll be there in a few minutes."

She put on a swipe of lip-gloss and made her way downstairs. The heavenly smell of roast lamb and some sort of pastry met her as she reached the bottom of the stairs and turned into the kitchen.

While the rest of the cottage had been meticulously maintained in its original eighteenth-century form, the enormous kitchen was a page out of a chef's glossy coffee table book. Along the far wall, a bright red cooker stood inside a fireplace alcove that still had the original spit mechanisms in place. Along the back wall of the house was a deep double-sized farm sink with a modern goose-necked faucet under a wide window that reached up to the ceiling. Inside the deep access on each side of the window were the original folding door panels for closing out the winter cold. In front of the sink stood a large waist-high butcher block table that probably had gotten those curved valleys in its surface from the knife of a real butcher in a real butcher's shop. The other wall was taken up by a commercial-sized refrigerator, more counter space, and a professional eight-burner stove.

The near end of the kitchen was taken up by a large wooden table. Along the inside wall stood an ancient Welsh kitchen dresser packed with china plates, cups, and figurines. The well-used table paired with six Windsor chairs could easily seat ten without blinking an eye.

"Oh, good, you're down." Glenda was adding butter to a huge bowl of mashed potatoes. "Savannah, pet. Would you mind filling the water glasses?"

"I'd love to." Savannah opened both refrigerators and realized that neither side was a freezer. "Where's the ice?"

"Ice? Oh, of course, you were born in Florida. We don't use ice; the water from the tap is perfectly chilled. Use the pitcher on the table and then refill it."

The table was set for five but instead of cloth place mats, the mats were a stiff fiberboard with a scene of St. Albans Cathedral on the front. Savannah picked one up and found a layer of cork on the back. The knife, fork, and spoon were wrapped in the embroidered napkins. Two wine bottles of a French cabernet sauvignon were open. A large basket was filled with dinner rolls and wrapped in another embroidered napkin.

"The table setting is fantastic. Do you embroider?"

"Heavens, no. I can barely mend. My sister-in-law, Ian's mother, is the textile artist. She inherited that talent from her mother. I received this ensemble as a wedding gift, and her Mum also gave me a set for more formal occasions. I'll show it to you this afternoon. As an artist, I'm sure you'll appreciate the intricate needlework."

Savannah cleared the sudden catch in her throat and her heart warmed. It wasn't normal for her to have a gushy reaction, but Edward meant a lot to her. "This is where Edward learned to cook, isn't it?"

After setting the copper roasting dish on a waiting hot pad on the table, Glenda smiled. "Yes, and a wonderful student he was. Not at first, mind you. Like all teenaged boys, he didn't take to cooking immediately, but as he got better, something clicked. From that point on, I couldn't keep him out of the kitchen."

A great clattering of rapid steps on the stairway heralded Edward's entrance into the kitchen.

"That and I learned a great many other things in this kitchen." Edward pulled the chair out for Savannah. "This is where I finished all my homework while Mum created the most amazing dishes out of nothing but simple, fresh ingredients and exotic spices. Her catering business is still chugging along even though she has tried to retire."

Glenda waved a hand at the table. "My friends are experts at making a fuss if I try to refuse work, but now I only take on the jobs I love. That's right. Sit there, Savannah, next to Pa's place with Edward next to you. We'll put Ian on the other side, next to Pa, so he won't misbehave."

Savannah looked at the contents of the Welsh dresser. "This is a beautiful collection. Goodness, what a huge teapot. Do the pieces have a history?"

"That enormous teapot belongs to Ron's side of the family. It was a wedding present to his grandmother, then to his parents—as his dad was the oldest son. Finally, it came to us when we married since Ron was their oldest son. We never use it."

The shower had helped Savannah feel more awake

and energized, but the novelty of last night's whirlwind round of fancy food and drink had delayed their settling down to sleep in the airplane's comfortable flat beds. Then, her slumbers were cut short by the hustling of the cabin crew to serve a full English breakfast and then prepare for landing an hour before touchdown. She was basically operating on three hours of sleep.

She jumped when she felt a nudge on her calf, and took a peek around the edge of the table. Right next to her was a tan and white Corgi puppy with the most soulful brown eyes she had ever seen. Edward reached down and ruffled the adorably cute perky ears. "This must be Dora. Mum's newest member of the pack." He looked over to his mother who was taking another heavy red roasting dish out of the AGA oven. "Does Dora make number four or five?"

"Actually, Dora makes only three. We lost Daisy and Dolly this summer. I didn't tell you because you didn't know them very well and it was too upsetting for me. It was so unbearably hot and they were getting on, you know. Duff and Dana are still young at only four and five. They withstood the unseasonably hot summer very well, but I'm afraid we may have to install air-conditioning so that the doggies are more comfortable."

Edward lifted both hands palms up and shrugged at Savannah. "That's Mum. No AC for the humans, but for her precious Corgis? Absolutely."

"Nonsense—you were healthier for a little weathering."

"You should try to cook in here for an afternoon event for fifty in August. Talk about sweating buckets."

"Don't exaggerate, Edward. That's not polite." Glenda smiled even as she chided him.

Edward looked at Savannah and mouthed, *"I'm not exaggerating."*

Glenda put one hand on her hip and pointed at the adorable Dora. "Miss Dora, you know you can't be here in the kitchen. Go back to the sitting room like a good girl." Dora slunk out of the kitchen but stopped at the threshold to glance back at Glenda. "Go on, Dora. We'll have our coffee and pudding with you. It won't be long, luv." She turned to Edward. "Have you seen Ian?"

A loud flush followed by running water in the sink sounded from the powder room in the entryway. A few seconds later, Ian stood at the entrance to the kitchen. "Is it ready, Aunt Glenda?"

"Only just," said Glenda. "Go fetch your uncle Ron so we can sit down to eat."

Ian turned his head to the side and bellowed, "Uncle Ron! Lunch is ready."

"Really, Ian. Must you act the fool in front of our guest?" Then she tutted with the zeal of an experienced tut-tutter. Savannah put a hand over her mouth and pressed her lips tight to suppress the urge to bust out in laughter. Ian sat across from Savannah and took a huge swig of water to cover his expression.

Edward's dad entered the kitchen. "Smells good as usual, Ma." He came up behind Glenda and put his arms around her for a hug and quick kiss on the cheek. Savannah got the impression that this was a normal and much practiced greeting between the two. Then he sat in the only cushioned chair with arms at the head of the table against the wall. "Come on, Glenda. Sit down so we can pray and tuck in."

Another tut was followed with, "Don't rush me, Ron. I don't want to forget anything."

"Come now, it doesn't have to be perfect." Ian shook his head. "It's just us."

"Behave." Glenda swiped a hand in the general direction of the back of Ian's head.

This is what having an extended family is like. It's so comforting. I understand why Edward is so confident—he has this whole family behind him. It was only me and Dad after Mom died.

Savannah felt her cheeks lift in a warm smile. Her young life was so different. Her dad raised her by himself since she was ten. Memories of her mother struggling with cancer left her isolated and a loner. Glass art saved her.

This was exactly what she imagined Edward's family would be like in their home. Cheerful, affectionate, full of teasing that showed how much they cared about each other. She had met them on their last visit to St. Petersburg, but the circumstances had been strained by Savannah's efforts to clear herself as the prime suspect in the murder of a prize-winning glass artist. Ron and Glenda had returned home before she could get to know them.

The meal tasted even better than it smelled. There was roast lamb shank with a thin au jus gravy, accompanied by creamy garlic mashed potatoes. The colorful vegetable dish was piled with a selection of carrots, both orange and purple, cauliflower, broccoli, and sliced turnips. Edward's mother used a kitchen towel to remove a stack of dinner plates from a warming door in the top shelf of the AGA. She sat them on her place mat and settled in the arm chair at the foot of the table across from her husband. She loaded the top plate with a hunk of lamb, a great dollop of potatoes, and a heaping pile of vegetables. She ladled gravy overall and handed it to Ian. "Pass this down to your uncle Ron, dear."

As she loaded up the next plate, Ian held out his hands, but his aunt signaled for the next plate to be Savannah's. Edward took it from his mother and quickly plopped the loaded plate onto Savannah's mat. "Watch it! That is hot."

In a comfortable routine, Glenda filled Edward's and his cousin's plates and finally ended by serving herself. When her plate was filled, she looked over to her husband and nodded. Everyone bowed heads, then Edward's dad gave the quickest blessing that Savannah had ever heard and everyone tucked in.

After the first few bites, the menfolk piped up.

"Delicious lamb, dear."

"Aunt Glenda, this is great."

"Mum, I have sorely missed your cooking. This is fantastic."

Savannah caught Edward's mother looking at her with her head tilted slightly and her eyebrows raised. "How is your lamb, poppet?"

"Poppet?" Savannah crinkled her eyes.

Instantly, the men stopped eating and looked at her. Edward nudged her with an elbow.

"It's a term of endearment for a young person. It means Mum likes you."

"Oh, I know what it means. British television is

incredibly popular in the U.S. It's just that I never expected to be called a poppet."

"Yep," said Ron. The men returned to their meals.

Savannah gulped, "Oh." She wiped her mouth with the linen napkin. "Mrs. Morris, I've only eaten lamb a few times at Edward's pub." She paused and nudged Edward back. "I must tell the truth." She smiled at Edward's mother. "Yours is better." She elbowed Edward again who was pretending to be shocked. "It *is* better."

Savannah felt the release of pent-up breath in the room. Apparently, she had passed some sort of test.

It's one thing to have met Edward's parents while they were visiting him in Florida and quite another to meet them on their home turf. I'm being examined for partner material, I'm sure.

Edward pointed a fork at Ian. "Thanks ever so much for letting me crash in your cabin for this cruise. I can't believe you were able to get me added to your reservation so quickly."

"No issues, really. I have a schoolmate whose partner owns a travel agency. He transferred my cabin for your cruise's departure date in a jiff. It will be even more fun to cruise with you guys."

Savannah had mimicked everyone's fork and knife in each hand style of eating. It was awkward at first, but in the end, she found it quicker. "Don't forget, I'll be working and won't be able to spend very much time with you. I do expect you both to attend every single one of my demonstrations. No excuses!"

Glenda Morris looked around the table at everyone's clean plate. "Pass the plates down to me and I'll get our pudding. It's Spotted Dick."

Savannah's eyebrows lifted. "I've heard of that. It's made of what, exactly?"

Edward grinned like a Cheshire cat. "A lovely vanilla pudding with raisins."

Glenda returned with a tray bearing white ramekins filled to the brim with the classic dessert. The little cups were passed around and polished off in seconds. Savannah gulped down the rest of her serving and felt like she was a slow-motion sloth.

"If everyone is finished, Edward, you should show Savannah the back garden and take Dora, Duff, and Dana with you. They all need their walkies before we set off on the St. Albans' footpath. Along the way, we need to stop by the Red Lion Pub for Ian's graduation celebration. We'll only be taking Dora. The others mind the commotion."

Savannah scooted her chair back to leave the table, but when she stood, a sharp yelp from below startled her. She stepped back trying to avoid Dora the adorable, but instead crashed into the dresser behind her. This was followed by the awful sound of crockery falling to the tiled kitchen floor. She turned around in time to see the heritage china teapot hit the floor.

Complete silence filled the room.

Savannah gasped at the destruction and put her hands up to her flushed cheeks. "I'm so sorry."

Dora began to whimper and then started to shake.

Edward's eyes widened. Everyone at the table was frozen in shock.

Savannah broke the silence, stuttering. "I've destroyed your granny's teapot." She looked at Edward and then looked at Glenda. "I'm so sorry." She felt the tears threatening to spill.

Everyone's going to hate me for this. What a horrible thing to do.

"Are you hurt?" Glenda reached out a gentle hand across the table in Savannah's direction.

"Dora! Come here!" Edward commanded in a firm voice. He lifted Dora into his arms and stood up. "Dora, you know you're not supposed to be here. Mum, you've really been spoiling her."

"Is it the heirloom teapot?" Glenda's voice was heavy with concern. "Is it shattered beyond repair?"

Hundreds of tiny shards were strewn across the stone floor. Savannah picked up the largest piece. "The spout is all that is recognizable. The rest will be impossible to piece together." She slowly placed the spout back on the shelf in the gap where the teapot had been. "I'm . . . I'm . . . I'm so sorry."

Glenda took Dora from Edward's arms and kissed her on the top of the head. "You naughty, naughty girl. How will I ever forgive you?"

"What can I do? Can I get a replacement?" Savannah shook her head to clear it. "Sorry, how stupid of me. This can't possibly be replaced. I've destroyed something precious."

"Yes, you have, my dear," said Glenda. "But it was only precious to my mother-in-law, who sadly is no longer with us."

Ron cleared his throat. "Mum considered it to be my heritage, but she conveniently forgot that I didn't find much value in crockery no matter who it belonged to."

"That's right!" Edward picked up the matching

creamer from the cabinet and nodded down the table to his dad. Ron picked up the matching sugar bowl and nodded solemnly to Edward.

Edward and Ron lifted their hands over their heads and crashed the china to the floor.

Savannah jumped, and shock raced across her face. "What are you doing?"

"Savannah," Ron spoke with a deep voice. "Savannah, don't worry yourself for a second. Although Granny's teapot had pride of place on our sideboard, in truth, she was a horrible person. She ruled with an iron fist and a wooden ruler and kept us all in constant turmoil." He walked around the shards and folded Savannah into his arms. "Some*thing* never means more to me than some*one*."

Glenda clapped her hands. "Chop, chop, Edward. Get the broom and sweep this mess away. I've been waiting for ages for that damned teapot to fall."

Afterward, Edward's mother wouldn't hear of Savannah's offer to help clear the kitchen. Although Duff indicated that he did not approve of Savannah by giving her a wide berth, he was happy for Edward to clip on his leash. Dora and Dana gave her tail wiggles as she clipped on their leashes.

Edward's mother held the back door open as they wrangled the three dogs out. "Don't let them fool you into dropping their leads. They love nothing better than a good chase on the downs. We don't have time for that."

They went out the back door and Savannah felt the world tilt. She grabbed the door to steady herself and caught her breath. The wild riot of color was not at all what she expected in an English garden.

There were two halves to the display. Bold colors on the left side and soft pastels on the other. The bright contrasting colors reminded her of a surrealist's garden, and the soft side took an Impressionist painter's palette. The flowers that drew her attention were the pastel roses—tall, proud, spectacular roses.

"They're gorgeous." Savannah cupped a heavy pink blossom in her hands and sniffed deeply. "And they have a scent. I miss the wonderful flowers that were everywhere in Seattle sometimes. Listen, Edward. I'm so sorry about the teapot. I don't know what's wrong with me."

Edward folded Savannah into his arms. "You're simply suffering from jet lag, but Mum has indeed been trying to get rid of that horrible teapot for ages." He released her and they headed toward the back gate. "You know about the superstition, don't you?"

"What superstition?"

"If you break a piece of china, you'll have very bad luck. Even worse if you try to mend it. That's why Mum had us sweep up the pieces so quickly and put them outside in the trash bin. The broken pieces foretell bad luck."

Chapter 3

Savannah and Edward walked behind his parents and Dora, and headed uphill on Abbey Mill Lane toward St. Albans Abbey. Dora struggled to keep her lead training in mind and needed a pointed reminder from time to time. Apparently, Edward's mum had so much training experience with dogs that she didn't break stride to correct Dora's behavior.

"Where's Ian?" asked Savannah. She puffed a little heavily as the steepness of the hill increased.

Ron grumbled with thinly suppressed irritation. "Long gone. He said he had to meet his friends to get ready for his party. Humph. His idea of getting ready is to arrive. He'll show up late as well. Watch."

"Don't be such a fusspot, dear." Glenda looked over her shoulder. "Savannah, we usually visit the Abbey when we take this walk. We do have a little extra time. Would you like to see the stained glass?"

She felt a wave of relief. *Edward is right. She isn't mad at me.*

"Yes, yes. I would love that." She grabbed Edward by the arm and gave it a squeeze. "I researched it before we left. There's a mixture of modern and ancient. The north transept rose window is especially interesting and has caused quite the controversy since it was installed."

He tucked her hand through his elbow and patted it. "The locals have always called it 'the Abbey' even though it hasn't been an official abbey since the sixteenth century. The architecture dates from Norman times. It became a cathedral in 1877. It's our parish church. You're going to love the windows."

Entering via the Slype visitor's center, they walked through the south transept and paused in the crossing to view the longest nave in England. They continued across and gazed at the stained glass designed for the north transept rose window. Savannah whispered into Edward's ear. "The glass is modern. It was designed by an artist named Younger and unveiled in 1989 by Diana, Princess of Wales."

"So much blue and red," Edward whispered back.

"That's why there was such conflict. It doesn't blend in with the ancient panels, but some of the windows from the fifties haven't aged well. In fact, they look horribly dated. These colors are bold and the pattern is quite geometric, but it manages to blend perfectly into its setting." She turned to find Glenda. "Thanks for taking me to see it, Mrs. Morris."

Glenda smiled and walked over to a shrine that had a metal stand holding rows and rows of lit candles flickering in ruby votives.

Edward whispered to Savannah, "Mum was going to stop by here anyway to light a candle for our journey."

"Really? It's only a cruise. Nothing dangerous. For me, it's a job. An exciting job, but still merely a job."

"Well, the thing is that she's terrified of water. She never learned to swim and I think she's worried sick about both me and Ian sailing on the same ship. Somehow that seems to make her think it will be even more dangerous."

They left the Abbey and took the footpath down to the River Ver footbridge and then circled back to pause in front of a timber-framed octagonal building with a large sign over the door, YE OLDE FIGHTING COCKS. There was an oval plaque listing it as Britain's oldest pub.

Edward's parents turned in unison to Edward. Then Glenda waved her hand at him in a "do your thing" gesture.

"Fine." He smiled and tipped his head to one side. "I'm the one in the family that tells our visitors about this pub. In case you haven't gathered by the enormous billboard on the wall of the pub, our lovely St. Albans is a popular tourist site. Although this pub claims to be the oldest in Britain, the earliest date for which it can be proved to have been licensed is 1756—and even that date is not certain. My vote goes to the White Hart Hotel, which dates to 1470."

"No matter, dear," said Glenda. "Ian's celebration is out back in the beer garden."

"Right." Edward took Savannah's arm and led her in through a dark, heavily beamed hodgepodge of small rooms each furnished with tables, chairs, benches, booths, and stools. Everything looked old and comfortable. The mostly red oriental carpets were worn and threadbare. She glimpsed an upright piano in one corner and they passed by the small bar crowded with beer tap handles and bar cloths. On their way out back, she felt the momentary warmth of a cozy fireplace featuring a vast copper hood.

A beer garden was typical of most popular pubs. This one was uncovered, windy and packed cheek by jowl with wooden tables and sturdy chairs weathered to an ashen gray. About twenty people were seated along two long tables with plates of assorted cheeses and baskets of crackers. Another table had been set up with an array of food chafers offering meats, vegetables, and fried rice.

A harried server kept busy fetching drink orders from the celebrants, some of whom had been there for some time, as the empty glasses outnumbered the guests. Edward stepped in front of the server, made sure that he had her attention, and ordered drinks for Savannah and his parents.

Glenda waved to an older couple seated near the edge of the outdoor tiled patio. The woman waved back. "Hi, Glenny. I'm pleased you could make it. Sit over here with us. The din is a bit lower."

"Hi, Sissy. You look positively radiant. An empty nest suits you." Glenda and Ron sat down with the couple. "This is Edward's friend, Savannah Webb. She owns a stained-glass shop next door to his pub in America. Savannah, this is my brother Howard and his wife Kate. They're Ian's parents."

Savannah bristled at being introduced as merely a

friend, but smiled anyway. "It is so nice to meet you."
She shook hands with them both.

Edward whispered in her ear, "Don't take that the
wrong way, Savannah. Mum is making sure you aren't
pegged as my partner. She doesn't want you to be
subjected to all our friends' curiosity. She's protect-
ing you—something she's never done for any of my
other girlfriends."

Savannah felt her heart lift. *Wait. Other girlfriends?*

Edward scanned the crowd. "Uncle Howard,
where's Ian?"

"He should be here any second. He has the dramatic timing of Churchill. I don't know how he does
it, but he instinctively knows exactly when to make an
entrance."

"What's this? Is this a party?" Ian bounded from
the back door of the pub and positioned himself
between his parents. He pulled them both up to
stand beside him. "Thanks!"

Howard took a small oblong package wrapped in
brown paper and string from the inside pocket of his
jacket. "You're just in time for us to give you our
graduation present."

Kate smiled over at her husband and glanced over
the crowd until it quieted. She raised her head and
spoke in a clear voice. "I am pleased to welcome you
to our son Ian's graduation celebration. As most of
you know, there have been times in his young life
when we despaired at his wayward route."

She paused during the laughter. "But it appears
that after his melancholy was diagnosed and treated,
his path has come around to grab success by the ears."

Howard reached for his glass of red wine and

gestured for everyone to follow suit. "Let's raise our glasses to our graduate, and may his unusual path continue to surprise and inspire us all."

The crowd drank and chanted, "Hear! Hear!"

When the noise died down, Howard continued. "As most of you know, we're gifting Ian the modern version of the Grand Tour by sending him on a Mediterranean cruise. Along with that I have a bit of legacy to offer to our son and heir."

Ian turned to his father. Howard smiled. "Son, I know we haven't always seen eye to eye." The crowd laughed, and Ian pulled a crooked smile. "But tonight's celebration represents a milestone in your young life and this gift acknowledges your entrance into adulthood." Howard handed the package to Ian. "Your mum and I are extremely proud of you."

Ian flushed from his throat to his ears, then carefully put down his beer before slowly extending both hands to take the package. "I think I know what this is." He pulled on the string to release it and slipped off the brown paper to reveal an oblong, highly polished wooden box. He grinned, scrunched up the wrapping, and threw it at Edward, who caught it. "Yes! It's the pen." He opened the box and pulled out a black fountain pen decorated with gold filigree and held it up over his head. "It's my great-grandfather's pen!"

The crowd burst into applause and Ian hugged his surprised father and then gave his mother a giant kiss as well. "Thanks, Mum. I know you talked him into this, but I am so chuffed I can hardly speak." He retrieved his beer and held it high. He pointed his drink to his mother. "Cheers to family." Then he pointed it to his father. "Cheers to tradition."

Savannah tapped Edward on the shoulder. "What did Ian's dad mean by an unusual path?"

"Oh, uh, there were some problems when we were living in London. Typical trouble. Growing up rough."

The celebration settled into the comfortable mood of a late, late, late-night celebration. The kind when many participants' exits would be timed and noted in future gatherings with jibes such as "left a bit early," "couldn't quite keep up," and "stayed to the bitter end." The young people at the party would outgrow this stage soon enough. This was the time in their lives where all-night parties could be celebrated without too much suffering the following day.

Ian and Edward were only a few years apart. Ian had taken a long time to identify his goals, and his parents supported his late entry into college with joy. Whereas Edward had known from the start that he would never be at university. He was a natural-born chef and loved running his pub.

Edward nodded to his parents and he took Savannah by the hand. They all made their way to Ian's parents to congratulate them and thank them for the party. Edward clapped Ian on the back and spoke into his ear. "I know you'll be celebrating until they throw you out, but don't forget that Pa is giving us a ride. Our train from St. Albans to London St. Pancreas leaves at 5:00 in the morning. It's a direct train and we arrive at 5:35. Then we take the Tube from there to Heathrow Underground."

"Yeah, yeah, yeah. I know." Ian smacked his beer mug on the surface of the wooden table. The beer sloshed over and dripped onto Ian's trousers. "Bloody hell!" He swiped at the spots and then picked up his mug again.

"We can't miss the train." Edward enunciated each word. "You must be back at my house in time to leave at 4:45 sharp or we'll leave without you."

"I'll be there." Ian smiled his thousand-watt grin and returned to his friends.

Chapter 4

Savannah and Edward were standing in front of his parents' thatched cottage with their roll-aboard suitcases along with their backpacks. Edward was alternating tapping his foot with leaning over to look down the lane for Ian's oncoming car.

"You're driving me crazy. Aren't you Brits supposed to be calm? It says so on about a billion mugs."

"I'm not calm when it comes to Ian. We'll give him two more minutes and then we'll have to leave him to find his own way to Heathrow."

Savannah drew a hand through her curly black hair. "He's got plenty of time to make the flight. It departs at, what, 9:30?"

"Not the point. He said he would be here. You actually have to be at the gate at least thirty minutes before the flight takes off, and we still have to go through the international security check-in procedures."

Savannah felt like a marionette in a Shakespearean

dream. Maybe the effects of all the British accents—
or the jet lag—or plain over-excitement. Anyway, she
didn't fall asleep until just before the alarm sounded.

Edward looked at his watch one last time, shook
his head, and cursed under his breath. He opened
the cottage door. "Pa, it looks like we're going to go
without Ian. We have to go now so that Savannah
can get to her orientation meeting at the port in
Barcelona."

Ron backed the car out of their one-car garage
and they quickly loaded the luggage and piled into
the well used but pristine Rover. They had buckled
their seat belts when the small bright red MINI
screeched to a stop behind them. Ian rolled out of
the front seat and then pulled out a duffel, packed
tight as a tick, from the backseat.

"I told you I would be here." He grinned wide like
a playful monkey. "Can you pop the boot, Uncle
Ron? I can leave the MINI parked here, can't I? It
will save me the fee for the car park."

"If you must," Ron said. "Give me the keys in case
we have to move it."

Ian pressed the lock button, waited for the chirp
of the lock, then tossed the keys to his uncle.

The trunk of his uncle's car popped open and Ian
struggled to squeeze the duffel inside, then slammed
the lid shut. He slipped into the backseat beside
Savannah. He brought with him the distinct aroma
of an all-night drinking binge followed by a greasy
fried breakfast.

"Oomph!" said Savannah, and wrinkled her nose.
"You're smelling a bit ripe."

"Sorry. No time to go home and shower. You said you wanted to leave on time, right? Well, I made it."

"Fine," said Edward. "Let's go, Pa. We're not in the clear yet. There's no margin left if Savannah hopes to make her orientation meeting on time."

"Wait! Wait!" Edward's mum came out of the house at a quick trot with a small package held up high. "Edward, you almost forgot your"—she paused— "special tea."

"Tea?" said Savannah. She could hear the exasperation in her voice, because now there was a real chance they were going to be late. Not that they would fire her if she missed her practice session, but glass teams depended on each other's support in the production of their art. Unreliability was always punished by exclusion. It could get awkward.

"Oh, my God, thanks, Mum." Edward slipped out of the car and grabbed the little package out of Savannah's view, then stuffed it in his trouser pocket. He kissed his mum on the cheek and whispered, "You saved me. Thanks." He turned to Savannah, "I need this mixture to combat *mal de mer*. It's not very bad, but as long as I have this tea—no issues at all."

"Take care and have a good trip." Glenda waved as they finally drove off.

They arrived at the St. Albans train station in time, but only due to Sunday's light traffic. They picked up their tickets, sprinted to the platform, and arrived at the top of the stairs to see their train approaching the station.

"Just barely in time." As they boarded, Edward glared at Ian with a tightly clenched jaw. They stowed their luggage in the racks at the end of the carriage, then joined Savannah who had found a table in the middle of the carriage with seating for four.

"What luck!" said Ian. "It's the quiet carriage. That's good luck isn't it?"

Edward stowed his backpack in the overhead rack next to Savannah's. Savannah slipped into the window seat and Edward plopped into the aisle seat. Ian sat across from Savannah facing the back of the train. "How can you sit backward?" she asked. "I would get dizzy."

"No worries at all," said Ian. "I'm going to sleep. Since you're here, I don't have to worry about missing my stop." He took off his jacket, folded it into a lumpy pillow, stuffed it on his shoulder, smiled at them both, then promptly went to sleep.

"He's not a very good travel companion." She pinched her nose and waved her hand under it.

"More like baggage, actually." Edward lifted his eyebrows. "Not a great welcome to my family, luv. Sorry."

Savannah pulled Edward's arm around her shoulders. "Nothing can dull the thrill of my first train ride—not even a stinky cousin." She gazed out the window at small, stone-fenced pastures interrupted by small villages that provided a bird's eye view into their back gardens.

The stations began to fly by. They stopped for a few minutes at some of them and bypassed others. "I'm surprised at how much countryside there is for such a small country."

Edward slipped his arm around her shoulders and pulled her in closer. They watched the countryside swoosh by until the scratchy PA system announced their stop for London St. Pancreas.

"Hey, Ian. This is where we transfer to the Underground." Edward shook Ian with a fair bit of enthusiasm. They gathered their personal luggage and made their way out to the platform.

After they had stowed their luggage again and settled in, Savannah felt more comfortable with the train system. Ian had needed continuous monitoring as he slept everywhere—even leaning against the station wall on the platform.

On the hour ride to Heathrow, Savannah was shocked to realize that she, too, had slept on the bouncy carriage.

The two-hour flight was mercifully routine and they all slept until the captain announced their clearance to land. In Barcelona, they gathered their luggage and hailed a taxi to the cruise port.

The ship was enormous and resembled a docked fifteen-story hotel.

The intense activity level signaled the total opposite of relaxation. The organized frenzy reminded Savannah of riding the bumper cars at the Florida State Fair—lots of scurrying and crossed paths to move in a circle.

Edward and Ian handed in their cabin-tagged luggage to the porters and kept their backpacks. They approached the terminal building.

Ian stopped abruptly, causing Edward to stumble into him. "Hey, what's wrong? Have you forgotten something? Is it your medications? Don't tell me that because I don't think we can get our folks to drop them off before the ship leaves. You are still taking the antidepressants, right?"

"I'm still taking them. But, no, it's not that. I have a good supply; I thought I recognized someone from our dockland days leaning out over the railing there." Ian pointed to a large balcony at the bow of the ship.

"Really?" Edward's voice raised several octaves.

"It would be just too bizarre. I mean, that was back when we were young and in a massive amount of trouble. The images from back then are a mixed-up jumble in my memory. It was a terrible time and we were lucky to slip away so easily. It was ugly." He shook his head. "No, I must be mistaken. I thought it was that big guy that we only saw occasionally. He was such a bully. He always scared the devil out of us. Whew! What dark days they were." He started toward the terminal.

It was a chaotic mix of elderly travelers, young adventurers, and large families with rambunctious and squealing children. There was a feeling of anticipation and excitement that made Savannah feel excited in turn.

"This is where we part," she said. "You two are passengers and I'm an employee." She pointed to the door labeled STAFF ENTRANCE. "They told me to use this door."

Edward grabbed her hand and held it. "Hang on a tic." He turned to Ian. "Go on ahead. I'll catch up to you inside." He turned back to Savannah. "When will I see you?"

She gulped and kissed him on the cheek. "I'll text you as soon as I find out. Because I'm actually an employee of the Crystal Glass Company and not of the Luminary Cruise Line, I understand I can have meals at any of the public restaurants. I'll find out more in the orientation briefing. Now, go before I embarrass your formal British self with an outrageous public display of affection."

Edward released her hand. He hurried through the door to the cruise terminal. She watched him meet up with Ian inside the building. It was clear that Ian had no idea where he was and what he was supposed to do next.

Savannah hitched her backpack to a more comfortable position, grabbed the handle of her wheeled suitcase, and headed for the staff entrance.

She opened the door and was greeted by a young man wearing a white uniform who asked for her papers. He checked to ensure that she had all the right documents. "You need to wait in area four." He pointed her to another door that led to a plain room with four sections of metal chairs with a *4* taped to the back wall. The waiting people sat in silence with their luggage in front of them. Most were taking advantage of the time to check social media on their phones.

Her group was the smallest at three people, and all of them appeared to be entertainers. The other groups were divided into maintenance personnel and service staff, and she couldn't figure out what the third group was but they were better dressed and were accompanied with very expensive luggage. She noted that everyone had followed the explicit instructions for how much baggage could be brought aboard: not much.

Her instructions had been to pack very few casual clothes for the week but to include at least one formal outfit should it be required. Her demonstration uniform shirts would be supplied by Crystal Glass Works, and she had been given an allowance to purchase two pair of shorts, one pair of trousers, and incidentals.

The door opposite the one she entered opened and a small man, elegantly outfitted in an all-white uniform, came into the room and scanned it from end to end. He cradled a bulging portfolio with one hand and his other hand held on to the doorknob. "Savannah Webb?" he called as he continued to scan the room with a squinted concentration.

Savannah stood and raised her hand. "Here, sir."

He waved his hand. "Come, come. The sooner we get your orientation completed, the sooner I can get back on schedule."

Grabbing the handle of her suitcase and the strap of her backpack, Savannah strode quickly to the doorway and went through.

"I'm Sheridan Nathanial, but everyone here calls me Danny. Welcome to the entertainment staff of the cruise ship *Obscura*." He closed the door to the waiting room and led the way down a plain beige hallway in need of a paint and polish.

Ah, this is the behind-the-scenes look. Industrial beige and gray eau de factory.

Danny stopped at one of the doors off the hallway and opened it. They entered a small interview room and he motioned for Savannah to sit in a metal chair. He sat behind a plain folding table on another metal chair. "Hand over your paperwork, and we'll get this done and over with as quickly as possible."

Savannah pulled her paperwork from the outside pocket of her backpack, placed it on the slightly grimy surface of the table, and pushed it in front of Danny. She felt an urge to chatter, but suppressed it. Sometimes, that urge meant that she was uncomfortable and her nervous words could cause trouble.

Danny flipped through her packet and nodded as he looked at each document. "These are all great." He looked up. "It's a pleasure to see some organization skills." He shook his head as he returned her package. "You have no idea the sort of disarray I have to put up with. Anyway, let me get your cruise card."

Savannah raised her eyebrows as he rose. He turned back to look at her.

"Don't worry, everyone has been as green as you are now and most have not only survived it, but thrived. I'll show you around after we get all this administrative stuff finished."

Savannah filed everything back in her backpack, waited a few minutes, then pulled out her eBook reader. After half an hour, he returned with a badge. "This is your identification, cash card, access badge—everything. Don't lose it. Let's go. I'm running late."

Warm welcome, buddy—not my fault you're running late.

Savannah slung the backpack over her shoulder and grabbed the suitcase handle. They left the terminal building at a trot and headed out a back door. If he had hoped to further intimidate her—he failed. She was a runner with a longer stride than his.

Out onto the pier, Savannah stopped dead in her

tracks and tipped her head back to see the gleaming hulk in front of her. It was sixteen decks high and over a thousand feet long. She tightened her grip on her backpack as she felt like she was going to tip backward.

"Yes, it's pretty impressive. One of the biggest. I think it's the best. Chop! Chop! Keep moving!" Danny snapped.

They entered the ship through a loading door and Danny took his card out of his pocket. He handed it to a white-shirted security guard who swiped it through a security machine. The machine made a distinctive *bloop*. He stepped through the small access gate and motioned for Savannah to do the same. Her card made the same strange sound. "You need to swipe in and out each time you leave the ship at any port."

Savannah nodded and followed him down a wide, gray monotone corridor that was frantic with activity. Huge luggage cages were being dragged to service elevators. Large skids of food were traveling by forklift to the kitchen larders, and crew members were passing in and out of the security gate. The sound level had to be above a safe decibel level.

"This way," shouted Danny over the din. He opened a door to a staircase also painted a uniform gray. Savannah tucked in the handle of her suitcase and carried it up the stairs to deck 2.

My tai chi classes are again coming to the rescue. Of course, I would collapse in a dead faint rather than ask for help.

After a long walk down a plain industrial corridor, he stopped in front of a bare door. "Place your card here on the keypad."

Savannah did and the cabin door opened in to reveal a compact crew cabin furnished with a single bed and a tiny couch with a desk/vanity/TV across from it. She could see a minuscule bathroom and an open closet—if a school locker was your definition of a closet.

"Get settled. There's a phone on the desk. Call your team leader and he'll take it from here. Good luck." He left.

The reality of being a crew member hit her with a fluttery feeling down deep in her belly.

I'm here. I've never done anything like this before. I've never felt this nervous about anything related to glass before. Buck up. Start moving.

Savannah stuffed her suitcase inside the open closet/locker and plopped down on the couch with her backpack still on. She needed a moment to catch her breath after the sprint up the stairs and down the hall. She needed a moment to process everything that had happened in the last few days. She needed a moment to reclaim her self-confidence.

I'm here and I'm going to do my best. Removing her backpack and placing it on the couch beside her, she dug her paperwork out and dialed the number of her team leader. He said he would stop by as soon as he could.

Savannah sat on the bed and bounced. It was an excellent bed. She slipped off her shoes and stretched out.

I'll close my eyes for just a minute.

In that minute she fell into a deep sleep.

Chapter 5

Sunday afternoon, Barcelona cruise port, Spain

Savannah was startled out of her nap by a brisk knocking on her cabin door. A tall, sturdy, thirty-something man with thick black hair grinned, revealing a discolored front tooth. He stuck out his hand. "Hi, I'm Eric Barone, your team leader on this ocean adventure."

Trying not to stare at the tooth was more than her jet-lagged brain could handle. "I'm Savannah Webb. I'm so excited to work in the Hot Shop."

He grinned again, tilting his head so the front tooth was on full display. "It's okay. I know about the tooth. One of the things about working on a cruise ship is that there's no easy way to get to your dentist."

Savannah could feel the confusion on her face.

"Yes, there's a dentist here on the ship for the crew's routine care and emergency care for the guests, but my problem is merely cosmetic. The overlay came off last week and I won't be able to get to my specialist dentist until the end of my contract. That's three weeks from now." He winked at her.

"That's a long time to look that way. I don't think I could open my mouth."

"Management isn't very happy, but they're also not willing to send me home at their expense for a tooth. They're already burning extra budget just to send you out here."

"How have you been managing with just the two of you?"

"It's difficult because the pieces we create are challenging and typically require at least a two- and sometimes three-person team. The dreadful part is that the commentary is short-changed during the demonstration. That's what the audience enjoys most. Anyway, let me show you the Hot Shop and get you ready for this evening's show."

"Certainly." Savannah grabbed her room key, slipped it into her back pocket, and followed Eric to the forward staff elevator. He punched the button for deck 16 and they walked out into the open-air glassblowing studio.

"We have a little stage door to act as a barrier between us and the audience. The cruise director likes to limit our access to the public so that it makes our public appearances seem special."

"Does that work?"

He stood still and looked up in thought. "I guess it does. Seems silly to me. But the proof is in the results. Our auctions are standing-room only and the pieces sell for thousands."

"Auction?"

"Right. The organization that supports the Hot

Shop demonstrations is strictly nonprofit. That means that all artwork must be sold to benefit charitable organizations. It works out beautifully—we get to demonstrate glassblowing and travel the world while earning a substantial salary. It's a pretty cool gig."

He handed her a clipboard with a checklist already in place. "This is what you do beginning thirty minutes before a performance. If you know that the furnaces are already on, you can wait until fifteen minutes, but always check. The audience will get antsy if we take too much time in preparation. They want to see glass being blown."

Savannah took the clipboard and held up the Hot Shop logo pen tied to it with a frazzled piece of string. "Really? People steal your pens? Aren't they in all the cabins?"

"Well, yes, but those have the generic cruise ship logo. When we came up with our pen a few years ago, sales in the gift shops skyrocketed. That also goes to the nonprofit charity." He shrugged his shoulders.

"Still seems like a paranoid bank teller's solution."

"For us, it's the convenience. If something goes missing during a demonstration, it's a pain to get it replaced. You're going to find that this gig will keep you very busy. Go ahead and get the pre-show checks done."

Savannah smiled as she untwirled the pen from its tangled loops. "Busy is good."

"When was your training?"

Savannah wrote in the date and time on the sheet. "Let's see. That was less than a year ago. I had to drop out at the last minute for personal reasons."

Eric raised his eyebrows.

"My dad died unexpectedly. I took over the family stained glass shop."

She looked at the list of pre-checks and it hadn't changed much since her training sessions at Crystal Glass Works. "I enjoyed the training and it looks like they have duplicated everything on ship very closely." She started turning on the equipment, checking the air vents and fans, and making sure all the tools were in place.

Eric folded his arms and leaned against the stainless-steel table and offered suggestions when she looked for something that had been moved. The whole pre-check took about ten minutes. Then she signed the checklist and handed the clipboard back to Eric.

"Now don't get oversensitive. We do this before every performance for everyone's safety." He took the checklist and double-checked each setting and action.

Savannah crossed her arms and leaned against the stainless-steel table—unconsciously mimicking Eric's exact pose while he had been watching her. She could feel her body temperature raise, and her jaws tensed into gritted teeth.

Cool down. Like he said this is for everyone's safety. We're at sea most of the time. I've gotten used to working with cold glass that you can cut and grind with your fingers. This is working with molten glass. It's for safety, not a personal insult to my work.

Eric finished and stood in front of her. "Congratulations! You're the first one I've double-checked who has gotten every single task perfect. Well done!"

Savannah could feel the unwanted tension leave the back of her neck. "Thanks."

He wound the string around the pen, then put the clipboard back on a little hook by their stage door. "Now let's practice your demonstration piece. Since you're only here for this cruise, I think it best that you should make color variations of the same basic vase. Is that good for you?"

"Why?" Savannah frowned. "I've got experience in more than half a dozen demonstration pieces. Why am I to be restricted?" The tenseness at the back of her neck returned.

"I know how you feel. On my first cruise contract, I was limited to one style for the first week. It's because the environment is so different from a land-based hot shop."

"But I've had the training in the mock-up shop."

"Right, but we're at sea. The ship is moving when we perform. We need to get familiar with your movements, and, more importantly, you need to adjust your performance. A wave can bounce the ship at any time. We have these safety practices in place to protect ourselves. I'm sorry, but that's the way it has to be."

"Of course." Savannah pulled a hand through her black curls. "What was I thinking? This setup is so close to the Crystal Glass Works training hot shop, I forgot about that."

"No worries, we repeat this lecture for each new gaffer." Eric smiled. "Now, go ahead and make that fluted vase."

Savannah stood in front of the furnace and inhaled deeply. *This is my audition. I hope my emergency practice session over at Zen's Glass Shop was enough*. She exhaled and selected a container of bright blue frit and sprinkled it on the stainless-steel table.

Eric walked over to the rack of blowpipes that were being heated in a separate electric furnace and pulled out one of the smallest and lightweight pipes. "This should be about the size that will be comfortable for you."

Should I be safe and make the simplest fluted vase possible? Nope, I'm going to make a stunning fluted vase. If I'm limited to one demonstration piece—each one will be spectacular.

"Thanks, but I'm going to use one of the larger ones. My student specialty at Pilchuck was large pieces. I'm stronger than I look."

She got another container and sprinkled a large quantity of light orange frit on the table along the front edge, and for dramatic effect, she added four groupings of white stringers. She then picked up the second to the largest blowpipe and put it in the glass furnace to gather a small amount of clear glass on the end. She knew she hadn't had much recent experience, but at one time she had been a Pilchuck star student. There was a reason for that.

Savannah worked quickly and expertly, building up a large mass of molten glass that she first rolled into the blue frit, added more clear glass, and rolled into the light orange frit. The blowpipe was getting heavy, but she knew she was strong enough to handle the larger piece.

Working cautiously, but swiftly, she added another layer of clear glass to the vase and rolled it on the white stringers, picking them up into the molten glass in little patterned clusters. She continued to reheat and smooth the piece until all the new glass was incorporated into the work and it was the color mix she wanted.

She then signaled for Eric to take her place on the work seat. She took a pair of pinch pliers and pulled the glass out a couple of inches. While pulling, she twisted it to the left, creating a swirl effect. She exchanged places with Eric on the bench and used a wet wooden shaping form to round and elongate the vase. Then she picked up a stack of wet newspapers to additionally form and shape the glass.

The steam rising from the soaked paper made her smile. She reheated the piece, then added the last layer of clear glass and continued to shape the vase. It was now over eighteen inches long. Finally, she flattened the piece with a square wooden paddle with a handle called a battledore. It helped her finish off the bottom of the base.

"You should start the base now," said Eric.

Savannah frowned at the unnecessary direction. Unnecessary in her mind.

He gathered a glob of glass about the size of a golf ball and exchanged places with Savannah on the bench. Savannah reheated the vase by twirling it slowly in the furnace. They exchanged places again and Eric reheated the foot of the vase. In about ten seconds he moved back to the bench and pressed it into Savannah's vase.

Then they rolled the piece in perfect unison until she was sure it was attached. Then she took a metal pincher tool and scored the top of the vase at the place where it joined her blowpipe. Dipping her

calipers in water, she let it run into the scored groove.
With a nod to Eric, she tapped the blowpipe and the
vase detached from her blowpipe, with the vase still
attached on Eric's blowpipe.

Eric handed his blowpipe to Savannah and she reheated it in the furnace. After spinning it until it was
hot enough, she took it to the work seat and formed
a hole in the top of the vase. She repeated a series of
steps that reheated and formed a deep cavity in the
vase. After a final reheating, she snipped several cuts
in the lip and stood on a small bench. With a dramatic swirl, the lip of the vase flared into the shape
of a tulip.

She felt her confidence rise at the ease with which
she handled the heavy base on the punty. It was one
of her concerns that perhaps her shoulder and hand
strength had weakened during the time she had
been running Webb's Glass Shop. She hadn't been
able to keep in practice with only a few hours now
and then at the nearby McClellan Hot Shop. Her
grip felt strong and steady.

"Well done!" said Eric. "Now let's go for the last
step and get this beauty into the annealing oven."

Savannah scored the vase below the foot and again
dripped water in the crease. Eric put on a heavy pair
of oven gloves that reached his elbows. He placed his
hands under the vase and then Savannah hit the blowpipe with a sharp tap. Instead of landing safely into
Eric's gloves, the beautiful vase split above the score
line, then took a wild spin. Savannah felt a sudden
coldness in her core as the vase fell to the deck and
shattered into ruins.

Chapter 6

"Can you imagine the shocked look on my face," Savannah said to Edward and Ian at one of the outdoor tables. She had an iced tea in contrast to hot tea for the Morris men. "I was mortified. I could barely speak above a whisper."

"At least it wasn't at a performance," said Edward.

"Right, but Eric waved it off. He says misjudging the temperature of a work in progress is the most common cause for breakage. I can't think what got into my head to create such a complex vase."

"I'll bet I know," said Edward. "Could it have been perhaps a tiny bit of an insult to ask you to stick to a simple piece?" He took a cookie from the plate of assorted treats he had gathered from the dessert station.

"Hmm." Savannah twisted her lips to one side. "Busted. That restriction certainly raised my hackles. It was wonderfully kind of him to let me have a practice session without an audience—and then I go and mess it up. It was a terrible mess, by the way. That was a lot of glass to sweep away."

Ian took his third slice of chocolate cake and noticed Edward's raised eyebrows. "What? Look at their size. They're ridiculously tiny. Look, not even an inch square." Ian plopped the sweet concoction into his mouth whole. "Barely a mouthful," he mumbled around the cake.

Edward turned to Savannah. "When's your first demonstration? We don't want to miss it." He elbowed Ian.

"Oomph. Too right."

Savannah enjoyed being in the middle of the Morris boys' banter. "It's right after the sail-away party around the pool."

"Nope, I don't want to miss that." Ian reached for the last square of chocolate cake. "Not for the world."

Savannah smiled and shook her black curls. "The demonstration starts at six o'clock. It will be only about thirty minutes after pulling away from the dock. The seas are expected to be calm, so we should be good to go. I'd better get going. I haven't met the other gaffer and I'd at least like to say hello before we start swinging around molten glass." She leaned over to squeeze Edward's hand.

He quickly gave her a kiss on the cheek. "Break a leg."

She went to her cabin and put on one of the Hot Shop logo shirts and a pair of tan khaki slacks with her new deck shoes with low white socks. She reached the demonstration area a little early and grabbed the clipboard and started performing the checklist. She had nearly completed the list when she heard her name.

"Savannah," spoke a smoothly feminine Southern voice.

"We're here," said another voice of the same tone.

Savannah stood stock still at the sound of those very familiar voices. They couldn't possibly be here on board.

Turning around, Savannah saw the undeniable truth. Her octogenarian perpetual students had somehow managed to attend her demonstrations at sea. To date, they had signed up for every class that Webb's Glass Shop offered. But, still, on a cruise ship?

"Ladies! I'm stunned to see you. Delighted of course, but stunned." She greeted the Rosenberg twins who were placing small, flat stadium cushions on the first metal bench of the viewing area. "How did you manage—"

"We usually take at least two—" said Rachel.

"—and sometimes three cruises a year. We wouldn't have missed this for the world," said Faith.

Savannah shook her head. "Well, your record is intact for perfect attendance."

The twins tilted their heads toward each other and smiled.

Rachel leaned in to whisper to Savannah. "We know you always get involved with a crime of some sort."

Faith leaned in to whisper as well. "We're here to be part of your posse."

They both leaned back with a very pleased-with-themselves look on their faces.

"I don't think that will be happening here. It's a cruise. This is a vacation. You're very early. The show doesn't start for another half hour," said Savannah.

"We wanted to make sure—" said Rachel.

"—we didn't miss a thing," finished Faith. "Also, we heard from some of the other suite guests that your show is so popular there will be standing room only."

Faith looked around at the three empty rows of metal benches. Each bench had a long straight part directly in front of the Hot Shop and then the benches had shorter arms that angled to hug the six-foot-high glass partition in front of the demonstration area.

"We were so lucky to get a last-minute cabin on this cruise," said Rachel.

"Not only that, but we found out that we use the same travel agent as you and Edward. Jan Brown was so sweet." Rachel looked over to her sister. "We haven't met her yet, but she sounds wonderful over the phone. Very efficient."

"I think knowing you helped us get our suite," said Faith. "We said we knew you two. She laughed and said that it's a small world."

"Oh, the suite is gorgeous," said Rachel. "And it comes with a full-time butler. Can you imagine?"

"We've been saying for a long, long time that we need to start spending some of Daddy's money one of these days," said Faith. Rachel beamed a thousand-watt smile. "And now we're finally doing it."

"You'll love Albert. He's so . . ." Faith halted.

"Substantial?" finished Rachel.

They dissolved in peals of laughter.

"Don't frown, Savannah," said Faith. "He really does look like Don Corleone from the Godfather movies."

Savannah turned back to continue her demonstration preparations and also to get her pre-show nerves under control.

Just as the twins had predicted, several couples had taken seats in the first row on the right side and three people had claimed seats on the left side.

Edward arrived around the corner and his eyebrows shot up. "Ladies! What on earth? I'm gob smacked, but I guess this is one of Savannah's classes. You are in extreme danger of being labeled as serial glass groupies." He sat to the right of the twins.

Savannah smiled. "Thanks for coming. It's lovely to see familiar faces out there. You too, Edward."

He smiled and looked around. "Ian was supposed to be here as well. He might still be dancing at the sail-away party. It got quite noisy and then he found a group of new friends. Lots of fun for him, but I don't expect he'll show up for this demonstration."

"You're the one I want to see." She laid one hand over her heart and patted her chest.

Edward blew her a kiss. "Good luck! Watch your temperature *and* your temper."

Savannah turned to the sound of the stage door closing. Eric waved a hand and she returned to the stage.

"I see you have a fan club. Is that your young man?"

"Yes, that's my Edward. He and his cousin are along to celebrate Ian's graduation from Bristol University."

Eric squinted. "He looks familiar, but I can't place where I might know him."

"He's from St. Albans originally, but he moved to St. Petersburg, Florida, a couple of years ago to buy a pub. It's next door to my glass shop."

"Doesn't ring a bell," he said. "It will come to me eventually."

The stage door opened again and out came the third member of the team. Savannah walked over and stretched out her hand. "Hi, I'm Savannah Webb. You must be Alan Viteri."

Alan was a sturdy man with streaky blond dreadlocks tied at the base of his neck with a red bandanna. His faded logo shirt sported dime-sized holes and his tennis shoes looked positively ancient. In fact, there was a piece of duct tape around the toe of the left shoe.

"Good to see ya." He shook her hand, bobbed his head, and turned to Eric. "What's the plan?"

Eric made a fist and pressed it to his forehead. "Alan, we discussed this last night and again this morning at breakfast. Don't you remember what I said?"

"Come on, Eric." Alan splayed his hands out palms up. "You know my memory is shot. The only place my brain works like it did before is here in the Hot Shop. You know that. Now what's the plan?"

"Sorry. I know that. I get frustrated sometimes because I worked with you so much before the accident."

"Those memories are gone," said Alan with a matter-of-fact tone.

Eric slapped Alan on the back. "No worries. We'll perform in the same order as we have always done. One of you will be first. I'll always be second, the other of you will be third, and if we need to fill time, I'll do another. Alan, you'll be first with one of your angelfishes, then I'll create one of my goblets. Savannah will create a fluted vase and if we need another piece, I'll make a platter."

Eric looked at Alan. "Got it?" Alan nodded.

"I need to hear you say it out loud, Alan," reminded Eric. "I need to know you heard me."

Alan scrunched his brows. "Right, I'm first, then you, then Savannah, then maybe you. Right?"

Eric said, "Perfect."

He turned to Savannah. "Got it?"

Savannah nodded. "Yes, understood."

"Good, I'll do the narration for Alan and you can be his assistant. You can narrate for me with Alan as my assistant. Then I'll assist you while Alan narrates. Okay?"

Savannah nodded again and then Eric said, "Let's get this show on the sea." Eric clipped the battery pack to the back of his shorts and fixed the microphone to his head. He tapped the little black foam-covered microphone. "Testing, testing. Can you hear me there in the back?"

Savannah turned to look at the audience, and sure enough, it was standing room only. The cruisers in the back shouted yes followed by some thumbs-up. Then Eric began a practiced introduction speech.

Alan pranced—actually pranced—over to the rack that held the various colors of glass.

"Anyone here know what that stuff is that Alan is pouring onto the table there?" Eric asked the audience.

Rachel and Faith both raised their hands and shouted, "Frit."

Eric nodded. "Yes, to the ladies down in front. Frit is crushed glass that will be melted into the angelfish that Alan is going to create for us today. He's using both black and white, which will give the body a speckled appearance. He's also going to use some thin rods of glass sometimes called stringers to make some stripes."

Savannah wondered if this much detail was a way of guiding Alan through the demonstration. He seemed a little out of it. Eric must be overwhelmed with taking on a cruise ship beginner along with shepherding Alan.

I need to at least stop him from worrying about me.

The demonstration progressed with no problems and Savannah was relieved that her fluted vase was even larger than her practice piece and landed safely into Eric's gloved hands.

After the performance, Eric fielded questions from the audience.

"What happens to the pieces that you make?"

"I'm glad you asked. Since we are the nonprofit arm of Crystal Glass Works here on board this beautiful ship, we aren't allowed to sell our work."

There were audible groans from the audience.

Eric raised his hand. "However, we are permitted to auction them to the highest bidder for the benefit of several charities. This week, the charities are United Way, Make-A-Wish of America, and City Year."

Someone from the back row yelled out, "When is the auction?"

Eric stood taller to look at the man at the back. "It works like this. On the last evening on board, there will be an auction in the same event space as the art auctions. We'll display our pieces up here for the duration of the cruise, then we place each of the pieces we have created this week up for bid. Any final questions?"

Eric paused. "Thank you for coming and I hope you enjoyed our demonstration."

He unhooked the battery pack and microphone headset, then walked out to stand in front of the access gate. He talked to the audience members who had additional questions or wanted to thank him for the show.

Savannah and Alan began cleaning up the Hot Shop in preparation for a complete shutdown for the evening. When no one remained of the audience, Eric slapped Alan on the back. "You did great! Perfect performance."

"I told ya. See you at family lunch tomorrow." Alan scooted through the stage door.

Eric walked over to Savannah and gave her a pat on the back. "Good job. It looks like you've got your rhythm back."

"Thanks. Like the cliché, it's like riding a bike."

Eric nodded. "It looks like you used to ride a racing bike. That was awesome."

"What's family lunch?"

Eric shook his head. "It's a way for us to stay connected during our three-month contracts. We try to eat together like a family at least once a day. It helps keep us semi-sane."

Savannah glanced over at the stage door. "I'm curious about Alan. What's wrong with his memory?"

"Boy, that's a sad story. Last year on this very same itinerary, he was hit by a car while riding one of those iconic Vespa scooters."

"In Italy? Like in the movie, *Roman Holiday*?"

"Yes, it was a complete miracle that he wasn't killed outright."

"Was he wearing a helmet?" asked Savannah.

"Thankfully, yes. It's not the law in Italy, which just mystifies me beyond words." He scanned the work area and found one more frit container to put away. "Anyway, he suffered a closed brain injury. If he hadn't been strong and fit, he likely wouldn't have survived."

"Who hit him?"

"The police never found out. It was a hit-and-run. Anyway, his short-term memory is erratic and sometimes nonexistent. His doctors call it a Swiss cheese memory. Some things are fine, but some years and some events are gone."

"He performs well, though."

"That's muscle memory. We all have that."

Savannah glanced out and saw Edward waiting at the edge of the seating area. "Are we done for the evening?"

"Yes, we'll meet for lunch at the buffet at one o'clock tomorrow to go over plans for the day's work. But, you're free until then." He looked over to the waiting Edward. "Just don't get caught in a stateroom. That's against the rules." He said the words sternly, but then winked.

Savannah walked around the audience glass barrier and gave Edward's hand a quick squeeze. "Whew! I'm glad that went well. I didn't want to break another vase."

"Are you off duty now?"

"Yep. I'm hot and sweaty. I'll shower and change

into something clean. You go to the main dining room and I'll get dinner with the crew to get a little better acquainted. Where do you want to meet afterward?"

"How about on the stern? I love watching the wake of the ship highlighted in the moonlight."

As agreed, Edward met her at one of the large outside tables overlooking the stern of the ship on the same deck as the buffet restaurant. He approached the table with two little old ladies trailing along right behind him. They had changed into matching outfits that featured large tropical fish on long flowing dresses and their feet were decked out with bright orange espadrilles.

Edward smiled ruefully. "Rachel and Faith wanted to see you after the demonstration, but they had a spa appointment. We had dinner together in the main dining room, so they asked if they could tag along for a few minutes. I thought that would be fine with you."

"Of course, what spa treatment did you have?" She looked at the sweet faces that were flush with a rosy luster in their cheeks and a bright sparkle in their eyes.

"We had facials and manicures." They both spread out their hands and wiggled fingers polished with a scandalous scarlet red.

Rachel tapped Edward on the arm. "That cousin of yours didn't show up for dinner. Is that a problem?"

"Not really. He's his own man and I'm betting he's finding the freedom from studying for his exams to be intoxicating as well as the unlimited beverage package. I told him to meet us here."

Faith piped up. "Do you think he will?"

"Yes, I pulled the 'I am the biggest cousin' card. He'll be here."

Faith leaned over to Rachel. "Tell her."

Rachel leaned away. "We don't have to—I wanted it to be a surprise."

"What surprise?" Edward pulled out two chairs for the twins to sit. "I'm in charge of all surprises, you know." He stared at each one of them through his eyebrows.

"Oh, it's nothing that big," said Faith as she settled into the chair.

"I think it's big," argued Rachel.

"I disagree," replied Faith.

"Oh, stop! We're annoying everyone." Rachel patted Savannah's hand. "We're going to buy one of your pieces at the auction," said Rachel.

"Here you are! I've been looking everywhere." Ian grabbed a chair from the nearest table and pulled it up between Savannah and Faith. He sat his nearly full pint of beer on the table with enough force to cause the beer to slosh over. "Oopsy!"

Edward leaped up. "I'll get a napkin."

"You're drunk, young man." Faith poked him in the shoulder with her red fingernail. "That's disgraceful so early in the evening."

A crew member hustled over and efficiently mopped up the spilled beer and handed Ian a cloth napkin. Edward also returned with a dinner napkin to help. Ian sat holding his beer and watched the activity. "At least I didn't spill it on any of the ladies." He raised his glass to Savannah and to the twins, then took a deep swig. "I've had a bad shock and need the fortification." His speech was slurred and again his arm wobbled before he placed his pint glass onto the table.

Savannah took the beer and held it away from Ian's grabbing hand. Ian glared at her and she glared back. "You've had enough for a while. What shock?"

Ian leaned back in the dining chair and balanced it on two legs. "It's one of my primary-school mates. He's not what I would call a mate. He made my life miserable—the bully."

Edward sat down after giving his sopping napkin to the server. "What? I don't remember any bullies."

Ian slowly turned his head and made an obvious effort to focus on Edward. It was apparently hard work. "Not for you. You were a big lad, remember? Nobody messed with you. It wasn't the same for us little cousins."

"Who is it?"

"I'm not going to tell. He hasn't changed one bit." Ian struggled out of the chair to a nearly upright position. "I'm getting another drink. Mum and Dad spent all this money for me to enjoy meself—and that's what I'm going to do."

He lurched away toward the bar on the other side of the ship.

Savannah placed a hand on Edward's arm. "He's completely plastered. Is he going to be all right?"

"He's a grown man. At least we don't have to worry about drunk driving. He can't get off the ship until our first port."

"I hear from the crew that an unexpected storm has formed within the last few hours," said Savannah.

"It sometimes happens at this time of year. They call it a medicane—Mediterranean hurricane. We might miss our first port due to high winds and choppy conditions."

Rachel frowned. "I'm worried about Ian. He seemed so angry about meeting this school bully."

Faith frowned as well. "Let's hope this doesn't end badly."

Chapter 7

Monday, at sea

"You should stay," said a drowsy Edward, pulling on Savannah's arm as she slipped out of his single bed.

"Now, don't be difficult." Savannah slipped out of his grasp. "Ian should be back any minute. None of the porters will be in the hallway and I can get back to crew quarters without being seen." She planted a warm kiss on his forehead and pulled the covers over him. "Go back to sleep. I'll see you at breakfast with everyone else."

He closed his green eyes and snuggled down into the white bed linen. "Don't forget to turn the magnet around. I'll see you tomorrow. I mean today. I mean at breakfast." He drifted off.

Savannah quietly opened the cabin door and peeked both ways down the length of the corridor. As she had been told by Eric, none of the porters were in sight and for the first time since she boarded, the ship seemed so peaceful.

She flipped the smiley face magnet from upside down to right side up as the signal the cousins had agreed to use to indicate that they wanted privacy.

Once she made her way into the elevator, she relaxed. No one would know where she had been. She punched the elevator button for the top deck to get some fresh air before heading to her cabin, and walked to the stern. She stopped short when she saw the Rosenberg twins leaning against the rail only a few feet from a still swaying Ian.

Feeling like a coward, she retreated to the elevator. Savannah didn't really want to answer their pointed questions about the whereabouts of Edward. They were always accepting and supportive about her relationship with Edward, but entirely too curious. Avoiding them was easier than answering a barrage of questions. She made her way to her room.

When morning dawned, she met Edward and the Rosenberg twins in the foyer of the main dining room for breakfast. Edward gave her a side hug. "How's your cabin?"

"Perfectly fine," said Savannah. "Not as luxurious as your digs, but a little noisy. Even with the door shut, I can hear everything that happens in the hallway. But, as soon as I fell asleep—nothing. Where's Ian?"

"I expect that he's a bit delicate this morning."

Savannah frowned. "Delicate?"

Edward grinned. "That's Brit for suffering a hangover."

"How long are we going to wait for him?" said

Rachel, tapping the face of her watch with a beautifully manicured fingernail. "This sea air is whipping up my appetite."

"We agreed to meet for breakfast, right?" said Faith.

Edward frowned. "He didn't come back to the cabin last night, but I more or less expected that he would find a shipboard companion—perhaps not this fast, but it's only going on nine o'clock."

Faith piped up. "But in our family, on time meant that you were actually late. We're always—"

"—at least ten minutes early," finished Rachel.

"Let's get a table for six and see if his new friend will be joining us." Savannah hooked Edward by the arm and they were seated.

Their waiter gave them each a menu and glanced at the two empty seats. "Are you waiting for the rest of your party or do you want to order now?"

Edward said, "We'll order now. We're not sure if they're having breakfast."

Edward leaned over to whisper in Savannah's ear. "He didn't take last night's meds. He really needs to take them."

Savannah reached over to put her hand in his. "He'll show up. Don't worry."

Rachel unfolded the linen napkin and placed her cutlery on each side of her breakfast plate. "He was up on the top deck with us late last night."

"It was actually early this morning," said Faith. "We've been a little jet-lagged and thought a little wave watching would help us relax."

"It certainly did. Once we got to sleep, we didn't wake up until a bit past seven," said Rachel. "That's very late."

"I think it was the sea air and the fact that we didn't actually sleep at all on the two flights from Tampa International Airport."

"Hang on, I'll ring him up. I still have my international calling plan." Edward pulled out his phone and waited. It seemed to go to voice mail, because Edward said, "Ian, we're at breakfast in the main dining room. Catch us up when you can."

"What about leaving a message on the cabin phone, too?" asked Savannah.

Edward nodded and left the same message.

The food was fabulous and filling with everyone ordering either eggs benedict, omelets, or freshly prepared Belgium waffles. The orange juice was freshly squeezed and the coffee hot and strong.

"I could get used to this kind of service," said Savannah as she drained the last of the orange juice from Edward's glass.

"We could get another glass, you know." He looked around for their server.

"No, I'm good, but aren't you concerned about Ian?"

"You read me like a book," said Edward. "I'm not worried especially, but he's pretty social and seems to have taken a shine to you. I'm surprised he's not here making you laugh."

"Do you think we should find him?" Savannah put her napkin on her plate and stood.

Edward looked at his watch. "Well, it's going on ten o'clock and he should have surfaced by now. I know he hasn't been in the room. His, um, vitamins haven't been touched. He's still young enough to bounce back rapidly from a party night."

"How should we do this?" Faith and Rachel said at the same time. They looked at each other, and each of them bit their lips.

Rachel picked at one of her beautiful fingernails. "I think we should make a serious attempt to find Ian. It's worrying me."

Faith picked up the concern. "I had a hard time falling asleep last night after we talked to him. Let's try to find him now so we all can enjoy our cruise."

"Let's do all the normal things first." Savannah put her hand in a stop position. "We've left phone messages, but we haven't put a note up on the message board."

Edward frowned. "What message board?"

"There's one down on deck 3 right in front of the Guest Relations counter. Eric told me about it as a method to keep up-to-date on any Hot Shop demonstration time changes. Let's do that. It's right here on the same deck as the main dining room."

"Great plan," said Rachel.

They walked toward the front of the ship and found the standing bulletin board.

Rachel picked up a blank sticky note and a pen from a slot in the stand. "What should I write?"

Faith blurted out, "Ian, get in touch, now!"

Rachel reared back from Faith. "That's too harsh. That won't work with a"—she looked directly at Edward—"young man in a delicate condition."

Savannah said, "Just write down this: 'Ian Morris. Please get in touch as soon as possible. Leave a message in our cabin.'"

"Good," said Rachel. She wrote that neatly on the note and placed it on the message board.

Edward looked at the note, took the pen from Rachel, and signed his name at the bottom.

Savannah tilted her head to the side. "Since there are four of us, we can cover quite a bit of ground at a time. Let's start on the top deck and we'll each take a quadrant and meet back at the center elevators and go on doing that until we find him."

"There is, of course, the obvious chance that he's in a stateroom with a paramour," Rachel paused for effect.

"Or he could be on one of the dozen elevators while we're searching," finished Faith.

"Even so, we really must give it a go," said Edward. He rubbed his hands together like he was trying to get warm. "Brilliant! Let's get started."

They made their way to the center elevators and punched in the top floor. Since each of them concentrated on their own section, it only took about ten minutes for each of them to finish their search and go down to the next deck.

After they had searched the top three decks and met back at the elevators, Savannah could tell that Edward was beginning to get worried. He wasn't an over-protective sort, but no sight of Ian was giving them all something to be concerned about.

"This is getting a little bizarre. We should have found him somewhere up here," said Edward. "Like every Brit I know, he loves the sun and we should have found him lounging by one of the pools."

"That's true, all right," said Savannah. "But he might be doing some shopping with his new lady."

"He also might be in the casino," said Faith.

"Does he like to gamble?" asked Rachel.

Edward rubbed his temples with both hands. "You know, I don't think he's ever been in a casino. That would be a new experience for him."

"Right." Savannah grabbed Edward's hand. "Not time to panic, yet. Let's go down to the casino deck, and if he's not there we'll scour the shops."

The four of them rode the elevator to the deck where the casino was located.

"Can you guys search the casino?" asked Rachel.

"I can smell the cigarette smoke from here," said Faith. "We're not so young anymore and we don't want—"

"—to risk an upper respiratory infection. We're, of course, a little bit susceptible after that long flight," finished Rachel.

"Of course," said Savannah and Edward at the same time. Savannah grinned at Edward.

"It's catching." She punched him in the arm with a soft fist.

They turned to the four quarters of the deck and each returned in less than ten minutes. There was no need to report their news verbally. They each walked up one flight of stairs and silently searched the main promenade deck.

By now it was after eleven o'clock and the daily character parade was in full swing. All the children on the ship were lined up behind barrier cords. Each child was desperately trying to get the attention of their favorite cartoon character by waving and screaming the name at the top of their powerful lungs. No adult can match the painfully high-pitched scream of an excited three-year-old.

The little search team reassembled in front of the central elevators. All but Edward. The twins were oddly silent and merely shook their heads in perfect unison to give Savannah the results of their search.

Savannah felt both worried and sick. Could the worst have happened? Could he have fallen overboard? If he was religious about taking his meds, then why did he miss a dose? There must be some compelling reason for his absence other than a liaison.

Savannah turned to the Rosenberg twins. "You ladies have been so helpful. You go have some fun. We'll see you later."

Rachel reached out to hold Savannah's right hand. "We're here if you need any help."

Faith reached out to hold Savannah's left hand. "Don't hesitate to call us if you need any help. Any help at all."

"This might be none of our business, but this could turn into exactly what it looks like," said Rachel.

"Yes." Faith put her hand on Savannah's arm. "We had a dear friend who managed to conceal a fatal illness from everyone close to her."

"In her mind, she had already imposed on the kindness of her social circle."

"And she couldn't ask for one more accommodation."

"So she booked herself a Caribbean cruise out of the Port of Tampa."

"And she never returned. The family took that same cruise on the first anniversary of her suicide and they had a memorial service in the ship's chapel."

"You never really ever know anyone."

"Ever," said Faith.

They both hugged Savannah.

"We're going back to the suite," Rachel said. "I'm feeling the need for a little nap."

"Not only that," said Faith. "You want to be pampered by the wonderful Albert. I have to admit, however, that a short nap on the balcony sounds wonderful."

"Oh, by the way." Rachel placed a hand on Savannah's arm. "I know how much turmoil is swirling, but don't forget we've signed everyone up for the Charity Walk."

Faith nodded. "Yes, we're probably going to just donate the money if things aren't resolved, but think positively—maybe this mess will clear up in time."

"Are you waiting for Edward?" asked Rachel.

"Yes, I am. You don't need to keep me company." Savannah paced in front of the elevators. *What was taking Edward so long?*

At that moment, Edward appeared and joined the huddle. "I finished early and then went down to check the room. He hasn't been there. I don't know what to say. Ian's been a little wild lately, but that's to be expected after so much work to get his university degree."

"Try calling him again," Savannah suggested.

Edward pulled out his phone and swiped left on the most recent number. He put the phone to his ear and listened. "Hi, Ian. Listen, chap. I'm beginning to get a bit worried. It's not like you to skip your meds.

Give me a call when you get this or call our room and leave me a message. I'm not mad. I'm worried. 'Bye."

Savannah took a deep breath. "We need to report this to the officials. They will know what to do from here."

Edward bent his head down. "I'm sure he must be somewhere on board. Maybe we should wait a bit longer."

"I disagree!" Savannah covered her mouth. "Oops, I'm sorry, honey. I didn't mean to be so forceful." She walked into his arms and squeezed him tight. He put his head into the crook of her neck. They stood like that for more than a minute.

Rachel coughed. "Do you still need us?"

Edward broke away quickly and Savannah stepped back as well.

"Ladies." Edward proceeded to kiss each of them on their rosy powdered cheeks. "You've helped us so much, and you've done more than we can ask of you. We're going to report Ian as missing to security and see what happens. We can't thank you enough."

Faith pressed her lips into a thin line. "Now, don't you go and be all independent here and forget your friends. We want to know what happens."

"Yes, you must let us know what they say," said Rachel.

Although she found it difficult, Savanah smiled. "We will let you know as soon as we know something, but don't wait for us."

After escorting the Rosenberg twins safely to the elevator, Edward turned back around and looked

Savannah in the eyes. "I'm not feeling very good about this."

"Then, let's stop talking and do something." She grabbed him by the arm and headed to the services desk.

Savannah practically ran down to the other end of the two-story promenade and approached the customer service counter. Three staff members were behind their stations, but there was a line of more than twenty customers.

Edward stopped short and Savannah nearly tripped over backward.

She turned. "What's wrong?"

"What if he's sleeping off the night in his new friend's cabin?"

Savannah grabbed him by both hands and looked directly into his clear green eyes. "Then the life lesson he's going to learn here is that you let your friends and family know where you are or they're going to tear a cruise ship apart looking for you. Right?"

A funny grin played across Edward's face. "Absolutely right. He knows better and if not, he soon will."

The line moved with agonizing slowness, but eventually they were in front of a young black man named Joel whose nametag listed him as from Jamaica. "Welcome. How can I help you, please?"

Edward turned to Savannah and raised his eyebrows. Savannah sighed and turned back to the man behind the counter. "Joel, we can't find a member of our party. We're very concerned. He was on the top deck last night, but none of us has seen him since. Is there a way for you to check on him?"

"Have you tried leaving a message on the door of your cabin?"

"No, but—"

"Have you left a voice message on his phone?"

"Yes, but it's going straight to voice mail."

"Have you asked your porter if he's seen him? They usually know everything about their guests."

The noise of the parade was beginning to rise as the band and dancing performers approached their end of the ship.

"No."

"What about a text or an e-mail?"

Savannah shook her head, unable to hear him over the parade. "What?"

Joel leaned closer to her and raised his deep voice. "What about a text or an e-mail? Also, we have a message board behind you. You could leave a message there."

"We did that." Savannah practically screamed.

Joel smiled with perfect teeth offset by beautiful black skin. "It is only going on noon. You are probably missing him between decks. I wouldn't worry."

Savannah looked over to Edward and frowned. "He's right," she yelled. "There are a few more things we could try." She turned back to Joel and shouted. "Thank you, we'll try a little longer, but just in case, where is the security office?"

"The security office is on deck 2. I'm sure you'll find him soon." Joel repeated his blinding smile and looked over her shoulder at the next guest in line.

She pulled Edward away from the customer service desk and they walked out onto the promenade

deck. The crowd was in the throes of the parade
finale and the noise level was too high to talk.

He frowned and led Savannah to the stairway.
"Joel's right. Let's do everything he suggested. If Ian
doesn't turn up for dinner tonight, then we'll have
no choice but to go to security."

"Because they're going to suggest the same things,
aren't they?" said Savannah.

"Right, but if he saunters into the dining room like
a carefree cad, don't be surprised if I don't knock him
into next week."

Chapter 8

"You seem distracted. What's wrong?" Eric asked Savannah while they were preparing for the next hot glass demonstration.

"Sorry, it's a family problem." Savannah began swiping a cloth over the surface of the stainless-steel table called a marver that stood near the glass partition closest to the audience. They used the marver table for shaping the glass that had been gathered on the end of the blowpipe. It was also where they rolled the glass frit onto the glass gather.

"Come on, we're your family, too." Eric picked out the two frit colors he wanted to use for his piece and put the container on the shelf under the table.

Alan popped over from checking that they had enough blowpipes in the warming oven. "Yeah, that's a rule here at sea. We're a family. If Eric didn't look out for me, I would have been fired by now. Trust him."

Savannah nodded and turned to Eric. "It's probably nothing, but we can't find Edward's cousin.

No one in our group has seen Ian since right after midnight on the first night of the cruise."

Eric was looking at tubes of stringers. He finally chose one and placed it beside his frit containers underneath the table. "He'll turn up. Lots of young guys underestimate their liquor tolerance on their first day of the cruise."

Alan sauntered over and added a container of frit to the collection under the table. When he stood up, he grinned. "I still do!" Alan looked quickly at Eric. "But I try really hard to remember that drinking is not good for me."

They laughed, and Savannah could feel the tension at the back of her neck slip away. She selected a lime green frit and added cobalt blue stringers for her fluted vase demonstration. For a dramatic accent, she gathered a handful of lemon-lime mille-fiori pieces. They were Italian in origin and resembled miniature glass flowers. She placed the delicate selections in a wide pattern to make them easier to pick up.

"He'll turn up." Eric did a double check on the materials that everyone placed on the stainless-steel marver table. Then he opened a small cupboard near the stage door and pulled out the portable audio system. He frowned and examined it carefully, then attached the battery pack for the microphone onto the back of his khaki shorts and clipped the microphone to his collar.

"Do you always wear a portable microphone?" Savannah placed both hands on her hips. "I didn't have one at Pilchuck Studio."

"Yes, I have to. My voice is thin and doesn't carry

over the wind and sea noise. I can't work without it."
He tapped the bulb and said, "Test, testing. One,
two, three, testing." He frowned. It wasn't working.

The audiovisual panel was also on the port side of
the ship next to their stage entrance door. He went
to the panel and checked the power. It was on. Then
he tapped on his headset microphone again.

No sound.

He frowned until deep furrows could be seen on
his forehead. He pulled the portable battery pack off
his shorts and checked the power switch. The little
light glowed red on the wall panel. He turned the
audio system off, then on and checked for sound.

Nothing.

Alan had been warming the blowpipe that he was
going to use and looked around to Eric, who was
fiddling with the panel. "What's wrong?"

"The sound isn't working."

"For Pete's sake, talk to the audience without it."
Alan spread his hands out palms up and jutted his
chin forward. "It's no big deal."

Eric mirrored the palms out. "It *is* a big deal for me.
My voice doesn't carry. I can't work without a mic."

Alan gestured for Savannah to come over. "How
strong is your voice? Can you talk for me instead of
Eric?"

"Sure, I've rarely used one of these fancy
microphone thingies before this. My voice projects
naturally."

Eric picked up the ship's telephone that was also
in the panel. "Great. You guys get started. I'll give the
ship's AV guys a call and maybe they have a replacement available."

Savannah shrugged her shoulders. "Okay. I'll assist Alan and narrate. That's how I was trained, anyway. Let's go." Alan started the demonstration while Eric was arguing with someone on the phone.

The center section of the front row was taken up by the Rosenberg twins dressed in electric orange throwback seventies style. On either side of them was another set of twins—gentlemen of about their age. They were white haired, wore white trousers with blue oxford button-down shirts along with those awful white patent loafers. Savannah noted that their large gold rings weren't alike. That should help her tell them apart. She wondered if this inclination to dress alike later in life was a twin syndrome of some sort.

Twins meeting twins on a cruise—you couldn't make that up.

She scanned the crowd and Edward was in the far back. She could see the wrinkles on his brow. He still looked worried.

She cleared her throat and began. "Good afternoon, folks. Can you hear me?"

The chatter of the audience quieted.

"Good afternoon, is everybody having a good time?"

The crowd yelled a rambunctious, "Yes!" Some of the guests lifted their fruity drink of the day high in the air.

Savannah laughed. "Can you hear me there in the back?"

She saw some thumbs-up from the last row. "We're having some audio problems today. So, while Eric is busy calling the experts to get it fixed, I'll simply yell!" She began the comfortable patter of explaining the process for the angelfish that Alan was making.

Alan finished his piece by tapping the blowpipe and it dropped neatly into Savannah's waiting thermal gloves. Everyone exhaled a sigh of relief and applauded. She walked along the front of the stage letting the first-row guests get a close view. Alan walked over to the annealing oven and opened the door for Savannah to place it upright, standing on its fins and tail. They both turned and bowed to another round of applause.

Savannah removed the gloves and helped Eric prepare for his demonstration piece. He had planned to make a goblet with a dolphin as the stem holding up the clear bowl.

Eric waved to her and Alan to stand close to him. In a whisper, with his back to the audience, he said, "No help is coming from the AV guys. They're having similar problems with the ice skating show. There are unexplained power glitches everywhere. They did say they would try to get up here as soon as they could manage." He looked at Alan. "Watch the stage door for them. If they see that we're in the middle of a demonstration, they might duck out. Don't let them do that."

He turned back to face the crowd with a broad smile. "Now for something completely different and quite difficult. My success rate on these goblets is running a bit higher lately. I usually lose about one in five. Now, however, I'm on a record-breaking streak. I've made twelve in a row and I'm hoping this will be my lucky thirteen."

Eric began gathering the glass for the goblet from

the furnace and started the process of blowing, heating, shaping, and reheating to form a lovely thin shape. For the dolphin, he used a piece of solid blue glass that he had warming in a special oven to bring it up to temperature. He and Savannah managed to affix the dolphin to the globe with no problems.

While Eric was pulling the blue glass into the shape of a dolphin, an audiovisual guy entered from stage left. He sidled around the front of the demonstration area and handed Alan a bullhorn. This apparently was the crew's solution to the audio problem. Alan looked at it like it had come from another planet. He mouthed a *really?* to the AV guy, then shrugged his shoulders and put it up to his lips.

"Testing. Testing one, two, three."

Nothing came out of the bullhorn. Alan looked down at the handle and found the power on switch.

"Testing!" blared out of the bullhorn as if they were in a football stadium. Everyone in the audience shrieked and put their hands over their ears.

Eric also jumped and nearly crashed his dolphin goblet into the side of the furnace. "Alan, put that thing down! I almost lost this."

Alan tiptoed gingerly over to stage left and placed the bullhorn down on the deck under the audio panel. He stretched out his hands as if to command it to stay and backed away slowly. He faced the audience. "We'll leave that there and I'll continue to shout a bit. Okay?"

The crowd chuckled, and the sounds of agreement were heard.

Meanwhile Eric was forming the dolphin by pulling

the blue glass with pliers, returning it to the furnace, and then adjusting it again. It finally met his approval and he held it up for the viewers to see. Alan announced that there was still the base to attach followed by opening the mouth of the goblet.

Savannah put a small gather of clear glass on a blowpipe and she and Eric attached it. He scored a channel in the glass close to Savannah's blowpipe and then dripped a little water in the channel. A sharp rap on Savannah's blowpipe caused it to separate, accompanied by a gasp from the spectators.

Eric shaped the foot of the goblet and then turned his attention to the opening of the clear bowl. He heated the entire goblet, concentrating mostly on the enclosed globe. He removed it and sat back on the bench. He used the pointed tips of giant tweezers to start a hole to form the bowl. He inserted the tweezers in the hole and gently pulled the opening larger and larger. It took three trips to the furnace to keep it to the correct temperature.

At last he was satisfied with the gentle tulip curve for the goblet bowl. Eric held his finished goblet high enough for everyone in the audience to see. There was a loud round of applause.

Eric sat back at the glassblowing bench.

Alan put his index finger in front of his lips and mimed a *shh* to the crowd. He signaled for everyone to cross their fingers and hold them over their heads. The audience followed his direction.

Eric took the giant tweezers and scored a groove between the blowpipe and the foot of the goblet. Savannah put on the oven mitts and pulled them extra tight up her arms. She glanced out into the crowd and saw a familiar head.

She lifted her chin. It was Ian!

"Savannah," Eric whispered with a hint of panic in his voice. "Pay attention."

She turned back to Eric and the beautiful dolphin goblet landed in her gloves. It wobbled from side to side for a second, then shattered into shards.

The crowd groaned like a weary old man.

Savannah stood back from the carnage, then looked at Eric. "I'm so sorry."

Eric stood up and looked at the crowd. "Obviously, thirteen is not my lucky number." A small rumble of laughter accompanied his pity-me look.

"I thought it was okay." Savannah pulled off the gloves and put them back on top of the annealing oven. Then she returned to stand over the shards.

"Sometimes, it's not something that we can even guess," said Eric. "I thought it was fine, as well, but I have seen that happen before. This is only the second time."

Alan joined them as if they were standing over a body. He tapped Eric on the shoulder. "Here, this will make you feel better. The AV guys came up with a backup portable microphone system."

His eyes lighting up, Eric clipped the battery pack on his waistband at the small of his back and slipped the headset on. "Testing, testing, one, two, three." A huge grin split his face as the sound carried to the back of the crowd.

Now it was Savannah's turn and she was hardly calm. She looked back to the final row for Edward, but he was gone. She certainly hoped it was because he had spied Ian, as well. But there was no time to think about that. Her turn had come and she was determined to make a beautiful fluted vase.

Eric was so grateful to have a portable microphone that he over-explained every step that she took in the process.

Alan was rolling his eyes and holding his sides tightly to keep from laughing out loud. It was a little funny and helped to push thoughts of Edward and Ian away while she concentrated on the glowing ball of glass. To make sure that the vase was a little bit larger, she made an extra gather in the furnace in between picking up the frit and the stringers.

Just as Savannah was using the giant tweezers to make the opening in her vase, she caught sight of Edward. At her next reheating phase, she risked turning her head toward where she saw him.

He shook his head and mouthed a *no*.

She furrowed her brow, confused. *Was that truly Ian? Am I just wishing so hard that I've imagined him?*

The next step in making her fluted vase was to step up onto the glassblowing bench and swing the blowpipe like a pendulum to let gravity lengthen the piece. She then raised it a few feet and swirled it so that it expanded into a blossom.

The crowd gasped and then burst into applause. Savannah quickly reheated the finished piece, removed it, and safely landed it into Alan's gloved hands. She gave a little flourishing bow and they were done for the day.

Several of the cruisers tackled her with questions

as they stood by the stage door while the crowd dispersed. A hummingbird of an elderly man came up and grasped her hand with both of his trembling ones.

"That was a lovely show. I love to see you girls hang in there with the men." He continued to hold her hand.

"Thanks; it's more about balance than strength."

He nodded and noticed that he was still holding her. He let go and stepped back. "I'll see you tomorrow."

Alan whispered into her ear, "I see the cavalier has found you."

Savannah continued to smile as the guests left the seating area. "Cavalier?"

"That's what we call him. He's one of those permanent cruisers who basically lives aboard for about the same price as a fancy nursing home. It's very popular with a certain set of seniors. He's been on this particular ship for about two months."

Savannah finally extracted herself from the glass demonstration viewers and grabbed Edward by the arm.

"What happened?"

"I took off after the guy and I lost him. He was the same general build as Ian, but why would he run from me?" Edward raised his hand in a tight fist. "My gut says it wasn't Ian and he's still missing."

Savannah rubbed his arm. "I think we're both wanting to find him so much that we're not assessing the situation correctly. Running away from us just doesn't make sense. I agree that it wasn't him."

* * *

The dress code for tonight's dinner was formal. Savannah wore a full-length black velvet gown that fit like a glove. Her panic-driven shopping trip to Dillard's at Tyrone Mall had unearthed the classic in a markdown rack that made the purchase a little less painful. She didn't like spending money for clothes she wouldn't wear often. She anticipated that her accountant would have a comment to indicate that a floor-length formal didn't improve the bottom line for her business.

Her late mother's heritage jewelry set the perfect tone with diamond earrings and an art deco sterling silver pin. The pin was shaped like a shield. She waited for Edward in the lobby in front of the main dining room.

She fiddled with the rhinestone catch on her tiny red evening bag that held only lipstick and her pass card.

"Savannah, dear," said Faith as she grabbed Savannah's hand and patted it. "I'm so glad we caught you before you went into dinner."

"We changed our table to one that could seat eight instead of six." Rachel smoothed the skirt of her purple satin gown with a lavender lace peplum jacket. "We have invited our gentlemen to join us."

Faith put her lavender gloved hand on Savannah's arm. "I hope you don't mind, dear. They have been very considerate and entertaining."

"It's nice to have interesting conversations again." Savannah smiled at their earnest expressions.

"There's no need to ask. Of course, they should join us. Have you seen Ian today? I thought I saw him at the demonstration."

The twins shook their heads in unison.

"We've been looking," said Rachel.

"But we haven't really been out and about very much." Faith looked sad. "We're finding the movement of the ship a little precarious."

"Let's be clear," countered Rachel. "We're not decrepit. We don't need canes or walkers yet."

Faith tilted her head to the side. "However, we did have some wobbly moments up on the top deck."

"I'm glad the demonstration occurred before that little bit of weather," Savannah replied.

Edward appeared looking like James Bond of the Sean Connery flavor. His tux fit perfectly, and he looked outrageously comfortable with a black cummerbund and expertly tied red bow tie.

Savannah could feel the deeply pleasant effects of his good looks right down to her toes.

He grabbed her hand and kissed it like Cinderella's Prince Charming. "You look brilliant—absolutely stunning." He gazed into her eyes for a long slow moment like he was trying to memorize every detail of her appearance for recalling later.

"Have you seen Ian?"

"No, and neither have Faith nor Rachel. I'm convinced now that he's alive." Their waiter arrived to seat them. "Hang on, I'll explain after we've been seated."

Edward tucked her hand onto his arm to proceed into the dining room. The Rosenberg twins followed. Their waiter led them to a location that was near the captain's table. Edward looked at Savannah with one eyebrow raised.

"We've been moved to join Faith's and Rachel's gentlemen friends. They obviously have some influence with the crew."

"But what if Ian—"

"The head waiter has taken care of that. If Ian shows up with his lady friend, they'll be led to our table."

Edward ordered a gin and tonic for himself and a glass of champagne for Savannah. The rest of the table ordered the ship's special drink of the day, Rumrunner.

"Before anyone else gets here," started Edward, "I know that Ian is alive."

Savannah turned to him so abruptly that she nearly tipped over her water glass. She caught it and set it upright. "How do you know?"

"I can't find his day-by-day pill box. He must have gotten into our cabin and now he has it with him."

Rachel leaned forward. "Is anything else missing?"

Faith leaned over as well. "Maybe his shaving kit or brush?"

"No, nothing else appears to be missing. So, the question is where is he?" Edward scratched his head. "Why didn't he leave a note?"

The four of them sat back in their chairs with a puzzled silence so thick you could slice it and spread it on toast.

Rachel pointedly stared at the four empty places at their table, then looked over to her sister. "What do you think has happened to our gentlemen?"

Faith squinted her eyes and pouted. "We may have

been just a tiny bit forward with them, dear. We can be a little larger than life sometimes."

Savannah quickly put the napkin over her mouth.

Rachel, "Yes, sister. We sometimes strike people the wrong way. I think we'd better tell Edward now, don't you?"

Faith nodded. "I think we've already waited too long. You start."

"Edward, we told you that we saw Ian out on the deck but there's more."

"More?" Savannah shifted her head around the arm of their server who placed a gin and tonic in front of her eye-line to Faith. "What do you mean? What happened?"

Rachel raised a finger, looking at the server. "One moment. Could you return in a few minutes? We're not quite ready to put our orders in."

The waiter finished serving their cocktails and left.

Savannah placed a hand on Edward's fidgeting leg and whispered, "Be calm."

"What do you know?" Edward's words had a crisp edge.

"We're breaking a solemn promise to Ian, but this situation has gone too far to worry about a promise. We had a conversation with Ian that was very personal," said Rachel. "He was looking demoralized and reckless."

"But it was also clear that he had had too much to drink," said Faith. She nodded to her sister. "Go on."

"Fine." Rachel took her napkin, fussily refolded it, and placed it on her lap. "He was in a mood."

"Or it could have been the drink."

"Faith, stop interrupting. Let me tell this."

Faith pressed her lips closed.

"Edward, your cousin appears to be having a crisis of some sort. He mentioned that he didn't feel that life was worth living."

"What?" Edward said loud enough to cause heads to turn at the nearby tables.

"Shush," said Savannah. "Let's listen to what they have to say."

Rachel started again. "He said that his prospects for a job were bleak and that he didn't want to be a burden to his parents any longer."

"That's ridiculous!" Edward took a long sip of his gin and tonic. "Ian's parents are well off and happy to make sure Ian gets a good start in life."

Rachel pursed her lips. "There's more."

Faith clasped her hands and put them in her lap. She straightened her already perfect posture a tiny bit. "He said he had been looking for a job for six months. He was keeping that part a secret from his parents."

"And you, too, Edward." Rachel sighed. "He said he knew his parents wanted him to be happy, and they fully supported his taking a little time off after graduation. But he wanted to get started in his career as quickly as he could."

"That sounds responsible," said Savannah.

Rachel continued. "The problem was he wasn't able to get a job at all. He interviewed every single company that specialized in his field of molecular neuroscience."

"But he said that he was rejected from each and every one of them." Faith brought her napkin up to the corner of her eye. "He broke down and began to cry."

"We didn't know what to do." Rachel looked over to Faith.

"Then he made us promise not to tell anyone about his confession," said Faith. "He especially didn't want us to tell you."

"He was so upset that we promised not to tell in order to calm him down."

Edward drained his drink. "So, what you're saying is that you think he actually might have committed suicide."

Rachel and Faith looked at each other. "There's one more thing," said Rachel.

Faith put her hand over Edward's and patted it softly. "Edward, dear. Ian said that he had forgotten to bring his antidepressants."

Edward stiffened. "He lied to me. I asked him straight out if he had them. Blast!"

"He said he was afraid to tell you," Rachel added. "He knew you would call his parents and then they would move heaven and earth to send them to him."

"It was only a week." Faith shrugged her shoulders. "He did remember to bring his homeopathic meds."

Savannah shot straight up, tipping her drink onto the linen tablecloth. "We can't wait any longer." She pushed her chair back. "I've had enough tiptoeing around Ian's feelings or broken promises. Let's go, Edward. We're reporting this to security, now!"

Chapter 9

"You agree, don't you?" Savannah swayed down the corridor with her feet wide to keep her balance against the pitching seas. She punched the elevator button for deck 2 and waited a moment. "What am I doing? It's only down one deck. Let's take the stairs."

Edward followed her down the wide carpeted stairway. "Of course, we should have done this hours ago."

"Did you know about his depression or about the jobs or about the medication?"

Edward shook his head. They followed the utility corridor to an office marked SECURITY. There was a window in the top half of the door and it basically mirrored the setup you'd find at your average shopping mall.

They entered a small lobby with two gray aluminum chairs in front of a counter. A workstation with an office desk was set up behind the counter. An officer was one-finger hunt-typing on a computer keyboard that overlooked a bank of a dozen display screens. Each screen was split into four camera views. The whole ship was under his surveillance. The hunt-and-peck typist walked over to the counter.

"Good evening." He smiled and spoke slowly with a strong Italian accent. "I'm Officer Gaffney. How can I help you?"

Savannah stepped up to the counter. "We'd like to report a missing passenger, Ian Morris."

The officer stood and pulled out a shelf with a keyboard from underneath the counter. The computer display was on the counter with its back to Savannah. "Can I have a few details, please? May I see your keycard?"

Edward stepped forward. "It's my cousin that's missing." He handed over his keycard to the officer. "Ian and I are sharing a cabin."

Office Gaffney slid the keycard over the scanner and it responded with a distinctive *bloop*.

The officer punched a few keys. "Cabin 6250, sir?" Edward nodded. "When did you see him last?"

Savannah tucked her hand in Edward's arm. She could feel the tense muscles through his tux jacket. "He was seen on the top deck in the wee hours of Monday with friends of ours."

The officer typed a few more words into some sort of form. Savannah wished she could see the screen. "Who were those friends?"

Edward answered quickly, "Miss Rachel Rosenberg and Miss Faith Rosenberg. They're both Americans from St. Petersburg, Florida."

"Oh, I see, the Rosenberg sisters. They're in one

of our suites." He looked up from the screen and asked Edward, "Did Mr. Morris seem well?"

"He was pretty sloshed. He was celebrating his recent graduation. This cruise is a gift from his parents. I don't think he's ever had unlimited access to drink."

"The gift was to the both of you?"

Edward placed his right hand over Savannah's, which was still gripping his arm. "No, I'm here with Savannah."

"I'm one of the glassblowers for your Hot Shop demonstrations."

"You're part of the crew?"

Savannah waggled her head. "Yes, but I'm only on board for this cruise. I have it in my contract to mix freely with the passengers, so I have a foot in both camps."

Officer Gaffney extended his hand palm up. "Let me scan your card as well."

Savannah gave him her keycard and the machine scanned it with another distinctive *bloop*.

"Thank you, Miss Webb." He returned the keycard and then turned the small flat screen around to face them. "Is this Ian Morris?"

It was the photo that was taken at the check-in station at Barcelona.

Edward nodded. "Yes, that's him."

Officer Gaffney returned the screen to face himself. "There's one handy tool I can use to figure out where our Mr. Morris has been." He used the mouse and then one by one punched in a few letters with his index finger.

Savannah grimaced as each finger pounded a key.

She wondered how many keyboards the man had destroyed. She folded her arms.

Officer Gaffney frowned, the wrinkles deep on his dark brow, and he bent his head closer to the flat screen. "That's odd. Let me try that again." He again used the mouse and pounded the keyboard. "Same answer."

Savannah leaned over the counter and managed to get a peek at the flat screen. It displayed a list of bars where Ian had ordered drinks.

"Ehi!" Officer Gaffney shifted his bulk to block her view. "Ehi! You can't see this."

"What does it mean?" Savannah straightened up. "We need to know."

"What I see, here, on this screen, is that Mr. Ian Morris bought many drinks. The last one was up on the top deck at the Full Eclipse Bar at a little after midnight as we left Barcelona."

"And then what?" Edward said with an edge of urgency. "Tell us!"

"There are no more records after that." Officer Gaffney began to wring his hands. "It doesn't look like Mr. Ian Morris has used his card since then."

"Exactly!" said Savannah. "That's why we are reporting him missing. Can we speak to your supervisor? Who's the security officer in charge?"

Officer Gaffney continued to wring his hands and stare at the flat screen.

Savannah pounded her fist on the top of the counter. "Hey! Move! Find the top man, now!"

As if scalded, Officer Gaffney left the counter and went to the back of the office through a plain door that they hadn't seen. Savannah and Edward caught a glimpse of a small office filled with officers scanning more banks of CCTV screens. Savannah saw at least four officers monitoring the closed circuit televisions before the door quickly closed.

Edward looked over to Savannah. "Yelling at the large Sicilian security officer was not the best political choice."

She shook her head. "Maybe not, but he wasn't moving fast enough. They have all those cameras. There must be a recording of Ian up on the deck." Savannah heaved a deep sigh. "Except that there are blind spots in the coverage of the cameras. Their security system is keyed to passenger activity. It's not trying to catch gamblers stealing money like a Vegas casino."

"I'm concerned that they didn't have a record of Ian coming into the cabin to take his pill container."

"Right. He must have found a way into your room without a key. Like—"

"When the cabin attendant is cleaning the room."

"Yes," said Savannah. "He could pretend he left something behind and the cabin attendant wouldn't think a thing about it. We need to have a little chat with him."

The plain beige metal door opened and a tall, muscular woman with a mass of long black hair walked up to the counter. She was wearing a highly decorated nautical white jacket and white trousers. Clearly a person of importance on the ship. She extended her hand first to Savannah.

"I'm Security Captain LuAnn Dalessio. You are

Savannah Webb?" Her slight accent was Eastern European, but her English was nearly perfect.

Savannah shook her hand. "Yes, and this is—"

Chief Dalessio turned. "You must be Edward Morris." She shook his hand and smiled warmly. Her slight lisp was charming rather than irritating.

"What's the problem?"

"Officer Gaffney didn't explain?" said Savannah.

"Yes, he did. But I would like to hear you explain it from your point of view."

Savannah and Edward took it in turns to explain the facts surrounding Ian's disappearance. They related their conversation with the Rosenberg twins at dinner, as well. When they had finished, they stood in front of the counter waiting for Chief Dalessio to speak. Instead, she nodded curtly and turned to the computer keyboard.

Her fingers sped across the keys and in seconds, she grunted with satisfaction. "Here is what Officer Gaffney found."

She turned the flat screen toward Savannah and Edward. As she had glimpsed, there was a long list of liquor charges that were time-stamped through yesterday afternoon and late evening. Chief Dalessio nodded and turned the screen back to herself. "You can see that the last purchase was different from all the rest. He had been drinking beer throughout the day and evening."

Chief Dalessio pointed to the last entry. "Then, here, he orders our most expensive single malt whiskey. It's quite pricey." She looked at Edward. "Is that typical of Ian's drinking habits?"

"No. The premium brands aren't covered in our

drinks package, either. I would have thought that he would keep to the brands that are covered." Edward's voice cracked. "I don't know why he would do that."

"You did mention that he had been despondent," said Chief Dalessio.

"I don't believe he would do anything drastic." Edward had lowered his voice. "But now that he's openly confessed his dark mood to the Rosenberg twins, that may have changed." His last words were barely above a whisper.

Savannah grabbed Edward's arm. "I'm not judging here, but has he tried to take his life in the past?"

Edward exhaled a low groan. "Yes."

Officer Dalessio halted her mouse movements. "When was this? Recent?"

Edward shook his head slowly. "It wasn't all that long ago, probably about six months—maybe less."

"Why?" asked Savannah.

"He was approaching his final exams at university and everything seemed to be collapsing in on him. He swallowed a handful of his meds, but regretted it immediately and called the emergency services in time for them to pump them out."

Savannah rubbed Edward's arm. "That must have been a terrible time for your aunt and uncle."

"They were stunned. Ian had hidden his troubles so well that even his parents were in the dark."

Chief Dalessio turned back to the computer. A few mouse clicks brought up a list of the keycards used for Edward and Ian's cabin. "Ian used his card at the cabin once Sunday afternoon and then once before dinner. He hasn't used it since then."

Savannah leaned on the counter to get a good view of the screen. "That matches what we've been able to determine. Could he be in someone else's cabin?"

She shook her head. "Of course, but unless you know who it is . . ." She turned her hands palms up and shrugged her shoulders.

Chief Dalessio turned back to the screen. She began typing. "Now, one of the things about this wonderful ship is that we have nearly every part of the ship under surveillance. Let me show you the midnight video recording of the top deck." A few mouse clicks. "Now, here you see him talking with—"

"A pair of elderly women? Twins?"

"Yes." Chief Dalessio adjusted the angle of the flat screen and pointed to Ian standing at the rail. "You can see him with a drink in his hand. He's obviously quite intoxicated. His balance is bad. He's having trouble drinking without spilling the whiskey. You can see that the ladies are trying to calm him down, but, right there he yells at them and storms down the deck to a spot just out of camera view."

"This is completely inconclusive," said Savannah.

"We also know that he—" Edward was stopped by Savannah's sharp look and a kick on his shin.

Edward quickly looked at Savannah and instantly understood that she didn't want him to tell security that he had also been seeing imaginary enemies. "I mean, he could have found someone to spend the night with, but we simply can't confirm that."

"Are there some other circumstances that can help us find Ian?"

Edward glared at Savannah. "He forgot to bring his antidepressants. He told the Rosenberg twins that he was afraid to tell me. He thought I would make a fuss."

Savannah reached for Edward's hand. "Right, they need to know that." She turned back to Chief Dalessio. "What else can we do?"

"First, you are to be commended for your actions. You've done the right thing by reporting him missing. I'll assign one of my officers to scan the tapes for any signs of Ian's movements from after that midnight drink through to the present time." She folded her arms in front of her chest. "I have to tell you that these cases end up in one of two ways."

"What are they?" asked Savannah.

"The first one is that they were sleeping off their hangover in someone else's cabin."

"And the second?" said Edward.

"Sadly, that he took his life by jumping overboard."

Chapter 10

Monday at Webb's Glass Shop

Amanda Blake had her first realization that, to some, she might be considered old. It was a shock. She was not yet thirty, but the computer installer who had brought a large box and a computer satchel on a cart to the shop seemed to be about twelve.

He put the last box inside the front door of Webb's Glass Shop and displayed a lively smile. He wore artistically torn jeans and a plain T-shirt under a blue plaid button-down shirt, and his hair was shaved. The finishing touch for the perfect hipster look was a pork-pie hat tilted at a jaunty angle. "Good morning, ma'am. I'm Will Leavy. You're getting our very best cash register system."

She saw his startled look as he scanned her bright lime T-shirt, Capri slacks, and matching lime streak in her hair. He recovered quickly. "Are you the owner?"

"Oh, no. I'm the manager of the shop. The owner is away. You don't need her for the installation, do you?"

"No, that's fine, everything is already arranged. I'll get started. Where do you want it?"

After months of irritating reliability problems, Savannah had finally ordered a new system to replace her dad's ancient cash register PC. It was so far out of date, even Legacy computer experts refused to show up for repairs. Today was installation day. It was also a day that Savannah could not be reached at sea. Though even if she had been reachable, there was the complication of a time difference.

"Right where we have the Legacy system on this glass counter. We use it for selling glass, supplies, craft classes, and studio time. Savannah said you would handle removing the old equipment, right?"

"Absolutely! That's in the agreement." He walked around to look at the current system. "Holy—" He clapped a hand over his mouth. "Pardon me, ma'am. I've never seen a system like this. This is ancient." He ran his hands along the worn keyboard, the large CRT display, and bent down to look under the counter at the large upright computer rack that whirred with cooling fans.

"This is like an archaeological find. It must be at least ten years old."

"That's why you're here. We've needed a new system since forever. It's very moody."

Will stood up. "You're lucky it works at all. Are you ready to shut it down for the last time?"

"With pleasure." Amanda performed the shutdown sequence and powered off the system. "It's all yours."

Amanda bit the corner of her thumb, careful not to damage her lime nail polish. She was worried about figuring out the new technology. This program

was significantly more complicated than the previous
software and would be a basic element in keeping
Webb's Glass Shop out of financial ruin. It didn't
help Amanda's nerves that Edward was gone as well.
He had installed the same system in his restaurant
pub more than a month ago and knew how to use it.

His bartender, Nicole, didn't like it very much, but
Edward loved the reporting features of the system
and knew his way around the various screens. Amanda
was glad that Savannah had ordered a one-on-one
training session to follow the installation. She felt relieved that the workshop scheduled for this week was
the beginning class for traditional stained glass. She
could walk students through their first stained-glass
piece in her sleep.

Feeling awkward, she watched him remove the old
cathode ray tube system. He carefully wrapped and
bundled it as if it were an Egyptian mummy. After
that, he replaced it with an all-in-one flat screen and
keyboard. It was so much smaller than the old system
that there would be plenty of extra room for clients
to set their purchases down on the counter while
they paid.

Will plugged in the new system, installed a Wi-Fi
box, an uninterruptable power supply, and plugged
them all into a fancy power strip. After that he stood
behind the counter and pressed the power button.
The monitor flashed on to display the welcome
screen. Then the cash register application displayed
its home screen in a blinding flash.

"Oh, boy! That's fast."

"Welcome to your modern system. I have a few

customizations to make in the setup file in order to hook it up with your Internet provider, and we'll be good to go."

In less than ten minutes, Will finished the setup and rebooted the system. "It's all done. Now, let me take you through the basic screens. It won't take long as everything is designed to be intuitive."

The bell over the door of Webb's Glass Shop rang. Amanda looked up to see one of her students arriving for the morning stained-glass class. "Good morning. Go ahead and get set up in the classroom. I'll be there in a few minutes."

Amanda turned to Will. "Can you give me the tutorial after lunch? This class lasts until one o'clock and then I'll have the rest of the afternoon to get familiar with the new system."

"Sure, I can do that," Will agreed quickly. He dug into his satchel and handed her an invoice to sign. "If you sign the invoice, that's my documentation that I've completed the installation. Then I can leave and come back this afternoon for your training." He handed her a pen. "It's no problem."

Amanda scrunched her forehead and hesitated. Then the ringing of the over-the-door bell announced more students. So, Amanda signed the form. She greeted the new students while Will gathered his tools and loaded them onto the cart with the Legacy system.

Amanda rubbed an itch on her left palm. "You'll be back this afternoon, right?"

Will turned on his thousand-watt smile and handed her a business card. "Absolutely. Most likely at about one thirty. That will give you a chance to have a bite before we start the training."

Amanda held the door for him and then her remaining students appeared. She enjoyed teaching and was soon immersed in the beginning student's instruction. Before she knew it, they were done with today's lessons and everyone was packing up.

Moments after the last student left, a regular customer came in to purchase several large, expensive sheets of glass that he needed for slumping into tall vase molds. He already had a kiln in his garage and stopped by regularly for supplies. He was experimenting with various colors to use in floral centerpieces at his daughter's wedding.

When Amanda took the wrapped glass over to the counter, she stopped short. "Oh, no. I forgot we have a new system." She inhaled a deep breath. "Well, this is where I find out if intuitive really means that using it is simple or that it is intuitive only to the designer."

She moved the mouse to wake up the monitor and the display revealed a menu screen. She clicked on the cash button and the screen flashed a bright red for a moment and displayed the menu screen again.

"Arghhh!" Amanda pounded her tight little fists on the counter in a staccato. "It doesn't work!"

Amanda wrapped the glass sheets in brown butcher paper and turned to the new cash system. The screen was black.

"Hang on a second," said Amanda. She wiggled the mouse.

Nothing.

"I'll try a reboot." She looked at the control strip

at the base of the flat screen and found the power symbol. She pressed it and heard the whirr of the internal fan wind down to silence. Then she counted to ten and pushed the power button. She crossed the fingers of both hands and closed her eyes.

The customer was beginning to fidget. He had already wandered around the shop looking at more glass, but now he stood in front of her at the counter.

When she didn't hear anything, she pushed the power button again, then crossed her fingers and added her little fingers as well. She whispered, "Please, please, please work." Amanda cracked one eye open to a silent black screen.

She looked at the customer and shook her curls. "I'm so sorry. We have a manual system as a backup. Are you good with that?"

"No, I'm afraid there's been too much hacking lately to my mind."

"Let me try something else." Amanda dived below the counter and ensured that all the wired connections were seated properly. She turned off the Wi-Fi box as well as the new PC. Again, she counted to ten and turned on the devices.

The Wi-Fi box came up with its tiny lights flashing then settling to steady, but the PC was still dark.

"Grrrrrr. It's not going to play today. Let me show you our manual system." She ducked under the counter and grabbed the folder that contained the forms and manual credit card slide machine. "We have lots of experience using a manual system." Amanda laughed.

"No, I'm not comfortable with that. I'll be back in a couple of days. You should have it fixed by then."

She thought about calling him back, but before she could get the words out of her mouth, the customer was out the door, leaving the doorbell jangling.

Amanda dropped her head to her chest in disappointment, then she called the number on Will's card. It immediately went to voice mail to the default message.

"Will? Are you there? This is Amanda Blake at Webb's Glass Shop. The system you installed this morning has shut down and isn't working. I've lost a big sale because the customer refused to use our manual backup system. Give me a call as soon as you can." She recited Webb's Glass Shop's number slowly. "Please call as soon as you get this. I'm in big trouble here. Call."

She felt her shoulders drop in dejection. Pushing the negativity aside, Amanda picked up her smartphone. *I hope Savannah doesn't lose confidence in me. No, she won't!*

She threw back her shoulders and began typing her daily message to Savannah.

Chapter 11

Tuesday, at sea

Savannah led a stunned Edward away from the security office. There was effectively nothing more they could do down there. He followed her like a puppy to the Passport Bar located up one level. She pushed him down into a chair at a corner table and went to the bar. She ordered two shots of Irish whiskey and asked the bartender to also deliver two pints of Guinness.

She handed Edward one of the shot glasses and he looked at it as if it were a moon rock. "Drink it down, right now." He looked at her with dull eyes that nearly broke her heart. "Drink it down."

Edward tossed back the shot and sat the glass on the table. "I'm going to have to call Aunt Kate and Uncle Howard." His green eyes were glistening with tears that he blinked away. Savannah knocked back her whiskey.

The bartender placed the pints of Guinness on

the table. Savannah looked up at the server. "Thanks, and could you bring him another shot of Irish, please?"

Savannah pushed the pint into Edward's hand. "Drink this, honey. You're in shock. Your conversation with Ian's parents is going to be difficult."

His electric green eyes turned to Savannah and he grabbed her hand in a tight grip. "I'm glad you're here. I'm such a lucky man." Edward had swigged about a third of the pint down when the bartender placed the whiskey on the table. "Is that all, ma'am?"

Savannah handed him her keycard. "Yes, thanks. We'll be fine now." She turned back to Edward. "We need to find a quiet place for you to call. How about the library? There's probably no one there at this time of day."

Edward nodded and sipped his whiskey. "They'll want to do something. Ian's parents won't sit around for news. Where's our first port?"

"I think it's Provence, France. I haven't been paying much attention to which ports we're visiting. My focus has been on the demonstration times. I can confirm that with the daily schedule handout from guest relations."

Edward nodded, then took another sip of the whiskey.

"Do you think you can persuade them to wait for an official statement?"

"No, they're strong willed and have always taken matters into their own hands. I can try, but most likely they'll join us in Provence."

Savannah paid the tab and they finished their

drinks. "You look a lot better now. Are you ready to make the call?"

"As ready as I'll ever be. My mum always told me it's better to run toward the problem rather than hide from your troubles."

Savannah took Edward by the arm. "She's a wise woman."

They took the elevator and as expected, they found the library completely deserted. They sat in two massive, soft leather chairs in the back. Edward dialed his phone.

"Hi, Aunt Kate. It's Edward. I have some bad news."

Edward pleaded for almost twenty minutes to prevent his aunt Kate and uncle Howard from flying out to Provence if they could catch the next flight. Apparently, nothing he said could prevent them from coming to find their son. Ian's parents were adamant that he could not possibly have committed suicide no matter what the ship's security team thought.

"I thought the cruise was full. How can they get a cabin?" asked Savannah as she and Edward left the library and proceeded to the lounge area at the stern. They sank into deck chairs and stared at the foamy wake.

"I don't know how, but I have full confidence that they will."

"Do you think he told them about his job interviews?"

"Probably not. They were so proud of him. You saw them beaming like the sun at his celebration, right?"

"Yes, I certainly wouldn't have picked that as a time to tell them that I was unemployable." Savannah leaned over in her deck chair and held Edward's hand. "I've only known Ian for a few days, but he seems the resilient type."

"It's the unemployable part that has him flummoxed."

"Why do you think he was rejected in his interviews?"

"I think maybe he was too forthright about his past."

"Is that possible?" Savannah swung her legs over and sat up in the deck lounger.

Edward cleared his throat and sat up so that they were sitting knee to knee. "There are some things I need to tell you about my past." He sat very still and pulled Savannah's hand into his. "I have a bit of a bad boy past."

She raised her eyebrows, disbelieving. "You?"

Edward placed his other hand over hers, cupping it like a captured bird. "Ian and I had a rough time when we were lads aged about twelve and nine."

"Everyone has a rebellious phase. It's completely normal." Savannah looked at him with a concerned smile. She reminded herself not to interrupt again. He was typically a very British flavor of reserved and did not share his feelings easily.

"This was a little bit more serious than rebellion. Ian and I were involved in a counterfeiting ring called the Ravens."

"In St. Albans?" Savannah slapped a hand over her mouth. So much for not interrupting.

"No, it was before we moved to a new house in St. Albans. Our dads worked on the docks, so we lived in a rough part of London. Our mums worked in food shops and that meant we were on our own after school."

He fell silent. To Savannah, it reminded her of someone replaying an old film in his mind. She said softly, "Go on."

He jerked. "Oh, sorry. Where was I?"

"You were saying that you and Ian were latchkey kids."

"Right." Edward squeezed her hand tight for a moment. "We fell into a bad group of kids that were part of an Italian family that were involved in some criminal schemes."

"Such as . . ."

"Running numbers, racehorse betting, and counterfeiting."

"What?" Savannah narrowed her eyes. "Impossible. I don't believe you."

"Yes indeed, counterfeiting. Ian and I would go around to different newsagent shops to collect winnings."

"But that's not counterfeiting."

"It gets worse." He opened her hand and traced the lines in her palm with a finger. "We were good runners and one of the wannabe leaders of the family took a liking to us, so he groomed us into willing tools in a finely tuned money-laundering scheme."

"How does that work?"

"We would go into a neighborhood newsagent shop—they were everywhere back then. Sometimes two or three per street. Anyway, we would go in and ask to change a fake five-pound note. Then we would get real change for the forged note."

"But wouldn't the owner catch on?"

"This was a long time ago. The notes were passed along quickly as change for a ten-pound purchase. We were assigned three or four a day in adjoining neighborhoods."

"How did you get there?"

"That was how they paid us. We were given rubbish bicycles that we paid for bit by bit but never seemed to actually earn enough to pay them off."

"That's mean."

"Of course it was, but they were just as mean to their own kin, so we didn't take it personal. Wait." Edward rubbed his temple and closed his eyes. "I'm trying to remember the big boss's name." He fell silent for a couple of seconds. "Right!" He opened his eyes. "It was Jimmy the Fist."

"That's a violent name. Didn't that scare you?"

"Sorry, it seemed pretty normal at the time. Besides, we had already lied to our parents that we had found the bicycles in a garbage tip and fixed them up with scrap parts."

That's sobering. Ian and Edward were skilled liars.

"Then things got worse. We were taught how to snatch and run with purses, wallets, shopping bags—anything really."

Savannah opened her mouth to interrupt. Edward squeezed her hand and placed his index finger over her lips. "I know you want to help. Please let me tell the rest straight to the end."

He swallowed hard and pressed his lips into a firm line. "Then three things happened at the same time. First, the pressure increased to get more and more bags each day. Second, our parents found out that we were part of that ring from someone that saw us when they were visiting out of the neighborhood. We didn't see the neighbors, so we were blissfully unaware that we had been ratted out."

He sat silent for a moment. When Savannah fidgeted, he held up a hand to stop her from interrupting. "The next thing was that I hurt a little old lady. I didn't mean to knock her down, but she had a firm grip on her bag and she pitched forward as I ran by on the grab."

He stopped again. They both sat still. Savannah reached over to squeeze his hand.

Then Edward resumed. "I turned back to look and she was lying on the sidewalk with her bleeding arm outstretched. She was crying out that her life was in that bag. Her voice sounded just like my granny's."

He stopped again. Savannah could see that he was playing the image over and over in his thoughts.

"I stopped cold. It hit me like a ton of bricks that she was right. Likely, she was on her way home from the bank with her monthly pension. She wouldn't eat if her bag was stolen. A cold sweat hit me as I realized what I had become. I went back, helped her up, gave her back the bag, then walked her home."

"Was Ian with you?"

"Yeah, we had been sent out together. He was across the street. It was completely by chance that we were on that street. It was a coincidence." His gaze wandered off into the distance again. Savannah didn't think he knew she was there.

She cleared her throat and he continued.

"The next part is very fuzzy for me. A long black car pulled over about three houses up from the old woman's and a man came out of the house shouting and brandishing his fist. The rear door of the black car opened, and a large man walked up to the shouting man and stabbed him in the stomach. We saw the flash of the knife. The shouting man went down like a rag doll."

"And then?"

"The shouting man hit his head on the front step of the porch and it split wide open. Blood was everywhere. But we later found out it was a typical family hit."

"Did you see the man in the car?"

"No, I only got a glance. But Ian got a good look at him."

"Then what?"

"That meant that the man in the black car got a good look at Ian. We both ran all the way home. I threw up when I got there and then told Mum everything. She made me wait on the front steps until Pa came home and then I told him."

They sat silent for several minutes. Then Edward continued. "My parents were wild with anger and disappointment. When I mentioned that the big boss was Jimmy the Fist, they figured out that he was the man in the black car. I would likely never be safe in London. They decided to pack me up to stay with a cousin who owned a pub out in the country. As soon as they could, my folks moved to St. Albans. Ian's folks arrived a year later. We never spoke of Jimmy the Fist again."

"You think he was still involved after you left?"

"It's likely he had to work for them until his folks also moved," said Edward.

"So, you think he met a member of the counterfeiting ring here on the ship?"

Edward held his head in both hands. "Yes, I do. Ian did say that he thought he recognized someone from the past. It was before we boarded the ship. I didn't see anyone I knew."

Savannah paused. "Do you think they will remember you as well?"

Edward lowered his voice to a whisper. "Yes, I do."

Chapter 12

After a fitful night's sleep in her cabin, Savannah powered up her laptop at the tiny desk in her cabin and clicked on the e-mail icon. The first in the list was sent from Amanda.

Hi Savannah! I have some good news and also some not so good news. I hope your cruise is super fun and you're enjoying being back at glassblowing.

The installation of the new cash register system occurred right on schedule and the whole thing appeared to be working perfectly until it didn't. After the installer left, the whole system failed. I've made numerous calls to the offshore service department, but it's a call center in who-knows-where. They promised to get an authorized representative to call me for an appointment within 48 hours—

this is not what I understood you bought for service.

I don't want you to worry. I have some friends I can call in to help diagnose the problem. I'm also looking into hiring a local service company who can respond quickly.

Although my research skills are monster strong, I admit that my computer hardware knowledge has now started to hold me back. If I had known more about basic computer hardware, I should have been able to at least ask better questions. Note to future goals: Take a basic computer class from the library.

Again, don't worry. We're using the manual system.

X O X O X, Amanda

P.S. Jacob says hi and that Suzy misses you.

Savannah opened a draft e-mail window and replied to Amanda that she had full confidence in her ability to manage the situation. It was annoying that the warranty part of the installation was not working, but if the replacement service handled the emergency efficiently, Savannah felt no loyalty to the installation company if they didn't respond when her business needed their help. She gave Amanda full authority to sign up a new company. At least this was an up-to-date computer and not a relic. They should be able to find any number of nearby services that could fix their problem.

After asking about Rooney, Snowy, Jacob, Suzy, and Amanda's mother, Savannah sent the e-mail, then dialed Edward's cabin to ask him to meet her on the top deck.

"Why did you want to meet here?" Edward was fully recovered and his slicked-back hair shone in the sun. "This is where the security staff think Ian went over."

"I think they're wrong. I wanted to see if there were any marks of a fall in this section. I'd like to be very sure of our belief before Ian's parents meet us at the port later this morning. We can examine each deck that we have access to for any signs of someone going overboard. I don't think we'll find anything, but I don't want to say that we haven't looked."

"I agree," Edward said with a serious edge in his voice. "I would never have thought of that. Brilliant."

Savannah had completed a sweep of the wooden railing on the top deck, when Edward turned toward the back of the ship. "What's that?"

"What's what?"

"Sounds like someone is crying." Edward tilted his head to locate the sound. He pointed back to the stern. "Over there."

They walked over to see a tall, lean young woman holding a tissue to her face. She blew her nose, crumpled the tissue, and stuffed it into the back pocket of her white short-shorts. Her light blond hair was blowing wildly over her face in the ship's breeze. She wore a simple navy tank and rich leather sandals. She didn't make a move to tidy her hair or wipe the tears streaming from her eyes.

"Miss," said Edward, "is something wrong?"

"I can't find him."

Edward and Savannah looked at each other, then turned to the young woman. Savannah moved to stand next to her. "You can't find who?"

She pulled a tissue from the travel packet she carried in her other hand. "I can't find Ian. The security police wouldn't help." She blew her nose again and stuffed the tissue in her back pocket. "I even told them we were engaged. I showed them my engagement ring." The young woman stuck out her hand and let the light catch on the small pearl ring. "But they said I wasn't a legal relation."

Savannah pointed to an angry welt on her arm. "Wait, how did you get that? Did you have a fight with Ian?"

The blonde covered the mark with her hand. "No, it wasn't like that. He wouldn't do that. Never."

Edward stepped over to stand close to her, and Savannah walked around to the other side of the weeping woman. Savannah glanced at Edward. He cleared his throat. "Excuse me, I'm Ian's cousin. Why on earth did he not tell me that he proposed?"

She used the heels of her hands to wipe her eyes and then turned her face into the bracing wind. "I was dating Ian back in my hometown. That's St. Albans." She looked up at Edward. "He didn't mention that a cousin was going to be on the cruise."

"We're even, then. Ian didn't tell me his fiancée would be here."

"Ex-fiancée." She sniffed and hiccuped. "We broke it off last week."

Savannah put her hand on the girl's arm. "My name

is Savannah Webb and this is Edward Morris. What's
your name?"

"It's Sally Maggio. I met Ian at the White Horse
Pub in St. Albans. We hit it off really, really, really
well. I thought he was going to be the one for me.
Really, I honestly did." She pulled out another tissue.
"And then my sister had to mess things up, of course.
That's what Ruth always does." Sally began to weep
in great gulps. Savannah put her arm around Sally,
who then let loose with deep sobs of misery.

"There, there." Savannah patted Sally on the back.
"I don't understand. What did your sister have to do
with Ian?"

"Everything," came as a muffled reply. Sally lifted
her head. "Ruth is my older sister and she's insanely
jealous of my boyfriends. She always charms them
away from me. Then she drops them like a hot rock,
but they never come back to me. It's spiteful, hateful,
mean, nasty, and bloody awful." Sally clung to Savannah
again and her sobs were so loud, people were beginning to stop and stare.

"Edward, let's take Sally somewhere quiet. How
about the secluded section on the front of deck
eleven?"

"Great idea." Edward led them to the elevator and
they went out the port side of the ship to a space with
a few lonely deck chairs and not a single person in
sight. They led Sally to a chair and sat on either side
of her.

Sally's crying had stopped. "Thank you so much
for taking me in hand. I'm grateful and it's thoughtful of you."

"Of course," Savannah said gently before glancing

at Edward. "Though we also want to know more about Ian's situation. Can you tell me more about you and your sister? How did you come to be on this cruise?"

"Again, that was my sister Ruth's doing. She talked me into this cruise with her as a bonding trip—a way to work through our issues and be close sisters again. There's only eleven months between us and some folks believe that we're twins. It worked out that we were in the same grade in school, so you can see how that keeps coming up."

"Yes, but—"

"Oh, sorry. I got off track again. Ruth made the arrangements through a travel office and we got on as part of a last-minute-deal special. I thought we were at last beginning to behave like adults and then Ian walked by while we were sunbathing beside the pool. I was so stunned that I yelled out his name."

Savannah prompted her, "And then what?"

"He stopped and looked at the both of us. He literally blushed red right up to his scalp. He obviously had no idea we would be aboard. Before I could explain, he blurted out, 'Can't you leave me alone?' and ran down the deck at a trot." Sally took a deep breath and pressed both hands to her face to stem the tears.

Savannah patted Sally's arm and they waited until she stopped crying.

"I haven't seen him since. I've looked everywhere."

Edward had turned pale and mottled. Savannah could tell he was embarrassed by the way he kept looking down at his feet.

"So, you don't know?"

Sally turned her red-rimmed eyes to Savannah, then Edward, and back to Savannah. "Know what?"

Edward cleared his throat. "Ian has been missing since the first morning of the cruise. No one in our party has seen him since he was out on the top deck that night at around midnight."

Savannah added. "We've left notes and voice messages, but we haven't heard from him at all. It's lucky that we ran into you."

"Did Ian's parents know about your relationship with Ian?" asked Edward.

"No." Sally's voice was calmer. "He was going to take me home to meet them, then Ruth pulled her dirty tricks."

"I'm afraid things have turned very serious," said Savannah. "The security team thinks that it's likely that Ian committed suicide by jumping overboard."

Sally leaped up to standing like a jack-in-the-box. "What?" she shrieked. "That's impossible. He wouldn't do that. I don't believe it."

Savannah stood and gently pushed her back into the deck chair. "We don't believe it, either; I'm only telling you what security said when we reported him missing."

"That's why we want to know more."

Sally sat silent. It looked like she was recalling a cherished memory.

Savannah tapped Sally's arm. "Please, can you tell us anything about that night? We need to know what Ian's frame of mind was."

"I lit into my sister like an angry Athena. I'm still furious that she would think this a joke. If it turns out that he took his life because of her selfish ways, I will never speak to her again. That's exactly what I'll do. She will be dead to me."

"We don't believe Ian jumped," said Savannah. "Do we, Edward?"

He shook his head from side to side.

Savannah continued, "There are conflicting opinions about his state of mind, but Ian seemed genuinely high spirited when we boarded. When did you last see Ian?"

Sally smiled. "It was up there on the top deck. He was walking by while I was watching the wake of the ship, being miserable."

"What did he say?" asked Edward after clearing his throat.

"He said he was embarrassed to have treated me so horribly." She looked at both Edward and Savannah. "That he should have been bold and realized that he had betrayed my trust by falling for my sister's charms. He said it was something that he despised about himself—that he didn't have the courage to do the right thing by me."

Savannah patted Sally's arm. "Did he seem unhappy?"

"Yes. Even though we talked about the situation, and he agreed with me at how horrible Ruth's behavior was for us both. He said that he was a worthless coward and not worth the air he was breathing."

Edward pressed his lips into a thin angry line. "That's absolute rubbish."

"That's what I told him. I also told him how much I loved him and that he needed to be strong so that we could overcome Ruth's actions."

"How did he take that?" asked Savannah.

"He said he was trying to work out some problems from his past, but he wasn't sure how that would affect our future."

Edward and Savannah frowned.

Sally leaned back in the deck chair. "Now, if you don't mind, I would like to be alone. I'm going to stay here until I figure out how to treat my sister."

"Where is Ruth now?" asked Savannah. "We would like to talk to her."

"She's camped at the smoking section. She's making a spectacle of herself, I'm sure. She's always the center of attention." Sally waved her hand in dismissal and pressed another tissue on her eyes.

Savannah and Edward could hear her sobs as they walked away.

"Do you think she's telling the truth?" asked Edward. "Could she have caused Ian to fall?"

"I just don't know."

The smoking section was easy to sniff out. The hard-core cruisers understood the idea of claiming one of the coveted sheltered lounge chairs nestled between partitions that reduced the sea breeze. Ruth was easy to spot. She resembled her sister in size but not coloring. Her hair was a burgundy red and her complexion was ruddy with a sheen of tanning oil. She emitted a strong coconut smell.

"Are you Ruth Maggio?" asked Savannah.

"Who wants to know?" Ruth shoved her large sunglasses up and parked them on the top of her head.

Edward took the lead this time. "I'm Edward Morris and this is Savannah Webb."

Ruth's eyes narrowed to a suspicious gaze.

"Edward Morris? Are you Ian's cousin—the one that went to Florida?"

"Yes, we want to talk to you about the last time you saw him." Edward looked around for a couple of chairs to pull over, but every single one had a dedicated smoker planted in it. "Can you—"

"He's an absolute snake. Don't talk to me about him." Her voice started rising. "I don't ever want to see him again." She began gathering up her cigarettes, lighter, and tanning oil, and stuffed them into a large beach bag. "I especially don't want to talk to you." She stuck her tongue out, then pulled her sunglasses back in place, stood, and left with her beach bag.

Savannah could feel her eyebrows shooting up toward her hairline. "That was an unusual response." She couldn't recall ever seeing a grown woman sticking out her tongue at someone.

Edward and Savannah left and returned to their favorite table at the pub. They ordered pints of Guinness. Edward spoke first. "Do you believe anything that they've told us?"

"I don't think we can discount the fact that Sally and Ruth were in the middle of a Dolly Parton song. You know the one. *Jolene, Jolene, Jolene, Jolene.*"

Edward sipped his pint. "I'm afraid you're right. At least we know why Ian was shaken when the Rosenberg twins saw him. He must have known that he would see the sisters again—St. Albans is a very small village—but there was no reason he would expect to run into them on this cruise."

"Right, and he can't really avoid them on the ship.

Even so it doesn't seem like a bad enough situation for jumping overboard."

"It still could be the problem with the primary school bully he saw. More likely it's something related to the counterfeiting ring. Maybe the thug tracked him down and started threatening him again. In his current vulnerable state, it might have been the last straw. Statistics state time and time again that one of the long-term consequences of serious bullying is suicide." Edward was silent for a few long moments, then shook his head to look at Savannah. "Maybe the two events have combined to be too much for Ian to handle."

Savannah checked her watch. "Ouch, it's nearly time for the demonstration. I've got to get changed and scoot up to the Hot Shop." She kissed Edward gently on the cheek. "Try not to worry. After the show, we've got to come up with a plan for locating Ian."

Chapter 13

After a speedy shower and change into her demonstration clothes, Savannah entered through the stage door to the Hot Shop after Eric but right before Alan. She was relieved that she wasn't very late. They finished their pre-demonstration checks and Eric signaled for a huddle. "Let's change the order this time and have Savannah go first with her fluted vase. I'll go next with one of my olive oil pitchers with a matching stopper. Alan, you'll bring up the rear this time, and could you make one of your mold-formed ornaments? We haven't done one in quite a while and you don't want to get out of practice. Okay with everyone?"

Savannah and Alan nodded. Then the three of them spent a few minutes getting their materials organized, pulling out multiple containers of frit and stringers, followed by making sure that the mold that Alan was going to use was clean and free of contaminants.

When they were ready, Eric started the program with his normal introductions, and Savannah selected a medium-sized blowpipe and opened the furnace for her first gather. She was trying hard to forget her worries about Ian, but sure enough, her concentration faltered for a moment and she burned her forearm as she pulled the blowpipe out of the furnace. She flinched automatically, but her body shielded the audience from viewing her mistake. Although it burned like fury, she had no trouble concentrating on forming her fluted vase.

As soon as she detached her finished vase from the blowpipe into Alan's waiting gloves, she walked over to her carryall and pulled out a burn ointment to apply to her forearm. Through painful experience, she knew she was in for a few days of irritation. But she didn't know of a practicing glassblower who didn't have a series of crisscrossed scars along their arms. It was the price of the art and her dues were being paid.

Savannah narrated for Eric's olive oil container. He was adamant about making them utilitarian rather than merely decorative. That meant that it not only needed to hold the oil without leaking, but also pour cleanly through a serviceable spout. Eric loved a challenge but it was a complicated piece that he fashioned out of plain clear glass.

The additional complication was that a stopper needed to be made to custom-fit the container. It had to be made immediately after the container was already in the annealing oven. One reason for this was to make sure the stopper had the same properties as the vessel, but the main reason was to check for fit while both pieces were still able to be corrected. Eric had done this many times, and as Savannah's first instructor had told her—you get good at what you practice.

After putting his blowpipe into the furnace to gather the glass for the stopper, Eric pulled it back out and frowned like Zeus. "The power's out! Alan, check the circuit breakers."

Alan ran over to stage left and pulled the circuit breaker door open. "Everything looks good," he yelled. "Is it heating?"

Eric was standing in front of the furnace. He opened the door and at a glance could tell that the molten glass was beginning to cool. "No, reset the whole bank."

Alan started from the top bank of circuit breakers, flipping them off and then flipping them on again. He did that for each row in the cabinet. "Okay, that's the lot."

Eric cracked open the furnace and stood for a long minute. "Great! It's back on." He turned to the audience. "Whew! That's a relief."

Savannah signaled for the crowd to applaud.

"I don't think I've ever created a successful stopper after the oil container has cooled. I need to have made the bottle right before the stopper." Eric gathered a small bit of clear glass and efficiently fashioned the stopper. It was a simple straightforward effort with no artistic flourishes. He didn't want to risk another power outage.

Eric had made at least two olive oil bottles each cruise for several months. He was a master. The crowd applauded loud and long after he finished.

It didn't hurt that I was able to explain what he and Alan were doing with some humor. Dad always said I had my mom's quirky sense of humor.

It was also good to bring some excitement to the performance by telling the audience when the risky bits were about to happen. After she turned over the wireless microphone to Eric, she assisted Alan in forming a spiraled ornament. The new part of the process was pressing a bulb of molten glass into a cast-iron mold that resembled a flowerpot with ridges on the inside. Alan had to stand on a bench so the molten glass remained in the mold while he blew some air into the form. After removing it from the mold he smoothed out the ridges on the stainless-steel marver table. Then he sat on the glassblowing bench and used a pair of pinchers to give the ornament a twist. He executed the process with confidence and created a blue and white ornament about the size of a large grapefruit.

Eric turned to the audience. "Thank you for your attention and your patience during our power issues. The pieces that we made today will be up for auction on the last evening of the cruise. We'll be hanging around for a little bit if you have some further questions." He bowed slightly, and the crowd stood and displayed their appreciation in applause. He removed the microphone from his head. "Thanks, guys, that was a great performance. Savannah, did I see you get a burn?"

"Yes, but it's relatively small. I've already applied ointment."

"Let me have a look."

Savannah showed him the burn.

"That is going to be painful for a few days. Because we're on a cruise ship, you must be extremely careful to avoid an infection. Get that taken care of down in the medical bay. You simply cannot walk around with an open wound. You must also wash your hands even more frequently. I'll bet the nurse asks you to re-apply the antiseptic cream ten or more times a day."

"Sure, thanks." Savannah helped the team square away the Hot Shop. "Don't we have a little break since today is a port day?"

Eric smiled. "Yes, we hardly ever give a demonstration while docked. Sounds a bit silly, doesn't it? It would be so much safer for us, but on the other hand, no one would be here."

Savannah smiled. "Are you going off the ship?"

Alan answered, "You bet. I know a small café that offers free Wi-Fi at monster-fast speeds. I download all the movies I can while I'm here."

Eric squinted at Alan. "I'll be hanging around the dock area. There is also a convenience store nearby that sells international phone cards at a great price."

Savannah caught up with Edward at the Passport Bar down on the Promenade deck after she went to the medical facility down on deck 2. It was a madhouse down there because it was also the boarding/exiting area for the port stop, Provence. She had to make her way upstream through the waiting lines of passengers who wanted to be first off the ship.

Edward had a nearly empty Guinness sitting in front of him with a full one waiting for her. She took a large swig. "Thanks, I needed that after that painful performance."

"What happened? I saw you flinch, but you didn't miss a beat."

"I burned myself on the blowpipe. I lost concentration for a second, so now I'll pay the price." She showed him the burn that had a thick coating of a burn ointment.

"Shouldn't that be wrapped?"

"I wouldn't let them do that. It would be distracting, which equates to dangerous while working the molten glass. It will be fine—I just need to keep it slathered in ointment. I heal quickly."

"The Rosenberg twins have invited us to dinner this evening with their new beaus."

"Beaus?" Savannah threw back her head and laughed out loud. "Did they really say that or is that a Brit phrase?"

Edward caught her infectious laugh and they both dissolved into a giggling fit. Savannah recovered first. "I'm sorry," she gasped. "It's really not that funny, but it sure took me that way."

"I think it's probably a near hysterical reaction to all the stress around Ian's disappearance." Edward wiped the tears from his eyes with the backs of his hands. "It's not a Brit thing, that's what Rachel called them. Anyway, I accepted for us. They said to show up at six o'clock. The dress code is smart casual."

"Edward," Savannah said in a musing tone, "I don't feel like we're our usual selves in this investigation."

"I feel the same. Could it be simply because this

investigation is uncovering my shirty past?" Edward also dropped his voice to a near whisper. "Has that changed your feelings?"

"No, but I feel a little hurt."

"Hurt? Why?"

"I guess I'm reacting to my whirling thoughts about your troubled youth. If we hadn't taken this cruise, would you ever have told me about your London days?"

"Fair question." Edward looked directly into Savannah's eyes. "I can't prove it now, I know, but I was planning to tell you about it before the end of the cruise."

"You're right. It's unprovable."

"I hope you believe me. It's crucial that we trust each other," said Edward.

"Well, I trust you, but now there's a little doubting voice in my head that will take some time to overcome. This has not turned out to be the relaxing cruise we were expecting."

"Plus, the fact is that this investigation is focused on the history of my family, not someone in the St. Petersburg art community," said Edward.

"That had occurred to me. Our other investigations were either close to me or associated with someone in the local art community. This is different. This is your family."

"I don't think I really appreciated the emotional trauma you must have suffered at the time." He paused and took her hand in both of his. "I had no idea."

"Maybe not, but you did all the right things."

"Meaning?"

"You didn't get impatient with my emotional reactions. You didn't stand in the way of my obsessive need to investigate. You stood beside me anyway."

"That's what I'll always do—I just didn't understand how important it was."

Edward folded Savannah into his arms and held her tight.

Minutes later, Savannah cleared her throat. "Did the ladies say six o'clock?"

Edward released her and gazed into her eyes. "Yes they did, but I am beginning to appreciate how important it is to savor the important moments."

"We are in total agreement, but the ladies will get anxious if we're not on time." She sealed their parting with a warm kiss.

Savannah hurried down to her cabin, and as she turned down the corridor she collided with Sally Maggio; they both fell to the floor in a heap.

Savannah recovered first and pulled Sally up by one arm. "Sally! What on earth are you doing on this deck? You aren't allowed here."

Sally brushed off the sleeves of her black blouse. "I was curious. I thought I saw Ruth down here, and her only mission, of course, would be to find Ian."

"Why?" Savannah shrugged her shoulders. "I don't get it."

Grabbing Sally by her upper arms, Savannah pulled her around to face her. "Do you mean you think she saw Ian?"

"Yes, and I think Ian saw Ruth." Sally wriggled out of Savannah's grasp. "Leave me alone. I don't want to talk to you."

Putting her hands out in front with the fingers spread wide, Savannah said, "Calm down. I'm trying to make sure you don't get into trouble for being in the staff area. You can actually be taken off the ship at port for violating your terms of passage."

"What?"

"Yes, indeed. Packed and disembarked at port. They have the right to do that. Didn't you read the terms and conditions? You signed them in order to come aboard."

Sally turned pale and looked up and down the corridor. "I didn't read them."

"No one does. Don't worry. I can get you back to the public area. Follow me."

Savannah took Sally by the arm and led her into one of the crew elevators. Luckily, it was empty.

They walked over to a crew access door. Savannah opened it wide and neatly pulled Sally onto the deck 14 jogging track. "You're fine here. Follow the track to the next set of sliding doors. That will take you to one of the public sets of elevators."

Sally let out a huge breath. "Thanks, I didn't realize that was such a taboo."

"No problem, but do me a favor."

"Sure, if I can," said Sally.

"Have Ruth call me." Savannah searched her pockets for a slip of paper but only found a café napkin. She at least had a pen and wrote on it. "Here's my cabin phone number and my cell number as well. Leave me a message when you find her. I want to make sure she hasn't seen Ian. Or better, I want to know if she *has* seen Ian."

Shaking her head in disbelief at the behavior of

the two sisters, Savannah went along to her cabin and changed into her only little black dress, wearing black pumps and topped by one of her handmade glass pendant necklaces. She met Edward at the elevators. He was dressed conservatively in a blue oxford shirt, tan slacks, and navy jacket. He looked her up and down. "I'm always surprised by how lovely you look in this dress."

"Well, if you only have one cocktail dress, it had better be well-fitting, versatile, and look expensive."

Edward kissed her on the cheek and then knocked on the suite door.

It was immediately answered by Albert, the Rosenberg twins' full-time butler. He was an amenity included with the cost of their suite. Albert was dressed in tails with a white bow tie and wore white gloves. His pencil-thin black mustache did nothing for the ruddy color of his face, but at least it matched his closely trimmed thick black hair. "Madam and sir, welcome to the penthouse suite." He stepped back to let them enter. "You will find the Misses Rosenberg in the lounge with the Messers VanGilden."

Savannah led the way into a large living room with floor to ceiling sliding glass doors, baby grand piano, two sofas, a full bar, and a gigantic television. A dining table was placed in front of a wall of mirrors. She could feel her eyebrows raise as she walked farther into the room. Each twin was seated on a sofa with one of the VanGilden twins. For a moment, Savannah felt disoriented with the surreal sensation that a mirror was splitting the room.

Faith Rosenberg popped up from the far sofa to

give her a hug. "Hi, dear. Please come in. Have you met our butler, Albert?" Faith whispered, "He's an absolute treasure. We couldn't begin to manage all the complicated arrangements for the entertainment, the specialty restaurants, and excursion venues without him."

Rachel also stood. "He's also fantastic about getting us meals from the specialty restaurants without actually having to go. I haven't eaten so well in years."

Faith said, "You recall that we have become acquainted with the VanGilden brothers?" She pointed to the nearest brother. "This one is Richard and that is his brother, Rickard."

Richard stood and shook hands with Edward and kissed Savannah's hand. "Pleased to see you. I understand that we missed you for dinner last night. It was a simple misunderstanding. We had invited the ladies to one of the specialty restaurants and we promised to have your main dining room waiter give you the news. It was simply a failure in communications. It was a dreadful faux pas."

Rickard agreed. "Yes, the meal at Murano on deck 5 is reliably spectacular but a little pricey. We used our sign-up bonus points to treat the four of us."

Rachel added, "The theme is Continental with a tilt toward new French."

Faith ticked off on her fingers. "We enjoyed an appetizer, soup and salad, fish course, sorbet, meat course, and dessert."

"One more thing, if you don't mind," said Richard. "We deplore being called Rich and Rick. We'll basically only answer to Richard and Rickard. Our parents named us after their fathers. We've fought against those dreaded nicknames since birth. Nightmare, really."

Rickard repeated the hand-kissing ritual with perfect ease. "Nothing really helped, as these ladies know."

Savannah felt a little dazed by their obviously practiced routine. "No problem . . . Richard and Rickard it is."

"Shall we sit at the table?" Rachel waved her hand toward the beautifully set table for six beyond the sitting room. "Albert is twitching to start our meal service."

The VanGilden twins each helped one of the Rosenberg twins sit across from each other on a long side of the oblong table. The gentlemen sat across from each other as well, leaving Edward and Savannah at the ends of the table.

After they were seated, Albert stood by Edward at the head of the table. "Would you care for a cocktail, sir?"

Looking up at Albert, Edward sat silent with a puzzled look on his face.

"He makes the most spectacular Cosmopolitans," said Faith.

"As well as perfect martinis," said Richard.

Edward broke from his reverie and ordered a dirty martini, and Savannah said she would try a Cosmopolitan. "You ladies are always saying how much you enjoy them. It's time I tried one."

Rachel cleared her throat. "I've also signed Richard and Rickard up for the Charity Walk on the last day of the cruise."

"It's a good way to get some walking in our last day at sea," said Faith. "Have you two been running at all? It's a wonderful track."

"I like the track," said Richard. "It has two clear lanes marked out."

"One for the runners and a separate one for the walkers," said Rickard. "Perfect for us old geezers to stay active but not get run over."

Albert stood at the bar and effectively entertained them with his practiced flourishes in producing the six drinks. When they had their drinks and Albert served two baskets of hot bread, Faith turned to Edward. "It's also a wonderful thing how concerned Albert is about Ian."

There was a crash as one of the serving platters that Albert was polishing bumped into the granite countertop of the wet bar, plummeted to the floor, and shattered to pieces. Conversation stopped, and everyone looked at Albert.

"Ladies and gentlemen, I apologize for my little accident. Please don't mind. It is nothing."

Faith pointed to the sleeve of his starched white shirt. "You're bleeding, Albert." A crimson stain was spreading from the cuff and wicking up the sleeve.

"*Dio santo!*" He shrugged out of his topcoat, avoiding the bloody cuff, then grabbed a napkin to staunch the bleeding at his wrist.

Am I to be constantly plagued by broken crockery? That broken teapot is jinxing me and everyone around me.

Savannah rose out of her chair. "Let me see."

Albert pulled his hand behind his back. "Madam, please, it's nothing to worry about. A tiny cut."

"Nonsense. I work with glass shards every day. You

might have cut an artery! It's possible for a sliver to work itself into your bloodstream. This is serious." She reached out her hand to him.

He huffed his irritation, but removed the napkin and stretched out his arm. Savannah took his wrist in her hand and examined the cut. "It's deep, but you missed everything important. Go down to the medical staff and get that dressed right away. Septic poisoning is a real danger with a bleeding wound."

"I can't leave during dinner service. I am still on my probation. Any time lost to an injury could count against me. I could lose my position." His face drained to chalk. "It took many years to work my way up to this level." He wiped the sweat from his forehead with his good hand. "Please, let me serve your dinner. Then, I promise that I will go directly to the medical team."

Savannah didn't believe him. "You know that's impossible. Blood and food never mix. It's lucky that you're nowhere near any open food dishes." She paused. "But I understand completely about not wanting to lose your job." She turned to Rachel. "Do you have a first aid kit?"

"Of course," said Faith. "We each have one. I'll get mine. One moment." She went into one of the suite's master bedrooms.

While Faith was fetching the kit, Savannah moved Albert to the bar and placed his wrist on one of the bar towels and used another as a compress. Faith returned with a white plastic zippered case with a large red cross on the sides. Faith placed the travel-sized kit on the wet bar.

"Here, Albert, keep pressure on with your other hand." Savannah rummaged through the well-appointed kit and withdrew antiseptic cream, wrapping gauze, scissors, and first aid tape. "How did you lose your grip?"

Albert flushed a deep red. "My mind wandered. I apologize." It took Savannah only a few minutes to bandage Albert ready for service. "Amazing, Miss Savannah. *Gratzi*." He flexed his wrist and put his coat back on. "You are so efficient." His little mustache wrinkled. "We haven't even lost the delivery timing for this bella perfect meal. It is being delivered right now. Sit. Sit. I have a pair of latex gloves to make serving super, super, safe."

Albert announced that the beginning course was charred beef with parmesan cheese, shaved asparagus with truffle mustard dressing, accompanied by slow-cooked Berkshire pork coated in a sweet and spicy glaze.

After sampling both, Edward commented, "I think the glazed pork would work well in my pub. I haven't heard of anyone else in town serving anything like this."

Savannah closed her eyes in pleasure after the first bite of the pork. "You won't be able to keep from running out of this every day. Do it."

Everyone was served a hand-selected dry-aged steak in their preferred cut. According to Albert, the beef was raised in Iowa and Nebraska. Each cut was dry-aged in a climate-controlled room for nearly four weeks to achieve the pinnacle of flavor, tenderness, and aroma.

Although everyone tried to savor the steak as long as possible, it was soon time for dessert. It did not disappoint. It was a chocolate cake with a molten fudge center and vanilla ice cream with a caramelized drizzle.

After declaring it the best meal she had ever eaten, Savannah left with Edward to check in with the security personnel to see if Ian had been detected using his keycard anywhere on the ship.

In the elevator going down, Savannah spoke. "That was a weird evening. Did you notice that Albert kept staring at you?"

"I did, but I thought it was because I dipped my cuff into the mustard dressing as soon as it was served. I wiped it off, but a mustard stain is usually permanent. I'm going to pick up a new shirt at one of the gift shops as soon as I can." They found Officer Gaffney at his normal position scanning the bank of CCTV screens. He stood up when they walked in. "No, nothing has been recorded from Mr. Morris's keycard. He can't possibly be on the ship," said Officer Gaffney.

Savannah spoke sharply. "Well, what have you done? I simply can't understand why there isn't more action. Don't you think this might be serious?"

"Patience, madam. We are following the accepted protocol for a missing passenger that is emotionally unstable."

"Oh, no." Edward put his hands over his ears. "This is a nightmare. I'm sure Ian was well and happy when we boarded this ship."

"Has a body been found?" asked Savannah.

Officer Gaffney turned a darker shade of red. "All the proper procedures are being followed."

Savannah turned to Edward. "That's a no."

"True, but we have made some inquiries with his local authorities and there was an attempted suicide, which a constable prevented. It turns out that, in fact, he was less than happy about many issues," said Officer Gaffney.

"What issues?" asked Savannah.

"I'm sorry, we can only discuss these personal details with Ian's next of kin. His parents are meeting us in Florence in the morning. They tried, but couldn't get an early enough flight to catch us at Provence. When they arrive, we'll brief them on the status of our investigation."

Edward frowned. "But I'm kin. He's my cousin."

"I'm sorry. You are not listed in his paperwork as his emergency contact. He had listed his father. We're going to speak to his parents tomorrow. They can share any information they want with you after that. My hands are tied."

"Can you at least keep Edward informed if there are any changes?" Savannah held Edward by the arm and started moving him toward the door.

"Of course," said Officer Gaffney. "We'll leave messages on your cabin phone."

Edward and Savannah left the security office feeling lower than ever.

Savannah pushed the elevator button. "Let's take a stroll on the upper deck. The fresh air may help us think of something we can do." Savannah held Edward by the upper arm in a double-handed grip. They stood at the railing near Ian's last sighting. "We'll be in Florence tomorrow morning. Have you tried Ian's phone again?"

Edward started, "It's been a few hours. Time to try again." The call went directly to voice mail and he left another message. On this one, he told Ian that his parents would be coming aboard to help the authorities find him. Edward ended the call and resumed looking out over the railing.

"Do you know what you're going to tell Ian's parents?"

"I have no idea." Edward's voice was low and lifeless.

"Well, one thing is still in our favor."

"What?"

Savannah pressed her lips together. "They haven't found his body."

"I don't see . . ." said Edward.

"This isn't the deepest water here. We haven't been all that far from shore the entire cruise. If he jumped over on our first evening, he likely would have washed up somewhere by now. Someone should be able to do the tide calculation thing that you see on television."

"This isn't television." Edward's voice turned soft.

"I know this might sound far-fetched, but it's true. Calculating the tidal effects on a human body is a real science."

Edward shook his head from side to side. "Of course, but who can we ask?"

"We can ask Jacob."

Edward crinkled his brow. "He's back in Florida. He can't possibly help us."

"Yes, he can." She gave Edward a serious look. "We can use the time difference to our advantage.

While we're asleep, Jacob can do the research for us and then when we get up, his results will be waiting for us.

"I think this is something that Jacob would love to do. He's already proved that he's good with sea charts and his librarian can help him find the tidal effects trends based on the ship's location in the Mediterranean Sea. If he doesn't think he can do it—he'll tell me straight out."

"That's at least something to try," said Edward. "Then we can give the results to security to make them pay more attention to searching the ship if the science says that he should have turned up by now." Savannah pushed away from the railing. "I've thought of something that Amanda can do to help us."

"Okay, what do you want her to do?"

Savannah grabbed Edward's arm and they started walking toward the elevators. "I want her to skulk around your past to find out about the Italian counterfeiting ring. She might be able to track down where any of the members are today."

Edward leaned back. "You don't believe me? You don't believe that I'm not involved anymore?"

"Of course, I believe you, but I'm not so sure about Ian's actions after you left for St. Albans, and you didn't keep in touch with the other members of the counterfeiting ring. You've already said that you didn't know what happened after you left. We should try to find out everything we can."

"It doesn't sound like trust."

"You know what I'm always saying . . . 'Trust but verify.' That's what I'm doing."

Edward puffed out a breath. "It doesn't sound like that to me."

Savannah put the palm of her hand over her eyes. "Is this one of those Brit/Yank conversations?"

"I think we're communicating perfectly," said Edward.

"Okay. I trust you."

"But I'm not sure. You tend to jump before you think and promise before you've thought things through."

Savannah bristled, then instantly sympathized. "You are perfectly correct, but it usually works out in the end. This has been an awful day and we're both tired and grumpy. I'm saying good night. I'll see you at dawn for breakfast." Savannah headed for the stairwell and sped down the decks to her Spartan cabin before she recalled that she hadn't kissed Edward before she bolted away.

I feel like a worm. I'm not being supportive to Edward, and now he thinks I don't trust him. Way to go. Some girlfriend you are.

Chapter 14

Wednesday, Webb's Glass Shop

Amanda printed off the last log sheet that Stephanie had e-mailed her for a manual accounting system. Although their previous antiquated system had been unreliable, it had never crashed completely. Looking back, she figured out that they had only two or three manual charges during any of the down times.

Webb's Glass Shop's accountant, Kevin Burkart, knew their Legacy system well and he had his assistant, Stephanie, create the forms for the shop to use until the maintainer could get their new system working. The new guy had dismantled the PC and placed the pieces beside the glass-cutting table.

The front door bell jangled at Kurt McNally's entrance. He was the owner of the local computer service only a few blocks away. "Hi, Amanda. I'm not too late, am I? I brought you a coffee from the pub next door. They knew exactly how you like it."

Amanda smiled and reached for the coffee.

"Thanks, I really need this. My mom had a poor night and the nursing home called me in to help calm her. I didn't get much sleep." She took a long drink. "Then, of course, we've had the big mess with the accounting system. Thanks for responding on such short notice. I hope you can finish it up today. I lost another customer yesterday. Did you find the part?"

Kurt lifted an Amazon box for her to see. "Yep, I got the exact replacement part I think is causing your troubles." He looked over to the torn-down PC. "I should have it up in no time at all."

"Why would a brand-new computer need a replacement part?"

"I think it's the power supply. That's how it behaves. If a computer's brain is its processor, its heart is the power supply. And having one that is underpowered, unstable, or just generally cheap is the most common cause of hardware failure."

Amanda frowned. With a pleasant shock, she realized that she liked him. He was thoughtful, easy to talk to, and seemed to enjoy her wicked sense of humor. "Well, don't rush it or anything."

He turned back to look at her and he smiled in perfect understanding. "No rushing from me."

"I'll be checking e-mails if you need anything." Amanda walked through the classroom to the small office in the back of the store. She sat at the ancient roll-top desk and booted up the computer. She wondered if Savannah would ever replace her dad's office computer. She shook her head. Of course not. It hadn't yet been a year since Savannah's dad had died and, although there were many changes in the everyday running of Webb's Glass Shop, this office was almost a shrine to John Webb.

She reflected on her reaction to Kurt. Her last relationship had been an emotional disaster. She had kept secrets, nearly lost Savannah's trust, and at the end of it lost all confidence in her ability to make good decisions. Perhaps Kurt represented a new start. New starts were good.

Amanda had worked through most of the routine business, then checked the e-mails to see one had come in from Savannah. Looking at the time stamp, Amanda determined that with the time difference, it had been midnight for Savannah when she wrote the message. Amanda read it quickly and lurched back in the oak desk chair, causing it to shriek like a barn owl.

Ian was missing!

Edward must be beside himself with worry.

Scanning the message quickly, Amanda could see that there was something she could do.

Good. Her Internet research skills had been helpful to Savannah's part-time role as an expert consultant to the St. Petersburg Police Department. Amanda wondered who would be foolish enough not to take Savannah seriously on the cruise ship. "They must not know about her past cases. Oh, well, they'll soon learn."

She reread the e-mail and began her task. Her concentration was so deep that when Kurt knocked on the office door, she jumped straight up and out of the chair. "Lordy! You gave me a scare."

"Sorry, sorry," said Kurt. "I thought I'd give you the good news . . ."

"Oh, wonderful." Amanda clapped her hands. "It's fixed?"

"And the bad news." Kurt frowned. "The new part fixed the power supply problem, but there's still a problem with the system."

Amanda felt her lips begin to smile but quickly adjusted to a concerned frown. "That's too bad. Do you need any special parts that might be difficult to find?"

"No, this is some sort of software initialization bug. I need to trawl through the systems files and I'll bet I find either a corrupted or missing data file. Do you mind if I stay to keep working on it?"

"Oh." Amanda felt her heart leap. She suppressed that and gave out a long sigh. "Well, I must have that system working. It's vital. We can't really run off the manual system for more than a few days. It's been two days already. Customers have begun to say they'll come back, but they really don't mean that. They're going to take their business to our competitor's shop downtown."

"Really?"

"Yes. People are busy and they don't have time to wait to buy supplies. They need them right then or their projects are stalled. Frank Lattimer's shop is downtown. He must be overjoyed to hear that we're having computer troubles. His prices are about the same as ours, but he stocks inferior quality supplies—disgraceful."

"So, you want me to stay?"

"Until it's fixed." Amanda smiled up at him. "Do you need permission from your office?"

"I'm my only employee."

"Perfect," said Amanda as she pressed her hands together as in a prayer. "Pretty please fix it?"

"I'm on it until it works." Kurt beamed a bright smile, spun on his heel, and left.

Amanda turned back to her research and began the deep dive that it would take to find the information that Savannah wanted. There were several complications to getting anything on Ian's background. He was British. The time frame was before social media had become mainstream. There was hope, however, in that most public records and newspaper archives had been scanned into searchable databases and were now accessible.

The schoolhouse clock in the office read nine o'clock when Amanda finished typing up her results in an e-mail to Savannah. She noted that there were several threads that she hadn't resolved, but noted to Savannah that she expected to find more answers tomorrow.

"I've got it fixed!" Kurt leaned against the office door and his expression broadcast his success. "You need to try it out."

"Okay, let me shut this old boy down and I'll be right out."

She quickly tidied up the office, powered off the computer, locked the back door, and grabbed her enormous handbag before going through the classroom to meet Kurt at the sales counter. "Oh, it's all done!"

"Yes, I put it all back together and it works great. I don't think you'll have too much trouble figuring out how to work it, but I wanted to give you the complete operational drill before I left."

"That's wonderful!" Amanda grabbed Kurt by the shoulders and planted a huge kiss on both cheeks. "You have no idea how great this is!"

Kurt looked dazed, his cheeks red where Amanda had kissed him. "Right, I have no idea."

Amanda plopped her handbag on the counter and rubbed her plump hands together as if warming them. "Now show me how to work this beast."

"It's pretty intuitive," he started, but Amanda interrupted.

"No, no, no! I've heard that before. I want a blow-by-blow tutorial followed by a full shutdown and then another full start-up. Then, and only then, will I allow you to take me for a drink at Queen's Head Pub."

Kurt grinned. "My pleasure on both counts."

Chapter 15

Savannah woke before dawn and looked out her tiny porthole. The ship was cruising slowly along a rocky cliff. Good. The ship hadn't docked yet. Watching the huge ship dock was one of the events that Savannah wanted to see.

But first, she wanted to fire up her laptop, check her e-mail, before she met Edward for breakfast and then heading with him to the secluded area on deck 14 to watch the maneuvers.

She read through Amanda's initial search results. Amanda had found an obscure article in one of the London papers about dockworkers who had found salvation from their crime-ridden lives in the arts. That obscure hint inspired Amanda to a surprisingly creative search that led to glassblowing as one of the recovery arts. Amanda thought that one of the glassblowers working on the ship might be one of those reformed scam artists.

Savannah leaned back in her chair. Eric or Alan

involved in the currency scam? That was a result from left field. She read the rest of the e-mail. Amanda couldn't confirm more until she had their personal details. Savannah replied with everything that had come up in casual conversation along with their full names, hometowns, and descriptions of both members of the glass-blowing team.

Given the difficulty Alan was having with his memory after the Vespa hit-and-run, Savannah wondered if it could be Eric. He was certainly large enough to be thought of as a thug, but she hadn't seen that kind of behavior out of either one of them. Was bullying something you could turn on and off depending on the situation? She resolved to watch both closer during the next demonstration.

She dressed as quickly as she could and dashed to catch the elevator up to deck 14. Edward was pacing in front of the elevator doors.

"I'm so sorry. I was such an idiot last night." Savannah's words tumbled out in a rush as she stepped into his arms. "I behaved horribly and added grief while you're already dealing with tons."

"It's all right," he whispered. "We were both upset."

"Have you heard anything?" asked Savannah.

"Not a peep." He hugged Savannah for a long moment. "I'm dreading this morning with my aunt and uncle."

"Let's not worry about that yet. I have some news from Amanda. But, first let's get some coffee and food." They picked out a hardy full English-style breakfast at one of the food stations with fried eggs, sausages, broiled tomatoes, baked beans, and grilled mushrooms. They both turned down the blood pudding but piled on the fried bread.

They found a quiet table for two. "Okay, spill it," said Edward after he had devoured one of his three fried eggs. "What did she find out?"

Savannah washed down her mouthful of mushroom with her heavily creamed coffee. "She found your primary school records in St. Albans."

"But that's too late!" Edward dropped his fork and knife on the table.

"Shh." She reached over and patted his hand. "Calm down and listen. She said that led to your primary school records in London—which is the same school as for Ian. That's where she's researching now. She has a lead on who was your teacher and was sending off an e-mail. She was a young woman at the time—a Miss Banks, I think?"

"Yes, I remember her. She was thin with buck teeth."

"Amanda also wants any names that you can recall from your London days. Anything can be a lead."

Edward scratched his hair just over the right ear. "It was a terrible time for me. I remember the big boss's name, of course. It was Jimmy the Fist. I never saw him but heard that the name came from the fact that his hands were huge. Our handler was a small squirrelly guy named One Eye. I think his real name was Terry. But he was really old at the time and it's not a career choice that enjoys a long life expectancy."

"Right, but really old to a youngster could be mid-twenties."

Edward nodded and scarfed up another mouthful of fried egg.

"She also thinks one of the glassblowers could be from your shared past as well."

"How did she find out about that?" Edward mumbled around a mouthful of traditional fried bread.

"I told her. You know how determined Amanda is when she's got a good source. She'll bulldog this until we have some real information."

"We can also ask Ian's parents." He picked up his fork and knife and returned to his breakfast, then said quietly, "I'm still dreading this."

"I know, but they will probably be better with us here than trying to keep them up-to-date through phone calls. They can also put more pressure on the security officers than we can. Worried next-of-kin pull a lot of weight."

They finished breakfast and went to the top deck to watch the docking of the large ship in a narrow slip. They waited until the drawbridge at the stern end of the ship had been extended and secured.

Savannah and Edward bypassed the overloaded elevators and took the stairs down to the deck where Kate and Howard would board. When they arrived, Security Officer Dalessio was waiting for them. However, the press of excited tourists meant that Ian's parents couldn't get onto the gangway against the press of the crowd. Savannah could see them waiting for the exodus to subside.

Savannah grabbed Edward by the hand. "Do you have your keycard with you?"

"Yes."

"Great! Let's go."

She pulled him into the disembarking queue and they zipped their keycards through the machine and walked down the short gangway with all the other excursion passengers. They turned and found Ian's parents.

The difference in their appearance from the celebration was drastic. Aunt Kate seemed a pale watercolor of the woman flushed with pride at her son's accomplishments. Uncle Howard's complexion had a gray, waxy tone. The seriousness of his look nearly broke Savannah's heart.

"Edward!" shouted his aunt Kate. "I'm so relieved to see you. We couldn't get by the crowd." She grabbed Edward and stepped into his waiting hug. "We know that they've got this terribly wrong."

"I wish we could be taking you to the nearest pub to meet with Ian, Mrs. Morris," said Savannah. "We're sure they have it wrong, but we don't have Ian yet."

Uncle Howard waited patiently for Edward to release his wife. He extended his hand for a quick handshake and put his other hand on Edward's shoulder. "I told Katie that you and your clever friend here would be able to help sort this out."

Savannah smiled. "Thanks for the confidence, but we're a long shot from solving exactly where Ian could be. This is a large ship and we've had no help from the security office yet."

"Well," said Uncle Howard. "We'll see about cooperation. What would you like them to do?"

Savannah held on to Aunt Kate's hand. She could feel the slight trembling. The poor woman was trying to hold things together under what must be a terrible strain. "It would be most helpful if you could ask them to give Edward and me access to all the recordings of Ian that occurred on that first day on board."

Uncle Howard nodded. "We can do that. Is there anything else?"

Edward took his uncle's arm. "Yes, we want you to tell them that we are acting as your agents and that all information is to be shared with us."

The flow of passengers had finally waned and the four of them walked up the gangway. They checked into the entry console.

"Welcome aboard, Mr. and Mrs. Morris. I'm Chief Security Officer LuAnn Dalessio." She neatly stepped in front of Savannah and Edward to separate them from Ian's parents. "Would you mind coming down to my office as soon as you're settled in your suite?"

"Suite?" Edward repeated. "Aunt Kate and Uncle Howard, where are you staying?"

Aunt Kate stopped in the hallway, put her hand to her forehead, and turned to them. "Oh, I didn't tell you, did I?"

Edward gave her a stern look. "No, you didn't."

"One of your friends—actually two of your friends— the Rosenbergs, kindly sent us a telegram to say that we could share their large suite with them. They said their magical butler found us. Wasn't that kind?"

Uncle Howard added. "We could hardly refuse. They said that they had more than enough room for us and it would be better for the investigation."

Savannah looked up at the ceiling. "Of course, that's typical of their famous generosity. They would do that."

"They said they knew you."

Savannah nodded. "Edward and I know them very well. They've been taking classes at Webb's Glass Shop for a long time. They are a little strange, but their hearts are in the right place."

Edward smiled. "You're in the best of hands."

"The magnificent Albert will certainly make you welcome." Savannah drew a hand through her curls. Edward and Savannah watched Chief Dalessio lead Ian's parents away for their briefing.

Savannah turned to Edward. "The Rosenbergs are trying to hire Albert away from the cruise line to work for them back in St. Petersburg."

Edward chuckled. "He must be terrified. What an unusual opportunity. I wonder how he would handle a working situation in the crazy state of Florida."

"I wonder how he's going to handle turning down the position without offending the generous Rosenberg twins. They are legendry over-tippers."

Chapter 16

Thursday, in port, Florence

Savannah and Edward were still annoyed that they had not been invited to the thorough briefing that the security office promised to give to Ian's parents. They went to the coffee shop and ordered double espressos while Savannah loaded up a plateful of pastries from the service counter. Edward used his keycard to pay for the premium drinks, and they sat in a corner table away from the other passengers.

"We know where they'll end up," said Savannah, trying to comfort Edward. "In the Rosenberg suite."

"I'm gob smacked that the twins would be so generous to people they hadn't even heard of until a few days ago." Edward drank his coffee and mumbled in the midst of munching a giant blueberry muffin. "I'm starved."

"Anxiety takes me the opposite way from you. I can't eat a bite right now!" She pushed the plate of sweets toward Edward. "Let's go up to the suite and wait for your aunt and uncle with Rachel and Faith. I'm sure they're anxious as well."

They drained their coffees and stood to make their way to the elevators. Two security guards appeared to block their way. "Mr. Edward Morris?" said the younger guard. His voice grated on Savannah's ears. It was thin and high.

Edward looked at him and the older, stockier guard. "Yes, what's the problem?"

"We are ordered to escort you down to the security office for questioning. It would be best, sir, if you follow along peacefully." The voice of the older officer was smooth and calming. Obviously experienced in the persuasive ways of encouraging intoxicated passengers to cooperate.

Savannah stepped in front of Edward. "Why do you need to talk to him?"

"Miss," said the older guard. "This is a matter for Mr. Morris alone. Please step aside." He firmly took Edward by the arm to the elevator.

"Don't worry, Edward," Savannah shouted. "I'm sure they just want to talk with you about Ian. If things get out of hand, I'll contact the British Embassy to let them know what's happening and then I'll phone your parents. I'm sure this is just routine. Don't worry."

Her last peek at Edward was of him standing over a foot taller, but still being held by each arm by one of the guards. The doors closed on Edward's concerned look.

Savannah turned around and was surprised by the thudding in her chest. *They can't be serious. The British*

Embassy threat was just that—an empty threat, but it sounded serious. Why would they take him *in for questioning?*

She went to her cabin and locked the door for privacy, then took a bit of time to think through her call to Edward's parents. She concentrated on telling them the circumstances without causing undue alarm. She told them she thought the situation would be resolved soon.

After that she made her way to the Rosenbergs' suite and knocked on the door. It opened and Albert said, "Miss Savannah. It is a pleasure to see you again. The ladies are expecting you." He looked behind her and down the corridor. "They were expecting Master Edward as well. Will he be joining us?"

"Not just yet, Albert. It's complicated."

When she entered the sitting room, she looked through and saw Rachel and Faith leaning against the railing out on the huge balcony. They were talking to Ian's parents who had apparently received what looked like a very short briefing. Savannah was about to slip through the sliding doors onto the balcony to update them on Edward's situation.

"It's nothing to do with Edward," said Uncle Howard. "There's no reason for the authorities to take that line and ask us about Edward. He would never harm Ian. They have been best friends for their entire lives."

Aunt Kate patted her husband's forearm in a rhythmic pattern. "Now, Howard. Let's not make things more difficult for everyone. There are many things we don't know about our young men's private lives. Edward and Ian have had a complicated relationship. They both began to get secretive long before we moved to St. Albans. Do you remember how confused we were at the change in their personalities?"

Uncle Howard shook his head. "What a terrible time. I was working long hours back then."

Savannah marched out onto the balcony. "They've taken Edward down to the security office for questioning."

"What?" said Rachel.

"Why?" said Faith.

"I don't know what to think. We've both been down there over the past few days pleading for them to start a ship-wide search for Ian." Savannah felt her eyes blur. "And their action is to question Edward? That's unbelievable!"

"But what basis could they possibly have for questioning Edward?" asked Rachel.

Faith shook her head. "It could be a straight-forward case of being the closest relative aboard when Ian went missing."

Savannah plopped down in one of the deck chairs and folded her arms across her chest. "I don't know what they're thinking, but they've gotten this wrong. However, they are a security office and they have ways to get information that even our Amanda can't get."

She looked at Ian's parents. "Did you tell the ship's security officers about Edward's and Ian's past?"

Uncle Howard walked over to his wife and held her in a side hug. "Edward told you about that?"

"Yes. Reluctantly, of course."

Aunt Kate looked up into her husband's soulful eyes. "We've kept this quiet all these years, but I don't see how that could possibly relate to what is happening now."

Uncle Howard's right hand thrummed a continuous rhythm that seemed to be trying to calm them both.

This is how a strong marriage works. They support each other, look out for each other, and depend on each other. Is that what I would like to experience with Edward?

"What did—" Savannah stopped when Albert arrived at the sliding door with a silver tray weighed down with sterling silver teapot, creamer, sugar bowl, cups, saucers, tiny spoons, and an extra pot of hot water. He placed the tray on the large round teak table and made a little half bow. "I'll pour, shall I?"

Rachel was the first to respond. "Of course, Albert."

Faith continued. "You're taking such wonderful care of us. We're going to miss you terribly when we go home."

He poured a cup of tea for each of them, asking if they wanted milk and sugar.

Savannah had to press her nails into her palm to keep her impatience under control.

After everyone was settled with a cup of tea, Albert performed another little half bow. "I will be back in a moment with scones, clotted cream, and strawberry jam." He somehow backed out of the balcony without tripping over the threshold.

"What did you tell security about their past?" Savannah said quickly.

Aunt Kate scooted her chair closer to Savannah's. "They seemed to already know about the trouble the boys were involved with. I don't know how they found out. What kinds of connections would they need for that? There were no arrests, but that was the topic they kept returning to every time we asked them about searching the ship."

Uncle Howard slurped his tea in a noisy rush. "I get the impression that they think Edward and Ian had an argument and as a result, Edward either accidently or intentionally pushed Ian overboard."

The twins gasped, "No!"

Albert cleared his throat. "Your scones, ladies and gentleman." He carried another large silver platter laden with about fifteen small plates of assorted scones, cucumber sandwiches, slices of cake, and decorated chocolates. As soon as he placed the tray on the table, Rachel sat tall. "That will be all for now, Albert. We'll serve ourselves, thank you. Please leave us until we ring for you to collect the trays."

Albert bowed toward Rachel and said, "Yes, miss. I'll be waiting to serve you. Press the service button and I'll return in an instant." He again backed out and they heard the door to the suite click shut.

Faith sighed deeply. "I love how that man makes me feel like royalty."

"A little too royal, sister. I didn't want him to over-hear the family troubles. We need *some* privacy now and then."

Savannah frowned, trying not to be annoyed by the twins. Though they were easily distracted from the situation by the finery of their suite, they *had* extended their hospitality to two complete strangers because of their fondness for Edward and Savannah. "I don't think Edward is feeling much like royalty right now."

"No, possibly not," said Howard. "But this business about security already knowing so much worries me." He glanced toward the entry door to the suite. "Could Albert be an informant?"

"That would explain a few things." Savannah scrunched her forehead. "Rachel, could you turn on some lively music?"

Rachel turned the TV on and selected a music station that was playing ABBA tunes. "How's that?"

"Perfect. I want to bring you all up to speed about everything that we've discovered, and I want to make sure we're not overheard." Then she stood. "I'm going down to talk to security. Maybe they've changed their minds about Edward."

When Savannah got into the elevator, the only other passenger was the gaffer, Alan. She smiled, but her mind was whirring. Amanda had listed Alan as a possible suspect in Edward's history with the counterfeiting ring. "Hey, Alan. Are you going ashore now? There's not much time left before we're at sea again." He had a large rucksack over his shoulder.

"Well, yeah. Uh, I know an out-of-the-way Laundromat near the dock. It's so much better than the ship's service and it means that I don't need to buy so many shirts. They get pretty faded by both the sun and the rough laundry by the end of each tour." He had pushed the button for the crew exit, which was the same deck as security.

When the doors opened, he flew out of the elevator and down the hallway. Savannah said, "See you at tonight's demonstration." He didn't turn around but waved a hand high above his head.

Savannah tilted her head. Alan didn't strike her

as someone who was particularly fussy about his clothing. It seemed a wasteful use of limited shore time to spend it in a Laundromat. What was the real reason? Was he meeting someone that he didn't want anyone to know about?

Savannah knew her visit wouldn't be welcome, but the faces of both Officer Gaffney and Chief Dalessio were expressionless. She felt a cold rock form in the pit of her stomach. This was bad.

"We cannot help you, Miss Webb," said Officer Gaffney.

The cold rock in her stomach grew into a frozen boulder. "I want to speak to Edward Morris."

"We cannot let you do that, Miss Webb."

"Why are you holding him down here? What has he done? I have alerted the British Embassy."

"That is a sensible precaution, Miss Webb." The rock in her stomach grew into a bigger boulder. If security agreed that it was a good decision to get the authorities involved, then Edward was in serious trouble.

"It is good that you're here, Miss Webb. We also have some questions for you. Please step this way."

"It's about time . . . I would have expected you to have interviewed everyone in Ian's party within the first hour of his being reported missing." She followed Officer Gaffney. "That's what would have happened back home."

"You are not at home, Miss Webb." Officer Gaffney opened a notebook and then asked Savannah, "How long have you known Ian Morris?"

"I met him on Saturday morning when he picked us up from Heathrow Airport in London."

Officer Gaffney laboriously wrote in his notebook for a good two minutes.

Savannah frowned. *He is completely unqualified to carry out an investigation. He's merely a security guard. I should feel sorry for him except that he's got Edward.*

"Where were you on the first night of the cruise?"

"After my glass demonstration, I spent the night with Edward."

Officer Gaffney looked up from his notebook. "That's not allowed!"

"Maybe not, but it gives Edward an alibi, doesn't it?"

"He says he was alone that night."

"That's being British—my statement is that we were in his cabin all night. So, unless you're also going to lock me up, I'm done with your questions. Can I see Edward?"

They refused to let her see Edward or even talk to him. The boulder of fear threatened to explode out of her stomach like in the *Alien* movie. She returned to her room and clicked the icon for her e-mail service. As soon as it refreshed, Savannah saw a message from Nicole Borawski, Edward's bartending manager.

Dear Savannah, For some reason, Edward isn't answering his e-mail or even responding to his phone's voice mail. There's a slight problem here at Queen's Head. The commercial dishwasher has flooded the entire pub. It happened after we had all gone home so it had hours and hours of time to flood the place to a depth of four inches.

I've closed the place for at least a week. I found a service to replace the dishwasher and another recovery outfit to remove the water. After that we need to dry out the walls, replace some of the supplies that were stored on the floor.

Luckily this was a gas station in its prior life and the floor is painted concrete, so no real damage there. The touch-up painting can wait until after the pub is open again.

It's useless to tell Edward not to worry, but there's nothing he can do from there. The credit card has almost enough reserve to cover everything, but the closure is the killer. Will work as fast as possible to get us even partially open.

Sorry for the bad news,

Nicole Barowski

Savannah let her forehead fall to the surface of her tiny desk.

Is the bad luck curse of that broken teapot haunting me? Things can't possibly get worse.

Chapter 17

Thursday, at sea

Savannah responded to Nicole's e-mail with as much positive encouragement as possible. She knew that Edward would be responding to Nicole's messages if he wasn't buried deep in the depths of the ship in an interview room. She sincerely hoped he wasn't in a jail cell. She tried not to let her imagination run toward a dungeon with clanking chains and growling inmates with tin cups. She failed.

She shook her head, then glanced at her watch. "Rats! I'm about to be late again. Eric is going to be annoyed."

She took a quick shower, changed into her Hot Shop shirt, shorts, and dockers. She ran as fast as she could to the elevator without knocking anyone down. It was clear from the smiles and chatter that everyone had returned from a great day in Florence.

When she opened the stage door on the demonstration set, she found Eric pacing with his hands behind his back. "There you are. I was beginning to think this would be a solo performance."

"Sorry, but I've been dealing with family issues."

"At least you're here. Have you seen Alan?"

"Not since he left the ship to do his laundry. That was this morning."

"Laundry? He never does his laundry in port."

Savannah started pulling out containers of royal blue and powder blue frit for the team colors of a Tampa Bay Rays baseball fan. "That's what he told me on his way off the ship. He had a large duffel-type backpack." She continued to perform the start-up tasks. "Have you called him?"

"Good idea." Eric pulled out his cell and she could hear the ringing tone followed by the voice mail message. Eric punched the end call button so hard she thought it might break the screen.

The audience was beginning to get restless on the crowded benches. Savannah waved a little hi to the two sets of twins in the second row behind the row of children. She felt sorry for Ian's parents, who had found a couple of bar stools at the back of the seating area. They looked pale and there were dark circles under their eyes.

Eric tried to reach Alan again, but this time the call went straight to voice mail. He punched the phone even harder. "I'm going to call the cruise director's office and have them page him in the crew area." He spoke into his phone for a few minutes, then put it on silence mode. "Let's get everything ready to give him as much time as we can."

They both finished the start-up tasks and Eric selected three graduated shades of orange and a final shade of red. "I'm going to try an ombré look with this platter." His eyes widened and his brows shot up. "I've managed it twice out of the last ten times." After that he stood with his hands on his hips. "We'll have to get started without him." Eric looked out to the audience for the first time and slapped his forehead. "This is children's day. I completely forgot."

"What's that?"

"The first row is reserved for the children from the six-to-nine age group who have made a drawing of something they would like to see us make. The child gets to take home the one I choose to make." He sighed heavily. "This is my most challenging demonstration of the entire cruise. I hope I can pull out an easy drawing this time. We need to stay simple since there are only two of us."

Savannah looked out into the audience. There were about fifteen children and each had a sheet of paper with a colorful drawing. Their counselor collected them and she waved Eric over to the side of the stage and handed him the stack.

"Good luck with your choice," said the cheerful counselor. "The children have been truly creative on this cruise."

Eric quickly shuffled through the drawings and after he had paged through to the last one, he looked over to Savannah and dropped his voice to a whisper. "These are great drawings—not a simple one in the bunch."

He walked over to the stainless-steel marver table and signaled for Savannah to follow. "I'm eliminating the ones that are impossible." He separated them into two stacks. Then he spread out the remaining six drawings and studied each one. He placed his hands on his hips and finally picked out the drawing of a beautiful little giraffe. "I can do this one—I think. I made a giraffe last year, so at least this won't be my first. I had trouble with the spots last time, but I think I can do better." He put the remaining five on the stack and returned them to the counselor.

Using the drawing as a color reference, he picked out his frit containers and placed them against the back edge of the stainless-steel marver table beside Savannah's. He explained the children's program to the audience and requested that the owner of the giraffe drawing stand up.

"It's mine!" said a little, pale redheaded girl. She stood and raised her hand as high as it would go. Eric asked for her name. "Colleen!" she shouted, then turned around to the rest of the audience. "That's my drawing." Everyone laughed and applauded as Eric handed over the microphone to Savannah.

Savannah began narrating Eric's creation of the little giraffe. It was difficult since this was a freelance creation and Eric was trying to recall how he approached it last year. He took his time. After each step, he would show the entire first row of children his progress. It was refreshing to see how interested they were. When he finished the last step before separating it from the punty, he held it up high for everyone to see. The audience loved it and clapped their delight.

Each demonstration piece was difficult for both Savannah and Eric. It took longer without a dedicated assistant, which meant more oven reheating. It required more concentration on Savannah's part to talk about the glassmaking while also assisting to create their pieces.

It was Savannah's turn next and she now regretted her plan for a complicated vase. However, the production went well. Eric seemed irritated at interrupting his patter with the need to assist Savannah during the creation of her fluted vase. She was pleased when it turned out to be the best so far. The vase would surely garner an auction bid of at least a thousand dollars.

Their final piece of the day was Eric's ombré platter. There were multiple frit pickups on the stainless-steel marver table. Savannah narrated calmly and was soon comfortable with just the two of them in front of the audience. She shared Eric's relief in completing the beautiful platter and placing it safely in the annealing oven.

"Thank you, ladies and gentlemen," said Eric at the end of the demonstration. "The little giraffe will be ready for Colleen to pick up at tomorrow afternoon's demonstration. Thank you." There was a large wave of applause and the usual lingering around to ask questions.

Finally, they were alone.

"Whew! That was the most difficult demonstration I've done at sea." Eric wiped the sweat from his forehead and stood under one of the air-conditioning vents to cool down. He lifted his T-shirt away from his body to let the air get to him.

"No one would have known. You looked calm." Savannah began the cleanup tasks. "That giraffe is perfectly adorable. Colleen is a lucky little girl."

"Do you mind doing the cleaning up? I'm going

to try Alan's room as well as his phone again." Eric pulled out his phone and stood near the stage door, so he wouldn't be overheard.

Savannah put the frit containers back on the shelf, wiped down the stainless-steel marver table, and swept the glass debris from the deck.

Eric returned with the clipboard in his hand. "No luck at all from his cell, but cell phones are not reliable at sea. It sometimes drives me crazy, but Alan didn't want to carry around a walkie-talkie. Honestly, neither did I, but I may rethink that since he missed this demonstration."

"Do you think it's because of his memory?" asked Savannah.

"I sincerely hope not. If he can't remember to show up to the demonstrations, he will definitely lose this job."

They finished the shutdown checks, then Eric hung the clipboard back on its hook.

"I'm going to call security about paging Alan. They don't like it—but he hasn't given me much choice." He opened the access panel near the stage door, picked up the phone receiver, and dialed security. He spoke in a clipped voice. "My name is Eric Barone. I'm the supervisor of the glassblowing team. Please page Alan Viteri. He needs to report to me up at the Hot Glass shop."

There was a long pause.

"What?" said Eric, straining his soft voice. "Say again," he said even a bit louder. "Are you absolutely sure?"

Another long pause. "Okay. Well, here's the thing. I'm on record as Alan's supervisor and I should have been informed as soon as you knew that he hadn't checked in. A call, a voice message, or a handwritten note under my door. I will be reporting this to the corporate office in my weekly report."

He turned around and slammed the receiver back in the cradle.

"What is it?" Savannah didn't like the grim look on Eric's face.

"Security knew that Alan didn't return from our Florence port."

"They knew?"

"Yes. They knew and didn't seem to think it important enough to let me know."

"That seems odd. They've been preaching at me to the heavens about proper procedure and protocols."

"Well, this is an absolute fail. If I hadn't called, who knows how long it would have been before they finally notified me that he missed the boat."

I wonder why you didn't call security before the demonstration. It only took a minute.

Chapter 18

Savannah was exhausted. She could feel the tired muscles protesting every move toward her cabin in the crew section of the ship. After powering up her laptop, she clicked the icon for her e-mail. While it was loading, Savannah moved onto her bunk and thought she would just rest for a moment.

The e-mail ping woke her up. "No!" Savannah looked at her watch. It indicated that two hours had elapsed. She sat up and groaned. The last few days of strenuous demonstrations had taken a toll. Every single muscle in her body complained at the unfair demands the glassblowing exacted on rusty skills. Savannah staggered into the bathroom and took two Excedrin. She turned on the hot water tap and wet the washcloth, then put it over her eyes until the tension in her temples relaxed.

The e-mail was from Amanda confirming that the glassblower Alan Viteri attended the same school as Edward and Ian before the Morris families moved to

St. Albans. She managed to track down Alan's family origins to a small neighborhood in Rome.

Delving into the newspaper records of Rome, Amanda found accounts of a counterfeiting ring associated with one of the powerful families. The reports of the articles were dated during Edward's and Ian's London dockland days.

Amanda reported that the accounting system was up and running perfectly now that Kurt had taken over the support contract. She reported that Kurt stopped by every few hours to make sure that the new system continued to work. He has also been showing Amanda some of the financial analysis tools that were embedded in the application.

After signing off there was another message:

Hi Savannah,I found a few obscure bits of information for you about Alan Viteri and the Moretti family. His father's side of the family and Alan dropped that name and simplified it to his mother's maiden name with no middle initial after they emigrated to London. His father's relations are connected to a centuries-old family organization that has been operating various scams in the neighborhood that surrounds the Trevi Fountain. Alan's parents moved to New York at about the same time as the Morris family moved to St. Albans.

It looks like whoever was running that operation had a lot of turnover.

On a personal note, I thought you might like to know that I have selected a hospice facility for my mom and will accompany her on the transfer to the new place tomorrow. I will not be in the shop for the rest of the day after my class leaves.

Jacob is going to take over. He will close both the Webb's Glass Shop and Webb's Studio at the end of the day. Jacob is becoming my rock. He's proving that he can take on more responsibility without having an anxiety crisis.

It was a difficult decision to move Mom, but she needs specialized palliative care that her current place cannot provide.

Mom will probably rally to keep everyone in high spirits and take her usual wise adviser role to all the nurses and aides.

The staff at the Abbey Rehabilitation Center is throwing her a going-away party today. I'm going to take Rooney in to see her for the last time. This is sad, but things must change, as her care needs change. Although, given the pleasure Rooney brings on his visits, I think we'll need to get Rooney trained as an ambassador for the residents.

Jacob says to tell you that he has finished with the nautical charts from the library and after reading about the effects of wind and tide on the day that Ian vanished, he is confident that the body would have turned up on the eastern side of Britain within twelve hours. He has scanned the chart and put an X on the location. I have attached the chart.

He says to also tell you that he's been studying
for his driver's license written test and he
thinks he will get a score of one hundred
percent. The officials have assured him that
he will be given an untimed test along with
access to a proctor if he needs a question to
be explained. He certainly has been studying
diligently for the exam.

He's also had me print out the deck plans of
your ship. He hasn't shared why he wants
them, but I'm sure he's going to help you in
some way.

Let me know if you need more research.

Say hi to Edward. Stay Safe!

X O X O X, Amanda

Savannah changed into her jeans and put on a
fresh white shirt. She gave her face a quick wash
and, for good measure, applied her brightest color
of lip-gloss.

She took a deep breath before opening the door
to the security office.

"Miss Webb. We've been expecting you," said
Officer Gaffney.

Savannah felt a pinch between her shoulder blades.
"How nice. I want to talk to Edward. You have no official reason to keep me from talking to him."

"Mr. Morris has been explaining your connection
with the local police department in your hometown."

"He has?"

"Yes, ma'am. It appears that we have our very own Nancy Drew aboard our ship." Officer Gaffney's eyebrows drew together in doubt.

The door from the inside compartment opened and Security Chief LuAnn Dalessio stepped beside Officer Gaffney. "Yes, Miss Webb. I've contacted your hometown and . . ." She looked down at the writing on a small tablet. ". . . a Detective David Parker highly recommends your skills for investigations that do not follow normal patterns."

Savannah stood still for a moment, taking it in. "And you want me to join your team in the investigation of Ian's disappearance?"

"Yes, we do," said Chief Dalessio. "As you can appreciate, we are more familiar with petty crime, drunkenness, lost children, and, sad but true, suicides."

"But Ian didn't commit suicide."

"We believe that you believe that, Miss Webb."

"There's more," said Savannah. "I had my apprentice back home make an analysis of the nautical charts where we were cruising on the night Ian is supposed to have jumped. With the wind and tide effects in that part of the channel, Ian's body should have turned up on the shores of Britain within twelve hours. That hasn't happened—Ian is still on board."

Chief Dalessio stood still and was obviously struggling with deciding. "I think I must trust you. We're extremely shorthanded for this cruise and the recommendation we received from Detective Parker is a gift. Would you be willing to help us work on the case?"

Savannah drew up to her full height and smiled. This wasn't the first time that Detective Parker had managed to make her unique skills known to others. "Yes, of course. So, you're willing to give me access to any data that you have regarding Ian and anyone else that I suspect?"

"Yes, of course. Anything that we have."

"When will you release Edward?"

Chief Dalessio sighed. "Ah, that's a little complicated. We won't be able to release him until it is proved beyond any doubt that he is innocent." She tilted her head slightly. "I must consider the ship's liability issues and the safety of the passengers. It's possible that he is involved not only with harming his cousin, but also connected with the disappearance of Alan Viteri. Worst case, he has killed twice."

"Oh, no you don't." Savannah stood even taller. "Edward is in no way, shape, or form associated with Alan's disappearance. I saw Alan myself AFTER you took Edward in for questioning. Alan was leaving the ship by the crew door and he had a large rucksack over his shoulder that he claimed was full of laundry. His exit can be verified by your system in two seconds. Do it now."

Chief Dalessio turned to Officer Gaffney. "Look up the crew exit database. What time did Alan leave the ship?"

"Actually, Chief. We already have that."

"And?" prompted Chief Dalessio.

"She's right. At the time Alan left the ship, Mr. Morris was already in our custody."

Chief Dalessio let her head drop. She inhaled slowly and turned to Savannah. "That takes care of any involvement with Alan's disappearance, but doesn't exonerate him completely. You must appreciate that I am in an awkward position."

"On the contrary, you are placing *me* in an awkward position. Edward is a principal member of my investigative team. I need him. His absence will greatly affect my efficiency."

"Good try, Miss Webb," said Officer Gaffney.

Dalessio turned a disapproving eye over to Officer Gaffney. "Patience, Officer Gaffney." Addressing Savannah, "I'm certain you can exonerate Mr. Morris faster than anyone on my staff. I ask that you do that before expanding your investigation to other related matters. That's fair, isn't it?"

Savannah considered Chief Dalessio's tone to be reasonable. It appeared that she had won the trust of Chief Dalessio, but certainly not Officer Gaffney. She turned to him. "Let me get this crystal clear. If I can prove that Edward is innocent, you will let him go?"

"Oh, yes," said Officer Gaffney. "And we require that you do that first."

"What about the keycard records? Have you verified his movements?"

"There seems to be a problem in accessing the records during the critical times. We have had some power shortages that have affected our logging systems."

Savannah pulled at her short curls with both hands. She heard herself growl, "When can I see him? At least *that* is permitted, right?"

"Of course. You are to be permitted to visit him anytime. Only after you have been searched, of course."

Quarrelsome idiot, thought Savannah. *I'm here to help.*

After a ridiculously awkward effort to search her for weapons, they led her through the main office to a corridor. Officer Gaffney pressed a keycard to the hotspot and opened the door.

Edward sat on the edge of a plain single bunk in a small cabin. He stood up. "Savannah! What's happening?"

She stepped into his arms and returned his strong embrace. "I'm here to assist these officers in their investigation of two missing passengers."

"Two?" He released Savannah but continued to hold her hand. "Who else?"

"One of the glassblowers. Alan Viteri didn't return from Florence."

"But he could show up when we dock in Rome. Trains are cheap and flights are sometimes even cheaper." Officer Gaffney shrugged his shoulders. "It wouldn't be the first time that crew have missed the boat. We don't wait."

"I'll accept that if you tell me that he has called his supervisor like a reasonable employee would do."

"We have heard nothing, miss."

Savannah turned to face Officer Gaffney. "Could you leave us alone to talk?"

"Oh, sure. Just give the door a knock and I'll let you out."

After Gaffney left, Edward sat down on the edge of the bed. Savannah sat next to him and kissed him hard. She didn't want him to doubt for a second that he was her love.

"How are Aunt Kate and Uncle Howard managing?"

"They're holding up rather well. The longer they're

in the company of the Rosenberg twins, the more they're convinced that Ian didn't jump. How are you?"

"Arghhh!" He lifted his head to look at the ceiling. "This is so maddening. I'm certain he's alive. I feel so frustrated to be locked up here and not able to help you find Ian."

"It's desperate times. First, I'm going to prove your innocence, then I'm going to ask the twins to help us."

Edward squinted and looked sideways at Savannah. "Did you say Rachel and Faith were going to help?"

"Yes, I know it sounds like a last resort, but if I can get you out of here, we will need some help covering the investigation sites here on the ship and then also in Rome."

"Why Rome?"

"Amanda e-mailed that she traced Alan's family to Rome, and we might be able to get some information about them from family and friends in their old neighborhood. The twins will be best there, as everyone loves to talk to them. Meantime, I'm going to look at all the tapes to ensure that Ian hasn't shown up on a camera."

"What about a search of the ship?"

Savannah stood up. "That's what I'm about to talk to Dalessio about. It's one of my primary worries. But I'll tackle that right after I find a way to get you out of here. Hang tight."

She kissed Edward again, then tapped on the door. It was instantly opened by Officer Gaffney, who was flushed around the neck.

"Have you been looking in at us?" Savannah challenged him with a bold stare. "You have, haven't you?" She shook her index finger under his nose. "Naughty, naughty." She walked back toward the offices. "I need to talk to Dalessio."

"But she's meeting with the ship's captain right now."

"Okay. I'll wait for her here. While I'm waiting, can you set me up to see all the video feeds?"

"Sure, but you're going to hate this." He pointed to an empty station with a three-by-three grid of flat screens. "Each screen can display up to nine images."

"How on earth do you stay alert?"

"Sheer discipline, of course. It's a boring task and it's easy to nod off while all the cameras are going. However, this task is part of my duties. It's a great job." He stood silent for a moment. "I don't want to lose it."

"You haven't done that, have you? Nodded off?" She noted his sheepish look. "Rats! You have! I'll need to go through everything."

I'm not leaving here until I've proved Edward innocent.

"Show me how to work the system." Savannah waved him over to the console. After a short familiarization lesson, Savannah felt comfortable with the video review system.

"Where can I get some coffee?" she said with a serious look aimed directly at Officer Gaffney.

He cleared this throat. "Don't worry, I'll get you some from the cruise staff kitchen. How do you take it?"

"Either as a cappuccino or with cream would be great."

He returned in a few minutes with a take-out cup. He placed it down on the desktop. "I had them make a cappuccino. Are you going to report me for napping?"

Savannah took a deep gulp of the coffee—a perfect cappuccino—then she looked up at Officer Gaffney. "Not if you keep bringing me coffee."

He smiled and scurried back to the reception room.

It took Savannah several hours to cover the areas of the ship where she knew Ian had been. As a last measure, she looked at the picture of Ian against the rail. His T-shirt had a distinctive circle logo on the left shoulder. It was a sports jersey. Of course, Ian loved soccer and his local team probably sold shirts as a fund-raiser.

She brought up a browser and searched for the St. Albans Football Club. The team was called the Saints and the colors were blue and red. It was an Australian Rules team, whatever that meant, but the main thing was the logo. It was the image of a rough-and-tumble player with a halo floating over his grinning face.

As she scanned the next few feet of video, she saw that the logo was also on the back of the shirt. Yes! She could use that to see if Ian appeared with his back to a camera any time after that evening.

The last few hours of images played like a boring silent film. Maybe it was because the novelty of the task had dulled. Savannah could now fully appreciate Officer Gaffney's problem. The endless view of passengers doing the same things over and over was mesmerizing. She had sent Officer Gaffney for coffee two more times and still had to pinch the palm of her hand occasionally to stay alert.

Then, just as she was about to concede that there were no sightings of Ian, she caught a glimpse of a round image on the back of a T-shirt.

Her heart leaped. Maybe this was it.

She manipulated the controls to bring the image into focus. Yes! It was the St. Albans Football Club T-shirt. Their distinctive logo was on the back of their promotional T-shirts. The wearer was heading away from the camera and into one of the doors that led to the crew stairways.

The time stamp indicated that it was just after the demonstration where she thought she had seen him.

"Officer Gaffney!" Savannah yelled over her shoulder. "I found him!"

No answer.

Savannah frowned. Where was he? She opened the door to the outer office and there was Officer Gaffney, snoring like a chainsaw. She shoved his shoulder hard enough to overbalance him.

Snort! He woke and lost his balance, then tried to compensate by pin-wheeling with his arms like an acrobat. He recovered before he fell out of the chair and smacked the floor. "What! What?"

"I've found Ian Morris. Let me show you."

She led the sleepy Officer Gaffney to the bank of flat screens. She pointed to the blurry figure about to enter the crew stairway. "Look, see that logo? That's the T-shirt Ian was wearing out on the top deck. That's him. He was right there behind everyone so I was the only one who could see him. Well, me and the other glassblowers, of course."

Officer Gaffney leaned over and squinted at the screen over Savannah's shoulder. "I can't quite make this out." Before he could complete his complaint, the power went off in the office and the computers all wound down to a deadly silence.

In a few seconds, a weak glow lit the room—the emergency power lighting came on.

Chapter 19

"What on earth is wrong now?" said Savannah.

Officer Gaffney shook his head. "That's weird . . . we never get power outages. I mean we have these wonderful engines generating all kinds of surplus power. This cruise has been haunted by a power gremlin during this trip that the electricians don't seem to be able to find."

The polished voice of the cruise director spoke over the PA system. "Please remain calm. We are experiencing intermittent power outages. Our engineering staff is working on the problem. We would ask you to remain where you are until further notice."

Savannah put her head in both hands. "I can't get a break." She released her head and turned to Officer Gaffney. "I saw an image of Ian that was time-stamped for when I saw him at the back of the demonstration a couple of days ago. Ian is alive. You must let Edward go. There's no basis for the charges."

"But the system is down . . . I can't verify it. I need to see it with my own eyes."

The door to the office opened and Chief Dalessio entered with a large flashlight. She swept the beam between Savannah and Officer Gaffney. "What's going on? What are you doing?"

"What's up with the power?" asked Savannah. "I found an image of Ian that shows him alive past the time when you thought he went overboard. I think this is enough for you to release Edward."

"Someone has been pulling breakers, according to the guys in the engine room. They should have everything sorted out in a few minutes. I need to see that image."

Savannah clenched her hands into fists, ready to pound the surface of the desk. Then before she could curse, the power came back on. The computers whirred and began booting up. In about ten minutes, Savannah was pointing to Ian's back with the distinctive team logo. "There he is. Edward is completely innocent. You must release him."

"You're absolutely correct," said Chief Dalessio. "Officer Gaffney, release him immediately."

"Finally!" Savannah stood up from the office chair and stretched her six-foot frame until she eased the tension in her back and shoulders.

Chief Dalessio folded her arms. "I am impressed with your persistence. I'm glad we took Detective Parker's advice."

Savannah responded with a curt nod.

Chief Dalessio frowned. "As if there isn't enough going on, I've got to track down who might have been responsible for this latest bit of nonsense with the power."

"What do you mean, latest bit?" asked Savannah.

"We've been plagued with multiple prankish instances of mischief. I don't understand why anyone on board would want to interfere in the smooth running of the ship. I've never seen anything like it and it started with this cruise. Anyway, that's my problem. I wish you luck in finding Ian. I wouldn't want to be in his shoes when you find him."

"Thanks," Savannah said as Chief Dalessio left the office. She turned to Officer Gaffney. "Well, come on. Let's get Mr. Morris out of here."

"There are a few paperwork issues that need sorting out. I'll let you know when he's released." Officer Gaffney began gathering a few paper forms.

"Nope!" said Savannah. "I'm staying right here until I can walk out with Edward."

Under Savannah's irritated glare, Officer Gaffney narrowed his eyes but lumbered through the paperwork faster than he had probably ever done. In less than ten minutes Edward was released.

After a rib-crushing embrace, Edward asked, "What's next?"

Savannah turned serious. "Quite a few challenges are on our task list—at least five." She counted off on her fingers. "First, we must tell Ian's parents that he's alive. Second, try to find Ian, which I think is going to be next to impossible. I mean, he's hidden from us this long and was only caught on camera the one time. He has likely switched shirts by this time."

"Still, we know he's on board," said Edward. "Have you kept calling him?"

"Every few hours or so until I was detained. Still no answer up until then."

Savannah frowned. "I wonder why he hasn't sent you a message?"

"It could be as simple as he hasn't been able to charge the battery."

"Logical."

"We still have to keep trying," said Edward.

"Agreed." Savannah continued. "Third, we need to search through Rome at our next port stop to verify Amanda's research and find out more about the Italian family that you and Ian knew who were behind the counterfeiting ring."

"Agreed."

"Fourth, we need to eliminate any concerns we had about Ruth and Sally. I've seen Ian on camera. He obviously isn't doing this kind of evasion to merely avoid a romantic misunderstanding. I believe he's acting through a genuine fear of being murdered. I would like to talk to the sisters again."

"Ruth should be easy to find. There can't be too many smoking areas, and she strikes me as a chain smoker."

"Okay, let's interview them and then if we're satisfied that they're in the clear, I think we must eliminate the threat before we'll entice Ian out of hiding."

"What's fifth?"

Savannah sighed. "Find a way to use the Rosenberg twins to further our progress. There's no stopping them when they're on a mission. We may as well use them to our advantage."

Edward agreed. "Let's go talk to them. They need

to know what we've planned. They can get out of
hand so easily."

"Oh, there's some bad news from Nicole about
the pub."

Edward rolled his eyes. "Just when I didn't think
things could get worse."

Savannah brought him up-to-date with the flood
and what Nicole had planned to do to solve the
problems.

"Well, she's doing everything I would have done.
Maybe I should sell the place to her and we could
spend several months at sea with you as one of the
glassblowers."

"What about my business? Would you—"

Edward stopped her with another kiss. "Just kidding, poppet."

Savannah smiled.

They arrived at the door of the suite a few minutes
later.

"Hi, Albert," said Savannah. "Are the sisters in?"

"Yes, Miss Webb. Go right on through."

The twins were sitting at the dining room table
with a map of Rome spread over the table.

"Edward! You're out of jail," said Rachel. She
reached up and pinched his cheek. "It's so good to
see you."

"Savannah! Why didn't you tell us Edward was
free?" asked Faith. She reached up and brought
Edward's head down for a smooch on his other
cheek.

"Just in time!" they said in unison.

"Just in time for what?" Savannah leaned over to
study the map.

Rachel pointed to a small area near the famous Trevi Fountain. "We were going to visit this little café right next to the fountain."

"We're going to have a very, very, very, long lunch," said Faith.

Savannah sat down at the table and looked at the sisters. "Oh, I get it. You're going to charm the owners into telling you about Alan's family. Right?"

The twins' eyes lit up. "Yes, but that's not all we have to tell you."

Savannah's eyes narrowed. "What have you done?"

"We noticed something about Albert," said Rachel.

Faith nodded. "Yes, it started after the dinner in our suite. Breaking that glass was the start of our suspicions."

Edward sighed. "Stop stalling. What have you done?"

The twins looked at each other and shrugged their four shoulders. Rachel answered, "We noticed that he had been taking a long time to answer when we buzzed the service needed button."

Faith finished, "So this morning after breakfast we decided to follow Albert and find out about these long absences."

Rachel rubbed her hands together. "We walked by one of the crew access doors and before he could close it, we saw him deep in conversation with Officer Gaffney."

Edward interrupted. "But that could be innocent. Albert is a senior member of the cabin stewards."

Rachel lowered her eyes. "Be still, I'm getting to the good part. They were arguing about money."

"Money?" Savannah rubbed her temples with both hands. "That makes no sense whatsoever."

"We agree," said Faith. "We didn't get any more out of them because he became aware of us and slammed the crew door shut."

Savannah sighed. "Rachel, Faith, I truly appreciate your enthusiasm, but you must promise me that you won't do that again. There's nothing at all that would point to Albert. I think you've taken your addiction to reading cozy mysteries far beyond the pale. Promise me that you won't try to tail any of the other crew members on the ship. I just can't add you two to my long list of worries right now."

"We were only trying to help," said Rachel.

"We didn't mean to add to your worries," said Faith.

"I know, but make that promise, please," said Savannah. "Both of you!"

They said in unison, "We promise."

Edward sat at the table. "First things first, ladies. Where are Aunt Kate and Uncle Howard?"

"They're resting," said Rachel. "Naturally, this has been a tremendous strain."

"On Kate's heart," continued Faith. "She's on some pretty serious medication."

Savannah looked over to Edward. "Why don't we track down the Maggio sisters and hopefully eliminate them from our investigation. It shouldn't take long and maybe by the time we're back, your aunt Kate will be feeling better."

"Good plan."

Cruise lines over the past several years had been slowly decreasing the permissible areas for smokers, and now there was only one place to smoke on board, where they had found Ruth previously. It was near the Mast Bar on the starboard side, deck 14, aft.

Edward led the way to the bar. "Do you want a soda or sparkling water? I'm parched."

"Perfect, make that with ice and a lime."

They took their plastic cups over to the smoking area and as expected Ruth was camped out like a claim jumper. This time, however, Sally was lying on the next lounger reading the latest *OK!* newspaper.

Edward found two plain chairs along the railing and picked up one in each hand. He placed them in front of the sisters and motioned for Savannah to have a seat.

"Hey, what do you guys want? Nobody asked you to join us." Ruth exhaled a long breath of smoke in Savannah's direction.

She coughed involuntarily. "Hey, no need for that."

Edward moved his chair to be right next to Ruth, deliberately imposing his large frame in her space. "We're here to get some straight answers from you."

"We've been working with the security police on board. They've given us authority to continue investigating Ian's disappearance. If you don't cooperate with us, we'll call them to come up and take you down to the interview room."

"I've just come from there," said Edward. "I promise you, the view is better from here. Answer our questions, or we call Officer Gaffney."

Ruth was in the process of blowing more smoke at Savannah but changed her mind—too late to keep from coughing up a storm. "Don't get your knickers in a twist . . . We'll tell you whatever it is you want to know."

"When was the last time you saw Ian?" asked Savannah.

Ruth looked at Sally and nodded a "go ahead" to her. "I already told you about that."

Savannah stood up. "Okay, Edward. They're not going to cooperate. Call Officer Gaffney to escort them down to security."

Edward made a show of dragging his phone from his pocket and lifted his finger high over the surface of the smartphone.

"No, stop!" Ruth lurched from her chair and tried to take the phone from Edward's hand. "I'll come clean. Don't call security."

"Then tell us what you know right now." Edward's voice carried and the other smokers had turned to stare.

Savannah patted his knee. "Calm down. I think they're ready. Right?"

Ruth and Sally nodded.

Ruth looked at Sally. "Go ahead. You're the one most affected."

Sally looked tragic. "After you talked to me, I confronted Ruth and we had a mighty row. We were lucky we didn't get thrown off the ship. But, suddenly it occurred to us that maybe we had caused Ian to jump overboard."

Sally caught her breath, then continued. "We both started crying. The thought of Ian overboard, trying to swim, failing, then drowning after he couldn't swim anymore. It was a life-changing moment for me," she said.

"I kept imagining how he must have felt to watch

the lights of the ship go farther and farther away from him with no chance to get back aboard." Sally shuddered. "It was horrible."

"That was when I admitted to Sally what a horrible sister I had been." Ruth spoke in a quiet, calm tone. "We held each other and cried for what seemed like hours."

The sisters looked at each other with eyes overflowing, which they wiped away.

"Then what happened?" asked Savannah.

"We were looking over the aft end of the ship when someone tapped our shoulders," said Sally.

"Was it—"

Ruth nodded. "You guessed it. It was Ian."

"We both jumped a foot." Ruth pulled some tissues from her pocket, handed one over to Sally, and then blew her nose. "What a shock to see him."

"How did he seem?" asked Edward. "Was he stable? Sober?"

"He was sober, all right." Sally swung her legs over to the side of the lounge chair and sat up. "Ian apologized to both of us. It seemed sincere, didn't it, sis?"

Ruth mirrored her sister's position on her lounge. "He was serious. Ian said that his life was in danger and that he needed our help."

"I believed him," said Sally. "He was always so carefree around us. This was an entirely different Ian. I felt like we were given a second chance to do right by him."

Ruth leaned forward. "He said that he was hiding from an old enemy and asked if we could help him."

"So, you got his medications from our cabin?" asked Edward.

The sisters fidgeted and squirmed in their chairs

and looked down at the deck. Sally looked at Ruth and motioned for her to answer. "Yes. It wasn't easy. We had to time it just right so that your room attendant wouldn't notice."

Sally leaned forward. "I distracted him while Ruth slipped in and got them. They were right where Ian had told us they would be."

Savannah put her hand on her forehead. "So that's why you were in the crew section. You were delivering the medications." Savannah leaned back in her chair. "Did I interrupt the delivery?"

"No," said Sally. "I had already done that. But you certainly scared me to death."

"Do you know who he's hiding from?" Edward asked.

Ruth reached for her pack of cigarettes, but drew her hand back. "No, we don't know anything about that. He told us to stay mum and he would see us back in St. Albans and explain everything."

Savannah and Edward exchanged looks. Edward reached out and squeezed Savannah's hand. "This is the proof I needed," he said while a slow smile spread over his face. "Ian is alive. It's safe to tell Uncle Howard and Aunt Kate."

Savannah and Edward reached the suite and Rachel let them in.

"Do you have news?" Ian's parents opened the master bedroom door. "We were resting when we heard you," said Aunt Kate as she looked at Savannah. "What's the news?"

"It's good news," said Savannah. "I found an image

of Ian on the ship. He's alive but hiding from someone. We don't know why."

Edward followed with, "Not only that, but we talked to the Maggio sisters who have seen him and filched his medicines from our cabin to give to him. So, he's not going without."

Aunt Kate put her hand on her chest and staggered. Uncle Howard quickly grabbed her around the shoulders and led her by the hand to a dining room chair. "I knew he was perfectly fine," she said, "but it's such a relief to know that he has been seen."

Savannah leaped up and grabbed a glass from the bar and filled it with water. "Here, Mrs. Morris. Drink this."

Aunt Kate took the glass. "Thank you." She drank with a trembling grip and placed the quivering glass down on the table. Then she reached up to briefly squeeze Savannah's hand. "You're so kind."

Uncle Howard sat in the chair next to Aunt Kate, but still held her by the hand with his arm around her shoulder. "Kate, take it easy now. Your heart isn't what it used to be."

She grinned at her husband. "Nothing is what it used to be, Howard. But I'm so thankful for these young people." She drank the rest of the water with a steadier hand.

Savannah's complexion blanched a shade, then she turned to Edward and spoke slowly. "Do you think he's avoiding you?"

"Me?" Edward reared back in shock. "That doesn't make any sense at all."

"With all the theories we've been batting around, I wanted to make sure that Ian wasn't blaming you

for his situation or maybe even his depression."
Savannah watched the reaction of Ian's parents.
They both looked confused.

Good, they trust Edward.

She grabbed Edward's hand and gave it a good hard
squeeze. "I didn't think that could be the case, but I
thought we all needed to hear you say it out loud."

Savannah crooked her neck to peer at Edward
and smiled. She focused her attention on the sisters.
"Now, what about that great plan, ladies?"

"Meanwhile, we can comb the neighborhood for
Alan."

Edward knit his brows. "You think he's there?"

"I think that's where he went from Provence. I
can't prove it, but I think he's part of the family that
ran the counterfeiting ring. It makes the most sense,"
said Savannah.

Albert approached holding a tray of drinks. "I took
the liberty of having some refreshments sent in." He
placed Cosmopolitans in front of Rachel and Faith,
a gin and tonic in front of Edward, Aunt Kate, and
Uncle Howard, and finally a Guinness in front of
Savannah.

They toasted to their belief that Ian was certainly
alive, but in hiding from someone he feared would
harm him. They vowed to pursue all clues and leads
to find the root of his predicament.

Chapter 20

Friday, in Rome

"What time is it?" Edward had his hands wrapped around a large coffee.

"It's seven o'clock." Savannah had consumed half of her cappuccino and only a few little flakes remained in evidence of her chocolate croissant. "We need to be one of the first people off. Our hired car will be waiting right next to the ship."

"How did you arrange that?"

"Simple, I e-mailed your travel agent. Jan had it arranged in a flash. Our driver's name is James."

"You are kidding me. How many clichés are we going to experience during this investigation?"

"Come on, hurry up!" Savannah headed for the take-out cups for coffee and filled two for their taxi ride into Rome.

James was alarmingly proficient at cursing his way around traffic snarls and dropped them off at the Trevi Fountain within an hour of leaving the ship.

They asked to be picked up two hours before the ship left port.

They both turned to see the fountain. According to a sixteenth-century author quoted on the website Garden Fountains, it was named after a virgin shepherdess who showed the spring to soldiers seeking water. Water flowed from the mouth of the dominating figure—Neptune, god of the sea—standing atop a shell-shaped chariot drawn by two sea horses and two gods. The horses represented the changing mood of the sea. The larger statue on the left was a representation of the goddess Abundance, above who was a bas-relief depiction of Agrippa, the son-in-law of the 19 B.C. emperor, shown approving the plans for construction of the aqueduct. On the right was the god Salubrity, topped by a representation of the virgin directing soldiers toward the water.

They stood in front of the fountain in silence. "I had no idea it was so beautiful," whispered Savannah. "It doesn't look like this in the movies."

"It doesn't sound like this, either." Edward wrapped an arm around her shoulders and they stood for a few more moments. "Okay, grab your coins. We're here. Let's do it."

They each dug three coins out of their pockets, turned their backs to the fountain, made a wish, and tossed their coins in the fountain.

"I hope this works to reverse the bad luck of the shattered teapot," said Savannah. "I want to come back here when things aren't in such a mess."

"Luv," said Edward. "Trouble has your scent and will stalk you to the ends of the earth. That's why we should always take our pleasures when we can."

Savannah smiled a crooked grin. "I do seem to find myself in trouble a lot, but I always get us out."

"That you do."

She grabbed him by the hand. "Let's do this."

The steep twisting cobblestone streets were a navigation challenge, but after a few wrong turns, Savannah and Edward were standing on the street that Amanda reported as the area where the counterfeiting ring originated, according to the ancestry documents she found.

They found the right house and Savannah knocked on the door. A young boy aged about ten answered and looked up into their faces.

"Hello there," said Savannah. "Do you speak English?"

His big brown eyes widened and a broad smile flashed a row of perfect white teeth. "Yes, ma'am. I learn good English in school. Good morning. How are you? Have a nice day."

Edward knelt to the young boy's level. "Could we speak to your mama or papa?"

In rapid Italian, the boy gave a shouted warning to someone behind him and slammed the door.

Farther down the street, Savannah saw Alan dashing around the corner.

"Christ on a bike!" she yelled. "It's Alan. Run!"

They gave chase, down to the first corner, and followed him up a steep cobbled street. They followed him down a tiny alleyway, but after the next intersection of five individual lanes, they lost him.

"Crikey!" Edward panted, leaning against a wall and holding his aching side. "You glassblowers are really fit." He continued to gasp long after Savannah recovered her breath.

"My morning runs with Rooney have certainly paid off."

"I thought we would be searching all day." He puffed. "At a leisurely walk."

"Well, we know this is the right neighborhood, anyway," said Savannah.

"Let's go back to the house and watch for the little boy," said Edward.

"Why?"

"If this is the kind of family that I think it is, we should be able to bribe him into giving us more information about where Alan might be."

"Bribe the kid to rat him out, you mean?"

"Ten-year-old boys are heartless—remember? I should know," Edward said with a grim tilt of his head.

"Right." They went back toward the house. There was the usual neighborhood café on the corner and they were able to get a seat that gave them a good view of the house.

After several cups of espresso, a cannoli each, and two more chocolate croissants for Savannah, another boy came walking down the street kicking a faded soccer ball. He tucked the ball under his arm and knocked on the door to the house. It opened immediately and the tattletale emerged to begin kicking the ball back and forth to each other along the street.

Edward left a generous pile of Euros on the table and they began to follow the boys at a safe distance. They led them to a small field with other players kicking, throwing, and practicing hitting the ball with their chests and heads.

Savannah whispered, "Now what?"

"Watch this." Edward pulled out his wallet and removed a one-hundred-Euro bill. He waved it in the air. "Do any of you speak English? I need a translator."

The players froze in mid-play. The boy from the house ran up to Edward and jumped in the air to reach the bill. "Hang on! Let me hear you speak."

"I can speak English!" The boy put his hands on his hips. "You're the ones who were at my house."

Edward gave the boy the bill. "That's for speaking English." He pulled two one-hundred-Euro bills from his wallet and held them up. "This is for telling us why Alan Viteri ran away from us and where is he going?"

The boy shuffled from one foot to the other. He eyed the two one-hundred-Euro bills in Edward's hand.

While the boy's eyes were on the Euros, Edward added a third one-hundred-Euro bill. Then he waved them under the boy's nose.

The boy cracked. "Fine, I'll tell you. Alan has never been nice to me. What do I care?" He grabbed at the bills.

Edward pulled his hand away. "Only after you answer the questions."

"Okay, okay." The boy stood still with his eyes glued to the money. "Alan said there was a new man on his ship that was treacherous. He said that he needed to find a way to disappear before that man recognized him from the old times." He snatched at the bills.

Edward pulled them back just out of reach. "Don't try that again. I'm better at this game than you are."

"But I answered your question!" he whined.

"There were two. Where is Alan going?"

"He's going back to the ship. He said he would have to pay a fine, but he needed to pick something up from his cabin."

"Do you know what it was?"

"That's three questions! No fair!"

"Life's not fair." He waggled the Euros again. "Do you know what it was?"

The boy hung his head down in dejection. "No, I don't. If I did, I would make you pay."

Edward slipped the bills in his hand. "Now, that's the truth. Thanks."

The boy darted away like a fish and returned to the ongoing game. He soon blended in with the other boys and they ignored Edward and Savannah with the insolence of all-knowing youth.

Savannah tapped Edward on the arm. "I think we'd better get back to the ship. With any luck, we can intercept Alan and find out who is after him. I'll call James to meet us at the fountain in ten minutes."

They made their way through the twisty cobblestone streets with only one wrong turn. As promised, James was waiting for them and gave them a return wild ride back to the cruise port and stopped with a squeal of brakes. Edward paid the fare and they looked for a café to wait for Alan to appear.

In less than five minutes, they were joined by the Rosenberg twins. Rachel and Faith sat at the outdoor table with lowered heads and shoulders slumped. "We're failures," said Rachel.

"Absolute failures," repeated Faith. "We had such high hopes of gathering some important detail—"

"—maybe even a vital clue in the investigation—"

"—that would solve everything for you."

"But, nothing."

Edward glanced at Savannah. "I think what you ladies need is an afternoon pick-me-up Italian style. They have a marvelous drink here called Limoncello." He waved his hand at their waiter and ordered four Limoncellos along with an assorted plate of pastries.

When the waiter left, Rachel straightened up in the café chair. "We did see something unexpected." She turned to Faith.

"Yes, yes," Faith continued. "We saw your glass-blower boss."

Savannah frowned. "Eric?"

"Yes," said Rachel. "He was in the kitchen talking to one of the restaurant's chefs."

"We only got a glimpse of him from the back, but it definitely appeared to be him. He was big and tall with thick black hair."

"By the time I got up and pretended that I was looking for the restroom, he was gone." Rachel folded her arms in front of her chest. "I used to be such a fast walker."

Faith reached over and patted Rachel's arm. "Those days are long gone. Let's be grateful that we can tackle this cobbled city without walkers."

"Funny," said Savannah. "Eric didn't mention going that far into town. He said he would be camped out at an Internet café. Why would he bother to lie? I barely know him."

"Maybe he's doing something against company policy," said Rachel.

"This could be completely innocent," added Faith.

Edward piped in, "Or he could be defending himself against a new glassblower who has an incredible curiosity about everything and everyone."

Savannah rolled her eyes. "That's true. I can be obnoxious."

Edward raised his eyebrows.

Rachel and Faith finished their Limoncellos and most of the pastries, then made their way up to the ship.

After the twins left, Savannah languished over a cup of cappuccino, thinking she probably wouldn't be able to sleep for the remainder of the cruise.

"Do you think it's odd that the Rosenbergs think they saw Eric?" asked Savannah.

"I think it's odd that he hasn't been more upset by the disappearance of Alan. So far, he has been much more relaxed about that than he was when the wearable microphones didn't work."

"You're right. Maybe we should pay more attention to our gut feelings. I could ask Amanda to do some background searches on Eric. I don't think that lead has been fully explored."

"Why not?"

"Indeed, why not? I'll text her now while we're *still* waiting for Alan." She pulled out her phone.

After that, they ordered sparkling water with a slice of lime. "No more coffee," said Savannah. "Even though the sun and this lovely breeze are threatening to send me on an unplanned nap."

Savannah's phone rang. It was Rachel.

"We've been back in our suite for at least an hour now and we haven't been able to raise Albert at all. We think maybe he's onto our investigation."

"Let me put you on speaker so Edward can hear."

Savannah punched the speaker icon and placed the phone on the café table. They heard the twins at a distance.

"No, I think this is the one."

"That's the call icon."

"You shouldn't have gotten a new phone right before the cruise."

"Our old ones weren't in warranty anymore. They were ancient."

"But they worked."

"Oh, here's the button."

"Savannah. Edward. Are you there?" said Rachel.

"Yes, ladies. We're here. What's the news?" asked Savannah.

"We can't find Albert anywhere. It is highly suspicious. We thought Savannah could call down to the security and ensure that he was on board," said Rachel.

"He's never missed welcoming us back to the suite. Something is seriously wrong," said Faith.

Savannah leaned over the phone. "Thanks for letting me know. I'll talk to Chief Dalessio just as soon as we get back."

They waited patiently until the crew began pulling apart the temporary tent that covered the gangway.

"He's not going to show," said Savannah. "That's worrying. I don't think we missed him."

"Neither do I, but we need to get on board."

They made their way up the gangway. Office Gaffney was on duty scanning in the returning passengers.

"Welcome aboard, Miss Webb and Mr. Morris." Officer Gaffney scanned their keycards. "Could you wait here in the entryway for a few minutes? I have a situation."

"Sure," said Savannah. She was curious. Officer Gaffney had been antagonistic toward her from their first meeting.

Officer Gaffney left the sign-in booth to stand beside a cloth-covered table staffed with two spa attendants passing out facial cleansing samples. He told the spa attendants to clear away their goodies.

Everyone watched as the remaining few passengers made a desperate sprint down the dock to avoid being left behind. Gaffney took one last look down the dock, then keyed his walkie-talkie. "That's all the passengers. We're clear."

The crew had obviously been waiting for that cue as the door was fastened closed and the lines were cast off. Officer Gaffney unplugged the scanning podium, covered it with a sturdy beige cover, and used some straps to secure it to the side of the ship.

Savannah and Edward stepped forward to speak to him, but turned around to alarmed cries from the spa ladies that were dismantling their display table. Savannah caught a glimpse of a pair of legs under the table.

"Step aside," said Officer Gaffney. "Let me look."

After dropping down on his haunches, he looked under the table. He poked the man. "Sir, sir. Do you need help?" When he pulled the man over to face upward, Officer Gaffney overbalanced and tried to windmill his arms to compensate. He landed on his rump with a howl and pressed both hands to his mouth.

One of the spa girls looked at the man's face and screamed, "He's dead!"

Edward and Savannah saw the face. It was Alan Viteri.

There was a deep crimson stain below the pocket of his white polo shirt.

Chapter 21

Saturday, at sea

"We need your cooperation more than ever now that there's a confirmed victim," said Chief Dalessio. "I'm also concerned about your safety, Mr. Morris."

Edward and Savannah had been called down to security after they had identified Alan as the dead man. "The killer has to be on board, doesn't he?" said Savannah. "Alan was killed right under everyone's nose in that small hallway."

"That does bring up an interesting scenario." Officer Gaffney drew himself up as tall as he could. "Is it possible that Ian was hiding from you, Mr. Morris? It is possible that Alan was your enemy as well?"

Edward pulled himself to his maximum height. "Are you still accusing me?"

"Let's not go down that road again." Savannah inserted herself between the two. Her strong arms pushed on the chests of both and they broke apart.

Her strength shocked Officer Gaffney. He wrinkled his brow in distress.

"How could that killing have been missed by everyone, Officer Gaffney? I thought you staffed an officer to monitor things twenty-four-seven."

"Unfortunately, with all the extra searches for Ian, we cut the number of security personnel at the check-in booth." Chief Dalessio pressed her lips into a thin line and looked daggers at Officer Gaffney.

Officer Gaffney shrugged his shoulders. "I'm doing the best I can."

Chief Dalessio continued. "The camera shows an unexplained ruffling of the table covering at the time a large and noisy family group came on board. They were completely inebriated and took the attention of everyone away from Alan's entrance. The recording shows that Officer Gaffney and even the spa attendants were completely distracted by trying to deal with the boisterous family."

"I saw some blood on Alan's shirt front but not loads." Savannah shuddered at the memory of the dark red stain. "How was he killed?"

Chief Dalessio made a *tsk-tsk* sound. "It was a deep, slim puncture like a stiletto or something with the shape of a stiletto—a traditional family execution."

"So, it relates back to Ian's and Edward's shared past." Savannah looked directly at Edward and reached out for his hand. "I think we need to do something to protect you."

"I strongly disagree." Edward narrowed his eyes and squeezed her hand.

Chief Dalessio held up her keycard and waved it by her face. "I say we go ahead and put him in the holding cell again. This time for protection, not suspicion, since neither of you were even on board when Mr. Viteri was killed."

Edward folded his arms in front of his chest. "No. That's not happening. I'm going to stick with our little group like glue until we've caught the killer."

Savannah closed her eyes and rubbed her temples with both hands. "You're driving me absolutely crazy." She dropped her hands to her sides. "But, I understand how you wouldn't want to be in the holding cell while we're trying to find both Ian and the murderer."

Savannah turned to Chief Dalessio. "I know you've been searching the ship for Ian, but we're going to try again. With our innocent-looking crew of searchers—especially the two sets of elderly twins, Ian won't know to be wary of them. We'll do that after tonight's glassblowing demonstration."

Chief Dalessio nodded. "You may be right about our uniformed searches. You might be more effective. It certainly won't hurt to try. Give me a call when you're going to start and don't let Edward go anywhere alone."

"No problem. I plan to stick him in the suite with Ian's parents."

Edward grinned. "So much better than the holding cell?"

They hadn't walked ten feet when Edward's cell pinged. He looked at the screen. "A text from Nicole." He scrolled through the message quickly.

"How's the pub?"

"She says that they found a company that is kind of like the ghostbusters for flood damage. They arrived yesterday with some giant industrial fans to dry out the furniture and the floors. The drywall installers are expected sometime today, and the new dishwasher has been installed. She's promoting a flood party with drink specials and a Noah's Ark theme."

"She's amazing. You're lucky."

"What have you heard from Amanda and Jacob?" asked Edward.

"Nothing horrible at all, but keep your fingers crossed. I still think that broken teapot is responsible for the bad luck at Webb's Glass Shop. The new cash point program has been repaired and now Amanda is taking a tutorial from the new service company. She has found an apparent genius, however, whom she describes as performing miracles to get it up and running. She's also getting us a quote on a maintenance program."

"Wow, I'm glad I had already upgraded my accounting system. I think that if she had to deal with the same problems that Amanda has endured, it might have caused Nicole to take a hike and never come back." Edward raised one eyebrow. "What does Amanda say about Rooney and Snowy?"

"Apparently, they are taking full advantage of Amanda's soft heart. Snowy has taken all the high spots on the furniture as ambush platforms. She pounces onto Rooney's back when he comes up to sniff her. Then she rides him like a screaming jockey until he lays down to let her off."

"That's all a trick to get more treats out of Amanda," said Edward. "We'll have to put them both on a diet when we get back."

"We will all have to go on a diet." Savannah patted her tummy. "That's the normal thing after a cruise."

"Which brings me back to your plan."

"Right, we're basically down to two suspects. It's got to be either Eric or Albert. Surveillance showed they were both on board when Alan returned to the ship."

"They've both been behaving strangely," said Edward.

Savannah ran a hand through her curls. "Now that I'm thinking about the two of them together, have you noticed how much they look alike?"

Edward nodded slowly. "Now that you've said it. They're both tall with thick black hair."

"They are neither slim nor bulky. Could the Rosenbergs have mistaken Albert for Eric?"

"Let's ask them at dinner. I'm starved. This endless parade of incredible food is making me crave more and more and more."

"Great, I'll change and meet up with you in the main dining room."

Chapter 22

Saturday, at sea

Savannah and Edward were in the main dining room sharing a table with the Rosenberg sisters, the VanGilden brothers, and Ian's parents. They had ordered, their drinks were delivered, and they were waiting for the appetizer course to arrive.

"Rachel." Savannah waved her hand to catch her attention. "When you and Faith were in the café near the Trevi Fountain, how sure are you that you saw Eric?"

Faith looked over to Rachel. "She's thinking along the same track as we are."

"What makes you say that?" Rachel turned to look at Savannah.

"I was struck by the resemblance of Albert and Eric today. I don't know why, but when you described Eric to us standing in the kitchen of the café, the image of Albert flashed through my mind first."

Faith cleared her throat. "We've discussed this."

"It could have been Albert instead of Eric. We've only seen Albert in his butler livery."

"In casual slacks and a golf shirt, he would have looked even more like Eric," said Rachel.

Edward drummed his fingers on the table. "There's one important difference here. Eric is on board and preparing for the demonstration."

"And Albert is missing," said Savannah. "I think Albert is the one who killed Alan and is searching for Ian."

"Albert's only been on board for a couple of weeks," said Richard.

Savannah tilted her head. "How do you know that?"

Edward shushed them to silence while the server placed their appetizers in front of them.

After the server left, Rickard said, "We've been cruising on this lovely ship for almost six months now. We noticed Albert only a few weeks ago."

"You've been on the ship for how long?" asked Savannah of the twin she thought of as Richy Rich even though she knew his name was Richard VanGilden.

Richard affirmed his twin's announcement. "We've been cruising for more than six months now."

Savannah's mouth dropped open. She recovered with a quick bite of her favorite appetizer, the garlic-laden escargot. She wiped her mouth. "How on earth does that work?"

Richard spoke first. "It's absolutely fantastic and a perfect fit for us. We used to have an old Queen Ann house in Upper Manhattan that our folks had left to us, but the upkeep was too much."

"We're the only children of our generation. They were in publishing and they had put back quite a tidy savings for us as well."

"We sold the house," said Rickard, "and turned the proceeds back over to the same financial adviser who had been managing our parents' money for their twilight years."

"Not one of those flash-in-the-pan get-a-quick-return kind of agencies. He really is looking out for us in a long-term way," said Richard. "We have also hired an online administrative assistant to manage all the booking and travel details."

"She's a living doll," said Rickard. "We chat on that live video thingy on the computer several times a week."

"But here's where this is going to help us," said Rachel. "These two know this ship inside and out."

"They also know most of the staff," added Faith.

"Oh," said Savannah. "You can help us search the secret, quiet, out-of-the way seldom used parts of the ship for Ian. It makes the most sense that he would be lurking in places where there aren't many guests."

"Bingo!" said all the twins, who looked shocked that they all thought so much alike.

"This is excellent news," said Savannah. "We need to start right after my show in the Hot Shop." She looked at her watch. "Let's see, it's six thirty now. He said seven o'clock sharp—one hour for practice—our demonstration for this evening starts at eight thirty—then I need to help Eric clean up. It will take longer with only the two of us—we need to meet back at the suite at ten o'clock tonight. Agreed?"

Everyone around the table agreed and they enjoyed their main courses of lobster and prime rib followed by the molten chocolate cake.

Eric was frustrated and irritated. Savannah thought that perhaps Alan's death was preying on his mind, and on top of that the porcelain overlay on his other front tooth had fallen out. He tried to hide it, but that triggered even more attention to his discolored teeth. His glassblowing practice suffered immensely for his lack of focus.

"Why didn't you get it repaired in Rome?" Savannah asked sympathetically.

"With my dental phobias? No way. It takes all my courage to go to my trusted family dentist." He sighed deeply. "I'll just have to manage."

As his third attempt at the complicated goblet crashed to the floor, he stood looking down at the shards. "Ready or not, Savannah. You're going to have to make our Best of Show piece. I can't do it."

"But I don't have one."

"What about that Day of the Dead Skull you sent in as part of your application?"

Savannah folded her arms. "You saw my application?"

"Yes, it was a courtesy, but yes." Eric began sweeping up the glass. "I liked the freshness of your approach. Can you do one?"

Savannah stood for a moment, mentally reviewing

the steps involved. "I need to make a few pieces ahead and store them in our heating oven. Otherwise, it would take so long to create each flower individually that we would overrun our performance timeline."

"Fine. Get started with the flowers. You don't need me for that, do you?"

"Nope. They're small and don't need transfers. I'm actually more comfortable doing them by myself."

"Good. I'm going to my cabin for a nap. I need to get my head on straight before the performance."

Savannah waved him good-bye and began making the flowers she would need to decorate the skull. It took more than an hour and by the time she had them safely in the warming oven, it was time to get ready for the demonstration.

Eric entered the Hot Shop with a serious look on his face. He obviously hadn't slept. "Thanks for agreeing to do the Best of Show piece. I appreciate it. I think we'll make that at the end of the show, so I'd like for you to start the program with a fluted vase. Then I'll follow with a simple but flashy fish and then your skull. How's that work for you?"

"Just fine. Let's do this!" Savannah finally felt confident of her glassblowing skills and knew that should Eric make a misstep, she would be able to carry on with the program.

The vase and fish creations were completed with little fuss and no emotional problems from Eric— or herself, either. She approached the white skull with self-assurance. She imagined this final piece as bringing the highest value at the auction on the last evening of the cruise.

She created the skull by gathering a large amount of molten glass from the furnace and then used five separate layers of white frit to give the piece a white cast. After pulling the globe into a skull shape, she began adding the color elements that would make it look like a true Day of the Dead Skull.

When she held up the skull on her blowpipe for the audience to see, they reacted with thunderous applause. She really felt their admiration in her chest. The last step was to break off the skull into Eric's waiting gloves.

She scored the skull at the base, dripped water in the crease, and tapped the blowpipe. It fell into Eric's glove safe as a newborn babe. She released her held breath once it was safely in the annealing oven.

Eric announced that the pieces would be available for sale at the auction and thanked everyone for their attendance. He also reminded everyone that the Charity Walk was tonight and would everyone who had entered remember to check in with the cruise director on the top deck prior to the start. The walk would begin at the stroke of midnight with the blowing of the ship's horn.

Savannah had been hearing about the walk since boarding, and she and Edward had bought T-shirts after the Rosenberg twins signed everyone up for the event.

"How is your investigation progressing?"

"Investigation?" echoed Savannah.

"Don't be coy. I heard through the crew grapevine

that you have been seen in the company of Chief Dalessio and Officer Gaffney. You've been called down there more than once. Why haven't you said anything about it? What's up?"

He must be suspicious. How can I deflect this?

"I didn't want to add any more stress to your current situation. It was hard enough to work without Alan. So basically, I tried to keep my investigation activities quiet. Does that bother you?"

"Well, I think I should have been informed. But we know how erratic compliance to procedures is with the security office. Have you found out anything about Alan?"

Savannah thought about the best way to use this conversation to close in on either Eric or Albert as the suspect. If she could safely plant a seed here—it might grow into a resolution.

She saw the Rosenberg twins at the guardrail and willed them to look over at her. They did. She waved a big *come over here* to them and she saw them start their steady pace across the deck.

"I am finally ready to identify the culprit. It seems that everything is connected to the neighborhood around the Trevi Fountain and what happened to the family members that didn't want to be in the family business or the family members that got kicked out of the family business."

"So, you think you're getting close."

She turned to greet the Rosenberg twins and looked back over her shoulder. "Yes, I've concluded that our prime suspect is Albert. I think he saw Ian Morris's name on the passenger list. Ian was the only witness to a long-ago murder that could identify him now. Ian could expose his carefully crafted new identity. Albert is the only one with a clear motive for murder."

Edward had walked up in time to hear Savannah's last sentence. He said, "Albert knows that I didn't see him back then, but as Ian is my cousin, he needs to eliminate me as well."

"The only trick is to prove it," said Savannah.

I really need to come up with a plan.

Chapter 23

Saturday, at sea

When Savannah went to her cabin to shower and change after the performance, she saw that she had received an e-mail from Jacob. He didn't communicate easily in either written or spoken words without a good reason. She clicked the mail icon.

> Hello Miss Savannah, Amanda told me about Edward's cousin hiding on the cruise ship. I can help. On the cruise ship's website are detailed images of each deck. Also, Amanda found some detailed drawings on the Internet that were used to build the ship.

> By analyzing them, I have identified a list of possible hiding places for Ian. The list is ordered by the probability of most likely to least likely.

I hope this is helpful to you in your current investigation. I like to help.

Jacob

P.S. Suzy misses you.

Savannah's heart swelled with pride when she read the e-mail. Her little investigative posse was right on target even across the seas. She copied down the list of places, tucked it in her pocket, and hurried up to the top deck to meet everyone.

To save time, she had called Edward and the Rosenbergs' suite to ask them to join the Charity Walk and meet her near the start of the race at 11:45.

Edward arrived a few minutes after Savannah stepped from the elevator. There were dozens of cruisers outfitted in their charity T-shirts ready to walk laps as a pledge to the United Way, Make-A-Wish of America, and City Year organizations.

Savannah announced, "It's important that we get Albert in custody before we even think about finding Ian. That's the only way he would be willing to come out of hiding."

"How are you going to find Albert?" asked Edward.

"Well, sweetie, I'm shamelessly using you as bait." She lifted one eyebrow. "If I could come up with something else I would, but if he wants to hide in this ship, it will be impossible to catch him. After all, Ian is still hidden and he started from scratch. Albert knows this ship exceedingly well."

The two sets of twins approached Edward and Savannah followed by Aunt Kate and Uncle Howard.

Savannah smiled at their outfits. They had all somehow managed to find white slacks and shoes that would not be out of place at any cricket match in England.

"Aunt Kate, Uncle Howard," said Edward. "Are you sure you want in on this?"

"We're just as fit as your friends. Younger, in fact." Uncle Howard gave Aunt Kate a broad smile and a side hug.

"We're ready to do whatever you need, Savannah," said Rachel.

"Us as well," said Richard.

Savannah did a double take. The twins had switched partners. *Concentrate,* she reminded herself.

"Why this race?" asked Faith.

"Well, Albert has basically been in the room for every visit that Edward and I have made to the suite."

"That is, until he disappeared after Alan was murdered," said Uncle Howard.

"True, but let me finish," said Savannah.

"He's right, Savannah," added Rachel.

"You're going to set a trap to lure him out," said Faith.

"Yes, is that the plan?" asked Aunt Kate.

Savannah's brow crinkled and she looked at Edward, then Ian's mother. "Yes, I have a plan to lure him out, but it depends on everyone playing their part without question." She looked at each of them in turn. "Without question. Agreed?"

Everyone either nodded or mumbled agreement.

Savannah took a deep breath. "Albert knows Edward is going to be in this event and there's one short stretch of the track at the stern of the ship that would make the perfect ambush. There's a hidden crew door where Albert could attack Edward, then get away. I used it to get Sally out of the crew area."

Edward scratched the back of his neck. "That does sound perfect. How do you plan to keep me from being killed?"

Savannah looked into his apple green eyes. "There's a blind spot that's out of view from the crew door. We're going to make sure that you have plenty of companions for the first five laps. Then for the sixth and final lap, we'll send you in alone. When Albert opens the door to attack, Chief Dalessio will be there to capture him."

"Does Chief Dalessio know about this?"

Savannah grinned. "Oh, yes, I wasn't about to suggest this until I was sure that she could support it. It's unconventional, but she agrees that it's the best idea anyone has to catch Albert before the next port stop."

"Why the first five laps with companions?"

"Simple. He needs to get frustrated, desperate, and then careless. This will be his best chance before we pull into our final port the day after tomorrow. With the cruise ship relatively empty and sniffer dogs available from the local police, they'll find Albert. He has to act now."

Edward gave Savannah a huge hug. "You're usually right."

"That doesn't mean that you should be careless. Be on your guard." Savannah kissed him full on the lips. They all moved over to the starting line and waited for the cruise director to start the race.

"Everyone get ready, now. The signal is the ship's horn."

Before the cruise director could finish that sentence, an ear-deafening blast split the air. The race began with some of the younger contestants sprinting out ahead.

Waiting until most of the passengers had started, Edward's team started the race by surrounding him into a virtually impregnable box. His protective team race-walked and soon everyone had finished the first lap. The next two laps went by quickly, but by lap four Aunt Kate had to drop out to save her knee.

"I'm so sorry," she told Savannah. "My knee replacement was more than three months ago. My physical therapist said I was ready for long walks, but I think I've overreached my capability."

Uncle Howard pulled up after lap four and began to limp. "Sorry, Savannah. I'm just not in good enough shape."

The fifth pass around the isolated part of the track was stressful. Everyone tried not to look at the crew door, but almost everyone did. It seemed to take forever to reach that same stretch of deck on the last lap.

"Okay, everyone," whispered Savannah before the vital turn. "Hang back here and let Chief Dalessio catch Albert. Good luck, the sixth lap is the lucky one, Edward."

Everyone hung back just before the turn to let Edward enter that section of the track alone. Savannah joined Chief Dalessio and Officer Gaffney just behind the crew door's line of sight. Savannah was expecting that Albert would open the door after Edward passed by and attack him from the rear. It turned out that this would be another lap of no action. There were several other runners just ahead and behind Edward. Savannah relaxed.

Instead, before she could react, the crew door opened to hit Edward on the shoulder and down he went to the deck holding his arm and howling.

One of the cruise runners jumped out of the way back into the pack that was following Edward. The pileup added another level of screaming and shouts to the chaos.

Albert plunged out of the doorway with a small stiletto, reaching out to stab Edward.

"Stop!" yelled Savannah as she grabbed Albert's wrist and could feel the bones of his wrist snap in her grip. "Stop!"

She forced her entire body weight forward and pushed him to the deck. Before she could shout again, he was being manhandled by Officer Gaffney and she sat up.

"Well, that didn't go to plan," said Edward, sitting up and rubbing his bruised arm.

"We caught him." Savannah returned Edward's half hug and then buried her head in his shoulder.

The rest of their group surrounded Officer Gaffney and Chief Dalessio and chattered questions to them in their excitement.

"Shush! We have him!" Chief Dalessio appeared to relish hauling Albert up by the scruff of his shirt to stand swaying with his hands handcuffed behind him.

Savannah shook her head slowly and began to laugh. "I can't wait to tell Detective Parker back home."

"What's so funny?" asked Edward.

"Don't you get it?" She bent over holding her sides, and tears streamed down her cheeks. "It's the ultimate cliché. The butler did it."

Chapter 24

Sunday, at sea

Savannah exited the elevator to meet both sets of twins, Ian's parents, and Edward. "Good news!" she told them. "Jacob has analyzed the ship's construction drawings and he determined where Ian might be hiding, accompanied by an estimated order of probability no less. In the kerfuffle with Albert, I forgot to tell you."

The elevator door opened again. Sally and Ruth walked out and stood just in front of the closing door. "We're here to help," said Sally.

"We overheard all the twins say they were going to search for Ian and we thought we should be part of the search." Ruth hung her head. "I feel horrible about the way I've treated Ian." She quickly gave her sister a side hug. "I'm especially ashamed of the way I treated Sally. I promised her I would help."

Savannah splayed her hands out. "Is that good with everyone?"

All agreed.

"Who is Jacob?" asked Richard.

Faith patted his hand. "Never you mind. He's a clever lad. We're going to do exactly what he says."

"Of course," Rachel agreed. "Jacob would have done an analysis for us on the first day if he had been along."

"Shush!" Savannah was looking down at her handwritten list. "Let's do the public area ones first. If we don't find him, then we'll get help from Chief Dalessio to search the crew-only locations. I'd like to avoid dealing with her if I can. I don't think she can be trusted."

Edward bowed slightly. "Agreed. Where first?"

"Let's start with the highest probability location, the Eclipse Theatre. It's on decks 4 and 5 and would be deserted in between performances and rehearsals. It's a large space." She looked at the others. "If we all go, it shouldn't take long."

Savannah was right. It didn't take long to determine that Ian wasn't hiding there. She looked at the list again.

"Jacob says the spa showers should be deserted during the evening after the staff leaves. It's possible that is where Ian is holed up. Let's split up and check both the ladies' and men's showers at the same time."

When they arrived, an attendant was putting the brochures and posters away from the lobby. "Do you mind if we have a look at the showers?" Savannah wasn't sure if the trim dark-haired girl understood them, but she nodded yes and they split up to search.

They met back in the spa lobby in a few minutes.

"Any luck, guys?" Savannah shook her head. "We didn't find anything."

"One of the shower stalls had been recently used. There was water on the walls," said Edward. "Let's check to see when the last male customer had an appointment."

"Early this afternoon," said the attendant. "That was the last gentleman guest to get a massage followed by a shower."

"Do you clean the showers after each client?"

"Yes, of course."

"Have you noticed that sometimes the cleaning is not done right away?"

"Yes!" She placed her hands on both hips in a Superman pose. "We thought it was the new girl not doing her job."

Edward spoke. "That smarty, Jacob, got this one right. This is where Ian has been cleaning up."

"Where do we try next?" Rachel asked.

"Let me see." Savannah consulted the list. "The next probable quiet public place is the adults-only solarium on the port side of the deck."

They took off and they stood looking at the packed tables.

"This doesn't seem right," said Faith. "There are lots of people here."

Edward took Savannah by the elbow. "What's next? He could have been here earlier, but there's no sign of him now."

"The next most probable place is down in the crew area," said Savannah. "I could check it out and meet you down at the pub. If I find him, he's going to want a drink."

Savannah entered the crew stairway and followed Jacob's directions down to the recommended level to search. This deck served as the ship's internal freeway to move items from the docks to the ship's stores. It was also the main portal for passenger luggage. She went to the bow of the ship where the merchandise cages were kept.

Good thinking. These cages are used to store the shopping merchandise that is displayed on the promenade each evening throughout the cruise.

She was careful to make no noise and crept her way to the bulkhead wall. When she examined the wall, she found a gap behind one of the cages that had a nest made out of jackets, T-shirts, and cabana towels.

She heard a sound along the wall.

"Ian. Come out now!" She waited.

Nothing.

"Ian, your parents are on board. They're desperately worried. The security chief told them that you committed suicide."

After hearing about his parents' being on board, Ian showed himself around the edge of the cage. "They told them what?"

"They're worried sick. You can't keep hiding and keeping them so upset. Come on out."

Savannah stood between him and any chance of escape.

Ian slowly walked around the cage and stood by Savannah. "I'm so sorry. I didn't mean for anyone to be upset. I meant to leave you a note where my pillbox was, but Sally didn't have time. Then after I hid for the first day, I couldn't risk being seen."

"That's weak, Ian." She grabbed him by the upper arm. "Anyway, we caught Albert so there's no need to hide."

"You caught Albert?" The relief rippled down his face.

"Not just me. The whole shipboard posse caught him."

Savannah continued. "He confessed under Security Chief LuAnn's surprisingly effective interrogation. He was responsible for tattling on us to her as well as the power outages. Let's go and meet your folks at the pub. You have some serious apologizing to do."

When Ian walked into the pub in front of Savannah, Ian's parents jumped up and grabbed him. Uncle Howard was pumping his hand up and down like a lever, and Aunt Kate had both hands clutching his arm while she wept.

It took quite a little while for everyone to settle, order drinks, and begin to behave like normal passengers on a sea cruise.

"I'm so sorry," Ian said for the hundredth time. "I couldn't think of anything else to do. When I saw Bert, I knew he wouldn't stop hunting me."

"Bert?" said Rachel.

"Our butler," said Faith.

Ian clasped his pint of Guinness with both hands and took a trembling drink. "Yes, he was part of the counterfeiting ring in London." He nodded over to Edward. "Your lot had already left for St. Albans, but I was caught up in the thrill of it. He knew about you, though."

"Why did he want to kill Edward?" asked Savannah. Ian furrowed his brow. "Apparently, he was thrown out of the family business because he couldn't keep boys in the ring long enough to make his cash quota. After you left, he was more hands-on with the rest of us."

"So, I made things worse for everyone?" said Edward.

"Way worse." Ian shuddered. "He was the poster child for bullying small boys. But in the end, the family recognized that he would never fit into the organization and cut him off. I would guess the cruise industry wouldn't really want a counterfeiting ringleader as one of its elite concierges."

Aunt Kate and Uncle Howard looked at each other. "Why didn't you tell us? We could have moved sooner."

"It was easier to play along and just wait for the move. If I ratted on him—he would have hurt you."

Edward pounded his fist on the table, causing everyone to grab at their bouncing glasses. "You could have said something when we arrived on board. You've terrified everyone. Why?"

"I didn't want him to know about you and Savannah. He was aboard for some reason and I couldn't risk leading him to you."

Savannah put a hand on Edward's arm. "Calm yourself. We have him now and Chief Dalessio is going to turn him over to the local police department tomorrow morning at our last port in Barcelona."

"Are you finished with your glass demonstrations?" asked Edward.

Savannah nodded. "I'm rather sad that they're over. I need to be at the auction this evening. Poor Eric will be embarrassed to speak much with his broken teeth, so I said I would do all the description banter for the auction."

"What time does the auction start?" asked Rachel.

"We're going to buy something," said Faith.

"But you ladies already have some of my pieces." Savannah was again amazed at how down to earth these wealthy little ladies behaved.

"Well, we have some of your stained-glass panels and a few fused glass platters," said Rachel.

"But this is the first opportunity we've had to purchase your glassblowing pieces," said Faith.

The group broke up with promises to attend the auction.

Savannah opened her e-mail icon and sent a message to Amanda and Jacob about the successful outcome of the capture of Alan's killer and their successful search for Ian. She pushed send and changed into her little black dress for the auction. She was just about to leave when she heard the ping for a new e-mail message.

> Dear Savannah, I am happy to know that
> my ship's search analysis was successful. I
> don't understand why you changed the
> search order.

Savannah shook her head. Of course, he would have had her start with the most probable site, but it wasn't a public area. She smiled. Some things would forever be a mystery to him. At least he was more relaxed about those incomprehensible social puzzles.

> Miss Amanda says to tell you that the
> accounting system is working perfectly.

The new analyst is training her to use all the new features. His name is Kurt. Kurt is good at customer relations. He checks on the accounting system at least twice a day. Miss Amanda says Kurt is not her boyfriend. Miss Amanda also says that Rooney and Snowy aren't playing Lion King anymore. They are playing tag.

I have good news. I have passed the written test to apply for a driver's license with 100%. Miss Amanda helped me practice taking the test in difficult locations. The test was not hard. Concentrating was hard. Suzy was permitted to be with me and she sat in my lap while I took the test.

When I become a good driver, I can help Webb's Glass Shop pick up and deliver commissions.

Jacob

P.S. Suzy misses you very much.

Savannah had never been to a cruise ship auction, but most everyone there behaved as if this were their natural environment. She was stunned to see how many glass pieces were up for bid. It hadn't seemed like they were making that many each day, but there they were—she counted twenty-two. She had to admit that she enjoyed seeing them on raised pedestals under dramatic spot lighting. It made her question her choice to leave glassblowing to run her dad's glass shop.

I must find a way to get the practice of glassblowing back in my life.

"Beautiful, aren't they?" Eric sidled up to her and rubbed his palms together. "Wanna guess on how much we make? The winner is who guesses closest without going over. Winner pays loser a hundred bucks."

Savannah laughed. "No, loser buys the winner a drink. Besides, you've done this many times."

"Okay, I'll guess first. Let's see, there are twenty-two pieces at about an average of four hundred dollars each. I'll guess eighty-eight hundred dollars."

Savannah pursed her lips. She knew that Alan's pieces would draw a large sympathy bidding war among some of his grieving fans. "I'll guess thirteen thousand. That's my final answer."

"What's a final answer?" Edward joined them along with both sets of twins.

"Savannah and I are betting on the final auction value."

He turned to see Rachel, Faith, Richard, and Rickard all with bidding paddles. "You have no idea what will happen with these four in the auction. Better get out now."

The auction began with the smallest glass pieces first. Either Eric or Savannah would explain the features and the bidding would begin. It was clear right away that even Savannah had grossly underestimated the enthusiasm that the glass collectors would spend to take home a cruise memory.

At the end, each of the twins had a piece, sometimes outbidding each other. The auctioneer turned to one of his assistants and she handed him a slip of paper. "Ladies and gentlemen, we have reached a new record for the glass auction. The amount raised for United Way, Make-A-Wish of America, and City Year is twenty-four thousand, six hundred and seventy-five dollars!"

Wild applause exploded in the small space.

Savannah could feel the color rise up her neck with the excitement of seeing her creations bring in so much money. "Drinks are on Eric!"

Chapter 25

Monday, sunrise near Barcelona

Savannah folded her arms on the deck railing and reveled in the beauty of a sunrise view of Barcelona. This was her favorite time of day—before passengers were strolling about—before the bustling of the breakfast buffet—before the crowds frantic to meet their departure flights. She held a mug of cappuccino and leaned against Edward, who was holding a cup of English breakfast tea with milk.

Edward couldn't be still. He kept looking at his watch and she was sure he gulped his tea without even tasting it.

"What's the matter?"

"Nothing, nothing at all. I'm just a little edgy after everything that has happened on this cruise." He drained his cup and sat it on one of the deck tables behind them. "This was supposed to be a relaxing time. It wasn't."

"We're going to have a great day! This is Barcelona.

We're going to visit every museum in town." Savannah frowned. "This is an incredible opportunity. Why are you so nervous?"

"Me?" Edward checked his watch and slipped his hand in his front pocket for a moment.

"What's with checking the time every five seconds?"

"I asked everyone to be here and they're a little late." He turned Savannah back toward the view of the dock the cruise ship was approaching with sedate speed. "I'll wait just a few more minutes and then . . ."

"Then what?" asked Rachel.

Edward grinned. "Ladies! Thank goodness. I was afraid my message was lost."

"We got a new butler," said Faith. "He's adorable. He looks about fifteen, but I'm sure he's nearly thirty. Such a wonderful opportunity for him."

Behind them were the VanGilden brothers, who each stood behind one of the Rosenberg sisters. "Thanks for including us," said one of the sisters. Savannah didn't see which one.

"Good show," said Rickard.

"Hey, cuz!" Ian poked Edward in the arm. "Is it done?"

Savannah frowned and looked around at all of them. "What's going on here?"

Aunt Kate and Uncle Howard arrived last. "We aren't too late, are we?"

"No," said Edward. He laughed. "I've been worrying myself silly here that I would be alone."

Savannah crossed her arms and began to tap a foot. "What is going on here? Are you all keeping secrets from me?"

Edward grabbed her arms with both of his hands. "It's not going to be a secret in a moment. Stand still, please." He reached into the pocket he had been checking and pulled out a small black box. Then he dropped to one knee and opened the box to reveal a ruby ring.

"Savannah," he started, but had to clear his throat. "Savannah, one of the reasons I needed to visit my hometown was to get this family heirloom."

Savannah put both hands to her face to keep from squealing.

Edward raised the ring up to Savannah. "Would you do me the great honor of becoming my wife?"

Everyone held their breath. Savannah was an independent strong-minded woman. This wasn't a sure thing.

Savannah lowered her hands. She could feel the seep of tears filling her heart and the surge of emotion in her chest. She pulled Edward up so that they stood eye to eye.

"Edward." She paused. "Love of my life." Another long pause. "Champion of my dreams." The silence around them deepened. "My partner forever." She smiled. "I would be delighted to marry you."

Everyone cheered. Edward removed the ring from the box and slipped it onto Savannah's finger.

She held out her hand for everyone to admire.

On cue, a waiter arrived with glasses of champagne.

"Pretty sure of the outcome, were you?" Savannah teased.

"I marshalled every weapon in my arsenal. I knew there would be only one chance."

Ian raised his glass. "To the newly engaged couple."

After she sipped from her flute, Savannah looked Edward straight into those green eyes. "This is going to be a fantastic adventure."

They embraced into a passionate kiss.

COMMON GLASSBLOWING TERMS

annealing—Cooling the formed glass product at a controlled rate of temperature change for the purpose of relieving thermal stress. The appropriate cooling curve varies with glass type and formed shape, especially thickness. Directly related to glass cut-ability.

battledore—A glassworker's tool in the form of a square wooden paddle with a handle. Battledores are used to smooth the bottoms of vessels and other objects.

bench—The bench is the center of the hot shop. It is where the artist works a piece and is where all the tools are kept. The bench has two rails spaced on either side going perpendicular to the seat; these rails are used to roll the glass pipes on.

bit—A mass of molten glass, usually small and freshly gathered from the furnace. In a team of glassworkers, the bit gatherer removes bits from the furnace, using a bit iron. Bits are also known as gobs.

blank—Any cooled glass object that requires further forming or decoration to be finished.

block—A tool made from a block of wood
hollowed out to form a hemispherical recess.
After it has been dipped in water to reduce
charring and to create a "cushion" of steam,
the block is used to form the gather into a
sphere before it is inflated.

blow pipe—An iron or steel tube, usually four to
five feet long, for blowing glass. Blowpipes have
a mouthpiece at one end and are usually fitted
at the other end with a metal ring that helps to
retain the gather.

blowing—The technique of forming an object by
inflating a gather or gob of molten glass on the
end of a blowpipe. Traditionally and in modern
furnace working, the gaffer blows through the
tube, slightly inflating the gob, which is then
manipulated into the required form by swinging
it, rolling it on a marver, or shaping it with tools
or in a mold. It is then inflated to the desired
size. In flame working, one end of the glass tube
is heated and closed immediately, after which
the worker blows into the other end and
manipulates the hot glass.

blown glass—The shaping of glass by blowing air
through a hollow rod into the center of a
molten glass gather.

casting—The generic name for a wide variety of
techniques used to form glass in a mold.

frit—Ground glass, ranging in particle size from
gravel-like to a fine powder. Frit is sometimes
used as a raw material in glass manufacture, and
sometimes as a coloring agent or for decorative
effect in hot glass crafts like blowing and fusing.

gaffer (corruption of "grandfather")—The master craftsman in charge of a chair, or team, of hot-glass workers.

gather—A mass of molten glass (sometimes called a gob) collected on the end of a blowpipe, pontil, or gathering iron; (verb) to collect molten glass on the end of a tool.

marver—A marver is a large flat table. The glass piece is rolled across its surface. It is used to not only shape the glass, but to remove heat as well. The rapid absorption of heat by the marver creates a stronger skin (surface tension) than the use of a wooden tool. Marver is derived from the word *marble*. Marble was originally used in the construction of this specialized table. Modern marvers are made of steel, typically stainless steel. Lamp workers use small graphite marvers mounted on or near their torches.

milli/millefiori—The Italian term, *thousand flowers*, used to describe mosaic glass objects.

noodle—A fettuccini-like glass shape used as a decorative element in the hot glass arts.

punty/pontil—A solid metal rod, around five feet long, used to hold an object being blown or hot-worked after it is removed from the blowpipe.

stringer—A spaghetti-like glass shape used as a decorative element in the creation of vessels in glassblowing.

GLASSBLOWING INSTRUCTION

Making gifts of glass is my favorite hobby. My husband and I have a large kiln in the small studio behind our house that we use to fuse glass. In addition, we have been creating a series of etched glass books with the covers of each book in the Webb's Glass Shop Mystery series. They are simply gorgeous and I always have one with me when I have an event at a library or festival. To see the process we use in making these books, go to the website sponsored by Kensington Books, www.Hobbyreads.com.

On occasion, we take classes to make blown glass pieces. There are several hot shops in St. Petersburg, and we have enjoyed participating in the "date night" workshops. Our first session was at the Morean Art Center on 719 Central Avenue. The format is simple—each couple will have a hands-on experience culminating in one piece of glass art. It is typically a solid sculpted paperweight or a blown-glass ornament made by the two of you in collaboration with an instructor.

Webb's Glass Shop is inspired by the real-life Grand Central Stained Glass & Graphics business owned by our good friends Bradley and Eloyne Erickson. Their website is www.grandcentralstainedglass.com.

You can find a class in your area by searching the web for fused, etched, or stained-glass classes in your city.

My husband and I have scaled back our glasswork to making gifts for friends, family, and book promotion. My current interest is in making glass beads in a technique called *flameworking*. It's a little intimidating, but I'm getting more and more comfortable with the process. George says he'll set me up a workstation in the studio. All I need to do is say the word.

Right now, I'm torn between telling him to go ahead or concentrate on writing the next book in the Webb's Glass Shop Mystery series. Since bead-making is the featured glass art in my next book, I predict that I will need to find a way to do both. I'll let you know what happened in this section of the next book.

Chapter 1

"They call it The Enigma," said Savannah Webb as she stared up at the dark blue glass structure ballooning out of the Dali Museum.

It stood proud against the warm evening light on the calm waters of Tampa Bay. The square concrete structure contrasted with the huge geodesic bulbous glass windows that oozed from the front of the building around to the other side. It fired the evening with an air of anticipation for a surrealistic experience.

"The building is as much an exhibit as anything inside." Savannah's balance wobbled and she quickly grabbed the arm of her boyfriend Edward Morris. She hadn't worn heels this high since, well, since high school. It was taking a little longer than she expected to find a comfortable stride.

Edward folded her hand securely into the crook of his arm. He lifted his chin as they approached the entrance. He wore the tux his parents had bought him when he'd graduated from University. It had been a good investment. One of the many advantages of growing up British—elegance and frugality traveled comfortably hand in hand.

Savannah relaxed and her balance returned. "Thanks for the arm. Pitching onto the concrete in a face splat is not the way I want to be remembered at this reception."

Edward squeezed her hand. "I'm the lucky one. You look spectacular."

Savannah smiled. Her dress choices had been small. As the owner of the venerable family-owned Webb's Glass Shop, her wardrobe was basically logo shirts with comfortable slacks or jeans. Luckily, this little black dress fit like it was born to party. Using bits of red, orange, and cobalt blue, she had created a statement necklace of kiln-formed glass medallions with a matching pair of small button earrings. She had also created a barrette that she'd clipped into her black curly hair.

"The building opened on January 11th, 2011. It's apparently an auspicious date that adds up to a lucky number seven. I wouldn't know, but the museum has been incredibly successful. So, who can say whether that choice was lucky or predisposed to shower the museum with good fortune? Not me."

"It looks like a bunker," said Edward.

"Well, with such a valuable collection inside, eighteen-inch-thick hurricane-proof walls seem like the minimum precaution. I love it—perfectly Dali."

Edward handed the invitation to the uniformed security guard at the members-only reception desk. A name tag declared him to be Lucas Brown, Security Manager. "Thank you for attending the opening reception for our special exhibition." He looked at his display monitor and picked up a bright red Tyvek wristband. "Welcome, Miss Savannah Webb of Webb's Glass Shop." He peeled off the backing and circled it around her left wrist. He looked back at his monitor. "And Mr. Edward Morris, owner of Queen's Head Pub, guest of Ms. Webb." He fastened an orange band around Edward's wrist.

Lucas waved a hand to his left. "Refreshments are being served in the café. The exhibit is on the third floor and the celebrated artist is receiving invited guests in the Community Room. That's the large room behind and to the right of the Gala café." The monitor beeped a message, which he bent over to read. Then he leaned over to Savannah's ear. "You are most particularly requested to meet the artist." He straightened back up. "Make your way through the gift shop and you'll find the circular stairway to the right of the café. The elevators are just beyond the stairway. Please enjoy yourselves!" He smiled briefly and turned to the next guest.

They walked through the extensive gift shop to the café. Edward flagged down a server holding a tray of bubbly flutes. He grabbed two. "Here, luv." He handed her a flute. "I know you love champagne."

Savannah smiled. They clinked glasses and sipped. She licked her lips, then smiled. "Delicious. That's an excellent vintage. They're not stinting on the caliber of the refreshments." She looked at Edward's puzzled frown over the rim of her flute. "It's pretty common to get cheap eats at these exhibits. The artists usually have to buy everything."

They each took a skewer of grilled shrimp from another of the many servers.

"Scrumptious." She grabbed his hand. "Come around to the outside. There's something back there I think you'll appreciate."

They took a left at the café and exited the building through two sets of double doors onto an outdoor space populated by Dali-inspired sculptures. The most prominent was a giant up-curled black mustache with a space in the center for posing.

Savannah pulled on Edward's hand and stopped at an opening in the hedges at the far back of the property. "This is it."

"Is this a maze?" He looked at the entrance with his arms out wide as if to hug the world. "I love them."

"I know. I can't believe you didn't know this was here." She smiled and stepped into the graveled pathway on her tiptoes to prevent her heels from sinking into the sandy soil below the thin layer of gravel. "Come on. The party can wait a few minutes."

It took less than five minutes of curving loops and whirls to make their way to the central circle of the maze. Edward pulled her into his arms for a warm kiss. "Thank you. I enjoyed my surprise."

"I know these things are popular in Europe, but pretty rare here." She had given him a key to her house last month. Since her father's murder, she was finding it hard to commit to a permanent live-in relationship. "We need to get—" She screeched and began to fall. Edward caught her around the waist and lifted her up to extract her heels from the soft ground.

"Those delicious shoes are a hazard to your ankles in this footing. I'll have you back in a jiff."

"No need." Savannah wiggled herself out of his grasp and carefully onto the path. "I think I stepped on something. I'm fine now." She straightened her dress and looked down on the path. "There it is. That's what tripped me." She bent and picked up a cardboard hamburger container. "This is a strange place to eat fast food. Who would do something like this? I'll put it in the trash can inside."

"Speaking of inside, we need to get going," said Edward.

They returned to the building, and Savannah tossed the wrapper into the first waste can she saw. They replaced their empty flutes with fresh champagne then climbed the white spiral stairway to the third floor and entered the main exhibit hall reserved for visiting collections. A ten-foot-tall free-standing banner announced the exhibit with a picture of Dennis Lansing beside a tall, bloodred, heart-shaped vessel etched with scribbled writing and images of lilacs and daffodils.

Edward stood in front of the banner. "What an unusual combination. My mother is fascinated with the Victorian secret language of flowers. She would know what they mean."

"That's a thing?" asked Savannah. "Really? Explain."

He grimaced. "Ugh! Mum gave me this lecture frequently. She couldn't fathom that I might not be interested. You might as well have the short version.

History relates that during the reign of Queen Victoria, the language of flowers was as important to people as being well dressed. For example, the recognizable scent of a specific flower sent its own unique message. Flowers adorned almost everything . . . hair, clothing, jewelry, gowns, men's lapels, home décor and china, and stationery, to name a few. A young man could either please or displease a lady by his gift of flowers. They had a silent meaning of their very own, and could 'say' what was not dared to be spoken."

The exhibit space was filled with about thirty glass vessels, each resting on a tall white pillar standing about four feet high. Overhead track lighting illuminated the glass from several angles to show off the deep colors and highlight the intricate etchings. Savannah tucked her hand into Edward's arm as they walked slowly through the exhibit. It seemed a little intrusive to overhear the quiet crowd admiring and commenting on Dennis's skill and talent.

When they were approaching the last of the pieces, Savannah saw a familiar-looking fiftyish woman in a plain black cotton shirtwaist standing in front of the large red glass vessel. "Mrs. Lansing? Do you remember me? I'm Savannah Webb. I knew Dennis from St. Petersburg High School."

"My goodness. Yes, I remember you." The small lady's bright blue eyes lit up her warm smile. She grasped Savannah's hand with both of hers. "Savannah, it's wonderful to see you here. I do so wish that things had worked out differently between you and Dennis. It would have made such a difference." Her phone pinged from within a pearl evening bag. She slipped it out and her face stiffened. "Oh, excuse me. I should have been downstairs by now. I've dawdled among the display pieces for too long, again. Dennis's wife will be annoyed." She left and they watched her hurrying down the spiral staircase.

Edward tilted his head and raised his eyebrows. "I am beginning to suspect that you have a certain history with this artist. Am I right?"

"Yes, but it was a long time ago. I was a freshman in high school. We dated for a few weeks."

"So, here in the States, as a freshman, you would have been about fourteen?"

"Yes, I was fourteen. It was at the very beginning of the school year. It will be nice to catch up with him and his career." She leaned in closer to look at the red vessel that was featured in all the promotional materials advertising the exhibit. It contained an etched image of a note in rounded loopy hand-writing. Savannah straightened up quickly. That was her handwriting! Dennis had included one of her childish love notes in his featured artwork. She felt a warm flush grow from her throat to her ears.

"What's wrong?" Edward slipped an arm around her waist. "Has the champagne gone to your head already?"

She ran a hand through her curls and smiled weakly. "Yes, that must be it. I've only had two small glasses. We'd better do our meet and greet before I become insensible."

"That's not likely. You're too strong minded for that."

They left the gallery and made their way to the ground floor.

Savannah slipped her hand through Edward's

arm. "I think we'd better get into the receiving line.
I want to tell Dennis how much I enjoyed his exhibit
and how much I appreciate his support of my etching class."

Edward placed his hand over hers and they walked
to the entrance of the community room. The chatter
from inside was spilling out into the hallway. There
were only a few people in line.

"Savannah! Savannah Webb, is that you?" said a
trim man with a red cummerbund and matching red
bowtie in an expertly fitted tux. "I haven't seen you
since I graduated. You'd just finished freshman . . .
maybe sophomore year. It's Charles." He shook her
free hand like a pump handle. He stepped back and
looked her up and down. "You've grown up. Definitely up." He smiled. "I'm still on the short side. You
remember me. don't you? I'm Charles King."

Savannah scanned the craggy face and tried to age
it back ten years. Nothing. "I don't seem to recall."

"I was a friend of our famous artist here. I used to
see you at Webb's Glass Shop when your dad was
running that apprentice program. Surely, you remember?"

Savannah smiled and shook her head. "I'm trying.
I think I remember a Chuck, but he was . . . well, he
was a big guy."

"Absolutely me. I was a big guy back then. Huge.
Obese, even. Yeah." He patted his slim waist with
both hands. "I got that fixed when I decided to go
into politics." He turned to Edward and pumped
his hand while slapping him on the shoulder. "So,
you're the lucky one who has captured our lovely
Savannah's heart. I'm Charles King, your state representative up in Tallahassee. Yep, I'm a local boy done

good. I hear good things about Queen's Head Pub. Nice to meet you. Too bad you can't vote. I have an election coming up soon. Are you going to apply for citizenship?"

Savannah snapped her fingers. "I've got it! You were a couple years ahead of me. I remember now that you were a close friend of Dennis's." She turned to Edward. "Dad and I attended the commencement ceremony that year because of that apprentice program that Dad established."

"Good girl!" Charles looked behind them and nodded to another guest. "I'll come by the shop to see you this week. It'll be good to catch up. Excuse me, I must speak to a major party supporter over there." He disappeared in a half run to greet a man and wife in elegant evening wear.

Savannah shuddered. "Ugh. I remember now that he was exactly that overbearing when he was our student council president. It was a testament to his persuasive powers that we would elect the fat boy over the football star."

Edward frowned.

"I know. Politically incorrect," said Savannah. "But he was quite the organizer. Ugh! Will high school ever be over? I didn't like it at the time, and I have few fond memories."

"Wise girl." Edward immediately responded with, "Oops, sorry. I didn't mean to call you a girl. I know that makes you angry . . . but in my defense, everyone does it."

Savannah's voice tightened. "It doesn't make it right. I'm no one's girl. I'm a woman fully grown." She tapped a pointed finger into his chest. With her three-inch heels, she stood taller than their equal six-foot height and she was enjoying the temporary advantage. "Remember that."

"Sorry, sorry, sorry." Edward chuckled. "Remember, I'm still a work in progress. British girls—young women, I mean—are quite different. They seem to be on a suicide mission to be more like bad lads for rude behavior. I am sorry."

Savannah closed her eyes then opened them again. "You're forgiven. I'm sorry for being so prickly. I'm glad that you know that about me." She downed the rest of her champagne and Edward placed both flutes on the tray of the nearest server passing by.

"Let's get in line to meet Dennis. I think he'll recognize me. I haven't seen him since graduation either."

"Same year as State Congressman Hot Air?"

"Funny, funny. You know I've watched that television program, *MP Minutes* on BBC America. You Brits have some clowns, too. Both our countries appear to lack for any kind of qualified political leadership, let alone a true visionary. An absence of ethics and brains seems to be the perfect formula to be a successful politician. That certainly describes Chuck."

A tap on her arm caused Savannah to turn to see Betty Lansing standing at her elbow smiling up to her. "Savannah, I didn't mean to be so abrupt in the exhibit hall upstairs. I'm glad we can talk a bit more. You have bloomed into a beautiful woman. I remember your father fondly. In fact, we were good friends while Dennis was in the apprentice program, but after Dennis graduated, your dad and I drifted apart. He was so focused on you and his glass business, I didn't have a chance."

Savannah eyed Edward and mouthed *help*. She turned back and took the woman's hand in both of hers. "Of course, I remember your visits. You talked to my dad for hours about Dennis's progress. Dennis was one of the first students to turn his life around." She turned to Edward. "This is my friend, Edward Morris. He owns the restaurant pub next door to the glass shop. You remember that old gas station? It was converted about ten years ago into a bar. Edward added a commercial kitchen and a passel of talented chefs."

Betty's eyes narrowed. "Yes, I think I recall, but my memory isn't as good as it used to be and I don't really get about very much now. Anyway, I'll let you young folks be. It was nice to see you." She turned away back toward the Gala café.

"I remember her exactly like that—nice—and then she would disappear."

"So I'm a 'friend'?" Edward air quoted the word *friend*.

"Please, don't read anything into what I say. I've had the dreaded second glass of champagne. It whips my words into a swirling mess. Beer doesn't do that to me. I need to stick to beer."

"Fat chance," said Edward. "Relax. Enjoy this."

They joined the short reception line to greet the featured artist of the new glass exhibition. Dennis Lansing wasn't wearing a tuxedo. Instead, he wore a unique Dali-like navy silk suit with an outlandish tie and beside him stood a woman dressed as a perfect replica of Dali's wife Gala.

Gala was famous for wearing the latest avant-garde couture designs to the eclectic performances that Dali arranged for the display of his latest paintings.

It spoke of an incredibly confident persona to pull off the Gala impression so well.

The line moved quickly. Most of the attendees seemed to be sponsors and Dali Museum members with no real connection to the artist.

As soon as Savannah and Edward reached the front of the line, the artist smiled like a Cheshire cat. "Savannah, Savannah. I'm so glad you could be here." He held her upper arms and gave her a quick peck on both cheeks, European style. He turned to wrap an arm about the woman next to him and gave her a side hug. "This is my long-suffering and inspirational wife, Harriet. She's my muse and my model just as Gala was for Dali." He raised his wife's hand to his lips as he continued to look at Savannah.

Harriet glanced at him wearing a much practiced closed-mouth smile.

Savannah tucked her hand into Edward's arm. "This is Edward Morris. He owns the Queen's Head Pub right next to Webb's Glass Shop." *Why can't I say* boyfriend? *Just because my last relationship ended in disaster doesn't mean that this one will, too.* "It's a major leader in St. Petersburg's new identity as a foodie destination." Savannah could feel a deep flush creep into her cheeks.

Why? Probably because it sounds juvenile. But I'm not bold enough to say partner or lover, either. Maybe I completely deserve to be called a girl.

Dennis smiled kindly at Savannah. She flushed even more.

She cleared her suddenly scratchy throat. "I'm so pleased you'll be coming over to my new studio to give a presentation to my etching students. Oh, and the personal tour of your exhibit is going to be the highlight of this week's workshop. I can't thank you enough."

Edward wrapped an arm around Savannah's shoulders and gave her a little side hug. "I'd be pleased to have you and your wife as our guests at Queen's Head Pub for a chef's table experience in the kitchen."

Harriet looked up at Edward. "Oh, that would be delicious! I've heard good things about the food and your online reviews are fabulous."

Dennis reached into the inside of his jacket pocket. "I have something for you that I think you would like to see."

Savannah had opened her mouth to respond when a woman in a royal blue, raw silk dress bustled up to Dennis and barged into the middle of the group of guests waiting to speak to him.

"Dennis, my darling, I must take you and Harriet away for a private tour with the governor of Florida, our senator, and naturally, of course, the mayor of St. Petersburg." She grabbed Dennis and Harriet by the elbow and literally dragged them away.

"But there are guests here who have been waiting." Savannah looked crossly at Harriet and Gina.

Gina looked back at the startled waiting line. "We can't keep the officials waiting, you know. We're dependent on city and state funding for some of our exhibits . . . this one included."

Edward frowned. "That was incredibly rude and the kind of treatment no one in this queue could possibly deserve. She should have apologized."

They both looked at the quickly retreating trio.

Savannah looked down at Edward. "She did say excuse me. Would you like more hors d'oeuvres or maybe another glass of champagne, I hope?"

"No." He wrapped an arm around her and pulled her close. "I'd rather spend the rest of the evening at home with you and your goofy dog Rooney. This crowd is giving me a chill."

"Good plan." She smiled and whispered over the mumbling in the line of guests behind them, "I guess we're definitely not A-listers."

Chapter 2

Monday morning

"Don't touch that!" Savannah Webb shouted at the pair of elderly twins over the high-pitched whine of the sandblasting equipment.

The loud warning did nothing to stop Rachel and Faith Rosenberg for a second. They were standing right next to the sandblasting cabinet on the outdoor patio of Webb's Studio. But like a cat who stares at you while knocking your coffee cup off the counter, one of them deliberately opened the access door on the side of the cabinet and sand whooshed out in a huge cloud.

All four class members tried to escape the powerful cloud of dust by ducking away, waving their hands, turning their backs, and covering their mouths. Everything was futile. The dust puffed out and covered everything within a ten-foot circle.

Savannah's shock delayed the release of her grip

on the sand-etching nozzle and she dropped the dish she was etching into the bottom of the cabinet. She quickly slipped her hands and arms out of the protective sleeves that extended into the sandblasting cabinet, reached around the side, and closed the access door.

After brushing the sand from her face and clothes, then spitting inelegantly onto the ground beyond the border of the small cement patio, Savannah turned to face the twins. They were both dancing a jig to slap the sand out of their newly treated lavender hair and the perfectly matched lavender capri pants, snug fitting camp shirts, and ballet flats. Their antics were surprisingly agile for the near-eighty-year-olds.

Savannah felt her scalp tingle as she heard her voice rise in both pitch and volume. "What were you thinking? I just talked everyone through all the safety steps."

Faith answered first. "But you didn't fully latch the door after the demonstration. It simply looked like it was latched."

"But it wasn't," continued Rachel. "Otherwise, the door wouldn't have opened."

Savannah looked at the access door and there was the safety latch swinging loose. She palmed her forehead and exhaled in a quick puff. "You're right. I forgot. Oh my goodness. I'm so sorry I shouted." She stopped for a moment, looked at the scene of dancing students, and began to laugh uncontrollably. One by one the students joined her.

"I'm glad you yelled," said Arthur Young, a middle-aged man who was a regular student of Webb's Studio.

The repurposed warehouse was Savannah's latest business expansion. It provided work space to intermediate level glass artists.

"It gave me enough time to back away." He stopped laughing abruptly. Then he widened his eyes and stood stiff. "Uh, I need to go—now!" He bolted for the back door, opened it, and rushed inside.

"Too bad," said Faith. "He seemed to be getting better. You know, with the Crohn's incidents."

"This may set him back a few weeks." Rachel shook her head slowly from side to side. "How annoying, but at least the bathroom is just inside."

Crohn's disease is a condition that causes inflammation of the wall of the gut. That can lead to diarrhea, abdominal cramping, and weight loss.

"Did you tell him about avoiding dairy?" asked Faith.

"He said he was just starting a new vegan diet. That's why he's been doing a bit better."

"Okay let's settle down." Savannah caught her breath and wiped the laughter tears from her eyes. "Luckily, we all had our safety glasses on, so no eye issues. Also, the breeze out here took the dust away quickly. How are you?" she asked the last of her students.

"I'm completely unscathed," said Edith Maloney. "What a good thing I was standing behind Arthur, who was also standing behind Rachel and Faith. Will this delay your instruction? I have another appointment immediately after class."

"Not really." Savannah scrubbed her hands through her short curly black hair to release a miniature cloud of dust. "I was going to demonstrate the fine points of cleaning the equipment later in the workshop sequence, but this accident provides an excellent opportunity. We'll just move it up to today's lesson. Oh yes, Edith, we'll definitely end class on time."

"That's a relief," said Edith. "I was so happy to see such an early class time."

"It's an experiment I'm trying for our more advanced classes. Also, starting at seven a.m. for a two-hour class helps avoid the heat of the day as well as the afternoon thunderstorms—extremely important factors when working outside in Florida's steamy autumn heat."

Savannah led the students through the detailed steps for proper maintenance of the sandblasting equipment. She explained the setup and they all took turns checking the compressor, the sandblasting cabinet, and the dust collector. After the equipment had been thoroughly cleaned and readied for operation, she showed them how to break it down. Then they moved everything into the storage room inside Webb's Studio.

"As you witnessed this morning"—Savannah glowered in jest at the twins—"sand etching can be unexpectedly messy. Storing the equipment inside, then setting it up on the back patio for use, is a sensible precaution. Cleaning the entire studio of sand is a task I don't ever want to tackle ever. *Ever.*"

Arthur raised his hand. "What if it's raining?"

"Good question." She paused and pressed her lips together. "It hasn't come up yet, but I think if I accept a commission that requires a short turnaround and need to sand etch in the rain, I'll buy one of those easy-to-set-up exhibit tents to use as a shelter. Typically, it's not likely I would need to go to such an extreme. Our Florida rains are either torrential or a fine mist hardly worth calling rain. The downbursts usually give us about a ten-minute rumbling thunder as a warning so I can drag everything inside."

Edith glanced at her Rolex. "I'm sorry, but I've simply got to leave for my next appointment." She looked at each student in turn. "Please excuse me." She grabbed her large pale green Prada purse and quickly stepped out the front door.

Rachel and Faith turned to each other and raised their eyebrows. Then they each turned to Savannah.

"Who is she?" Rachel asked. "We haven't seen her before and your requirements for this class were quite clear. It is aimed at the intermediate level student . . . not at beginner level."

"Yes," said Faith. "We've been to every Webb's Glass Shop class for years now. We're definitely advanced students."

Not so much in skill level but an entertaining fixture in each class.

Savannah nodded agreement. "You're right. She came with class experience from a school down in Sarasota. She had a letter of reference and brought several finished pieces for me to evaluate. She'll be fine. Why do you want to know? Has she said something?"

The twins looked at each other and shrugged simultaneously. "It seems strange that she would be making things hard for herself," said Faith.

"Sarasota is at least an hour's drive, but she seems to have urgent business in St. Pete," said Rachel.

Savannah shook her head. "She's going to make etched glass awards for one of the Sarasota charity events and it doubles as her class project. I think she only needs a few."

Faith patted Savannah on the shoulder. "If that makes you feel better, dear. Anyway, we'll see you tomorrow. I hope you forgive me for the kerfuffle."

"So, it was you." Savannah slowly shook her head and smiled. "I couldn't tell in the cloud. It wouldn't be a Webb's Glass Shop class without you two. Okay, everyone, I'll see you tomorrow at seven sharp."

The twins left through the front door and nearly bumped into Jacob Underwood, the apprentice that Savannah's dad had hired shortly before he died. She continued with his education as a tribute to John Webb's memory. Jacob was a little over eighteen, lanky and dark-haired. He was holding Suzy, his trusty brown, tan, and white Beagle service dog. Suzy was trained to assist Jacob to control the panic attacks that occasionally struck him when he was under stress. He walked up to Savannah and deliberately looked her in the eyes. "Good morning, Miss Savannah. How are you?"

"I am very well, Jacob. Thank you for asking."

A flash of relief played across his face and he looked down at the floor. "I'm practicing my social skills. Mom says I will need to be much better if I want to work with clients on glass commissions."

"What a good start, Jacob." Savannah's chest filled with pride. Jacob had what used to be known as Asperger's Syndrome and thrived in the routine—but creative—work of stained glass design and repair.

"Good customer relations bring repeat business, along with referrals from satisfied customers. A little practice making eye contact every day will make it more comfortable for you. It may never be easy, but it will certainly be more comfortable." She scratched Suzy behind her ears. "Good morning to you as well."

Suzy licked her hand, then turned her gaze back to Jacob.

Jacob smiled slightly, and without another word walked quickly into his workroom to perform his first task of the day. He sat in his chair and slipped rubber booties on Suzy so she could run free in the studio without collecting stray shards of glass in her paws. Suzy looked up at him with her pleading big brown eyes, and performed an awkward goose stepping circle, but she relented to the shoes and settled into the routine of Jacob's day.

Savannah realized she was smiling. Jacob's efforts to socialize were strongly encouraged by his mother, Frances Underwood, a juvenile court judge. Only last week, they met for a long lunch at the swanky Vinoy Hotel at Frances's expense to discuss specific scenarios for Jacob to practice. This was his first attempt at making eye contact.

A tap on her shoulder interrupted Savannah's thoughts.

Arthur stood behind her, grinning like a possum. "I'm staying for a while to work on my new project. This early class is a great way to get me up and out of the house. I think it will help me create enough pieces for the next Second Saturday Art Walk. I want to thank you for encouraging me to participate." He laughed. "Although, *prodding* is probably more accurate in my case."

"A big part of my long-term plan is to inform the more advanced glass students about the mechanics of managing the financial side of this business. There's so much to learn about pricing, marketing, and promoting yourself, and I want to share the knowledge."

Arthur nodded. "It's overwhelming and then there's the fear that your work isn't good enough." He turned and walked back to his private studio space two doors down from Savannah's office along the back wall of the building.

Savannah had no sooner sat in her office chair when the front door opened. In walked Officer Joy Williams of the St. Petersburg Police Department, smartly dressed in a brand-new, freshly pressed dark blue uniform.

Savannah walked out into the exhibit space to greet her. "Joy, I haven't heard from you for a couple weeks. The new uniform looks great!"

The darker hue lent a natural authority. For Joy, a petite woman of color with neat braids coiled at the base of her slim neck, Savannah thought it would add a significant boost to her official presence.

"Was I happy to get rid of those white shirts trimmed in green over those horrible green trousers? Absolutely." She twirled a little spin. "I'm so lucky. I'm one of the trial squad members to give the new model a shakedown run. I love the pockets, the fit, and it's got a wicking thing going so it doesn't lose its shape. I was concerned about the dark color absorbing heat. We do live in hot, hotter, and hottest Florida, but this new fabric keeps me cool. The best thing is that the dark color doesn't shine up like a beacon at night. This will save lives."

"It looks professional. Didn't we say we would meet for lunch?"

Joy rubbed the back of her neck. "I'm sorry. It's completely my fault. I promised we'd get together for a beer and a good chat, but I've been preoccupied in trying to make a good impression with Detective Parker. I haven't gotten a lecture lately, but that doesn't mean one isn't about to happen."

Savannah laughed. She had worked with Officer Williams and Detective Parker on a murder case a few months ago. Officer Williams was the first woman of color to join the Homicide Division. She had a right to be worried about her perceived performance. Although she felt welcomed and a valuable part of the division, she was acutely aware she was the first and that meant all others would be judged by her example. The future of many young women to follow depended on her ability to achieve success. She appeared to be handling the pressure well.

"Yep, I've been on the receiving end of more than one of those lectures," said Savannah. "They're extremely uncomfortable in the heat of the moment, but I've always learned something vital. Every. Single. Time."

"I know the feeling. Anyway, I'm stopping by to invite you to participate as a consultant on a current case. The body of a young man was found early this morning at the Dali Museum. There is definitely an art community connection and Detective Parker wanted me to ask if you would be interested in helping out."

"Oh my goodness. What happened? I was at the museum last night for the grand opening of a new glass exhibit. Was it someone who attended the party?"

"Yes. It was the artist himself, Dennis Lansing," said Officer Williams.

Savannah's hands flew to cover her mouth, then she let her hands fall away. A deep sadness struck her into breathlessness. "Dennis? But . . . I was going to . . ." She looked down for a moment, tried to calm her breathing, and pressed her lips together. "We were going to— Never mind. I was in the receiving line speaking to him when he was pulled away for a VIP tour of his works. I didn't get a chance to say much to him. We left early to spend some quiet time at home."

"You knew him?" Joy took out her notebook and began to scribble. "Was he the one you met in Seattle who was involved with your scholarship?"

"No, my Seattle boyfriend—" Savannah pressed her lips together and choked back a curse. She paused and then tilted her head. "Dennis was my very first boyfriend right here in St. Petersburg High School. We had been corresponding by e-mail after I found out he was the featured exhibitor for the Dali Museum." She looked down at the floor. "I didn't get a chance to speak to him in person until yesterday."

"So, first thing. Where were you in the wee hours of this morning?"

Savannah looked up and she felt a professional mask steal across her face. "I was at home asleep with Rooney and my boyfriend, Edward Morris." She watched Joy note down those facts and saw Joy's shoulders relax.

"That's good, but it would help significantly if I could confirm that with someone other than Edward."

"Of course." Savannah considered for a moment. "My neighbor across the street waved at me through the window when I took Rooney out for a walk."

"What time was that?"

"It was late, probably after midnight."

Joy nodded. "Good—not perfect, but I'll check that out. I still want to know if you can help as a consultant. It looks like your experience will be needed."

"The timing is disastrous. How do these things always happen when I'm starting a new class? Not only that, but I have a major commission due on Saturday, and this workshop is technically challenging. I think I may have to turn this down." She frowned and rubbed the center of her forehead. "Wait, what am I saying?" She pulled a hand from her forehead. "I can't believe this has happened to Dennis."

Savannah stood still for a few long moments trying to control the trembling of her bottom lip. "Working with you guys will give me a chance to help Dennis find justice. It hits me right in the heart. Of course, I'm interested, but since I knew him, you'd better get it cleared with Detective Parker. If he approves, trust me, I'll find a way to squeeze this in along with everything else."

Officer Williams opened her mouth to reply when her phone chirped. "One second. It's Detective Parker. I'll take this outside."

Savannah watched the trim young woman leave quickly and pull the front door closed. Savannah felt strongly connected to the police department due to her involvement in several murder cases. The most personal one was the investigation into the murder of her father and his trusted assistant about nine months ago. Since then, she had developed a reputation as an effective consultant who used wildly original thinking to help find justice for homicide victims. She felt connected to each victim's family. She understood their need for resolution and although it didn't make a dent in the loss, it somewhat answered questions for the families.

Detective Parker had hired her personally on the last murder investigation. It was a positive sign for him to extend an offer of assistance again. The consulting fee was always a welcome addition to her perennially depressed cash flow.

Officer Williams opened the door and walked up to Savannah with her dark eyebrows lowered. "Detective Parker wants to see you downtown at the crime scene as soon as possible."

"As soon as possible? Why?"

"The victim was propped upright on the green bench sculpture."

Savannah tilted her head, "Yes, I know the one. Edward and I strolled through the garden last night, but we didn't stay for the entire party. We left early. Why does he want me at the scene?"

"Detective Parker said a letter was found in the dead man's inside suit jacket pocket."

"So . . ." Savannah put her hands on her hips. "Oh, I remember. He was reaching into his jacket when the director pulled him away for a VIP tour. Honestly, Joy, why are you making this so difficult? What's wrong?"

"The letter is dated ten years ago and appears to

answer a request for a character reference for a permanent job. The letter recommended that the company not hire the applicant as he wasn't capable of honest, trustworthy behavior. It's signed by your father, John Webb."

Connect with Us

Visit us online at
KensingtonBooks.com
to read more from your favorite authors, see books
by series, view reading group guides, and more.

Join us on social media

for sneak peeks, chances to win books and prize packs,
and to share your thoughts with other readers.

facebook.com/kensingtonpublishing
twitter.com/kensingtonbooks

Tell us what you think!

To share your thoughts, submit a review,
or sign up for our eNewsletters, please visit:
KensingtonBooks.com/TellUs.